05/2017

THE DICTATOR

THE DICTATOR

A NOVEL

DAVID LAYTON

PATRICK CREAN EDITIONS
An imprint of HarperCollins*PublishersLtd*

The Dictator
Copyright © 2017 by David Layton.
All rights reserved.

Published by Patrick Crean Editions,
an imprint of HarperCollins Publishers Ltd

First edition

HarperCollins Publishers Ltd
2 Bloor Street East, 20th Floor
Toronto, Ontario, Canada
M4W 1A8

www.harpercollins.ca

Library and Archives Canada Cataloguing in Publication
information is available upon request.

ISBN 978-1-55468-677-3

Printed and bound in the United States of America

LSC/H 9 8 7 6 5 4 3 2 1

For Anastasia, with love

THE DICTATOR

1 Aaron had cleaned his father's teeth last night. Karl wore dentures, something Aaron had not been aware of until his father temporarily moved into his apartment.

Aaron had believed his father's teeth were naturally yellow, but yesterday morning, before his father positioned the dentures in his mouth, he'd glimpsed the horrendous collapse of his father's face as if gravity were a fist, and he was reminded of how extraordinarily violent the universe was and how with even the minutest removal of our physical ramparts, we collapse into ourselves.

The sight so worried Aaron that he'd purchased dental scrubs at the drugstore and, after his father fell asleep, had brushed his father's dentures over the bathroom sink. Holding the pink plastic gums in his rubber-gloved hands, Aaron could tell that despite his father's recent neglect, the dentures were of high quality, the dentine stain just right, the teeth themselves expertly proportioned, or rather disproportioned, to mimic the teeth of men who might still have any loitering in their mouths. Once they were brushed, he'd dropped the dentures into a glass of fresh water, torn open a wax-paper pouch and deposited a tablet that scoured away plaque and other bacteria that Aaron forced himself not to contemplate. He felt compelled to clean the glass by hand before returning it to his father's bedside table, because he didn't want to contaminate his dishwasher.

The entire procedure had disgusted Aaron, but in the morning, when his father walked out of the bedroom with a set of clean teeth tucked into his mouth, oblivious as to who had cleaned them, he felt an odd measure of contentment.

"Breakfast?" Aaron asked.

"Coffee."

"What do you want to eat?"

"Nothing."

Regardless, Aaron slipped bread into the toaster.

It had been like this over the past few mornings, his father asking only for coffee and Aaron adding toast and jam and butter, but today was not like the other days. Today he was flying to London and leaving his father behind in the apartment. *My* apartment, Aaron reminded himself. Just days ago, Karl had left the stove on in his own place, triggering fire alarms that might have been dismissed as a regrettable incident by the condo board, if he hadn't also been behind in his monthly fees. It would all have to be sorted out when Aaron returned home, a task he relished with the same enthusiasm as he did cleaning his father's teeth, but in the meantime, he wasn't going to rearrange his life for him.

Aaron threw some sausages into a frying pan, not the "fat white worms," as his father disparagingly called English breakfast sausages, but real ones with pepper grinds that fired the tongue. He cracked some eggs, cooked them in the sausage fat and then served the whole concoction to his father, who was already seated at the table, waiting impatiently. For a man in his nineties, he still knew how to put it away.

"A last supper," Karl said, observing the feast.

"We're having breakfast," said Aaron, frying himself an egg in a separate pan.

He toasted some more bread and sat down with his father. They ate in silence because there was nothing more to say, conversation having run out between them on the day his father had left him and his mother some forty years ago, and probably even before then. Karl kept his distance from everything, even his food, which he didn't lean into but reached out for with his knife and fork, upon which he built and speared precise architectural constructions of egg, sausage and tomato, an orderly consumption that provoked an immense irritation in his son.

Aaron watched his father bite into the food with teeth that he'd cleaned and sterilized the night before. If only you knew how intimate things are between us, thought Aaron. If secrets were what brought families together, they'd have been the closest family in the world.

"What smells?" Petra asked, emerging from her bedroom while rubbing sleep out of her eyes.

Aaron found it remarkable that his daughter was up so early on a Sunday morning. His father was an early riser, but even his presence here, at just past seven, was unexpected. It was as if they'd woken up purposely to condemn him.

"Want some?" Aaron asked Petra, pointing to her grandfather's sausages.

"I don't think so."

Petra had been a vegetarian, like Aaron, until she was fourteen, when he'd separated from her mother. She'd turned to eating meat after the divorce, as if to get back at him, but he was pleased there were still things she regarded as verboten.

"Morning, Grandpa." Petra leaned over and planted a kiss on Karl's cheek.

Notes of such honest, straightforward affection still startled Aaron, who had no recollection of even once giving or receiving such a kiss from his father. It made him feel like a stranger.

The two-bedroom apartment he'd rented after his divorce was meant to house only him and his daughter when she came for overnight visits. There'd been no thought of his father sleeping over, because up until a week ago, thoughts of any kind about him were few and far between. With Karl in the apartment, Aaron had slept on the couch when Petra came over.

"Can I make you some eggs?" he asked.

Petra eyed the packed suitcase beside the couch. "When are you going?" she asked, though she knew exactly when.

"In twenty minutes."

Petra looked out the sliding glass doors; clouds, gun metal in colour, floated across the sky like decommissioned warships. Due to his father's aged needs, the thermostat was kept at an altogether stifling eighty-four degrees. Even on the coolest nights, Aaron normally kept a window open, the late September air a soothing relief.

"I just want some coffee," said his daughter.

Aaron disapproved, but he wasn't about to put any bread in the toaster for her, as he'd done for his father. At sixteen, Petra would eat—or not eat—whatever she wanted. She'd consume meat, drink coffee, use white sugar, and generally reject just about everything her father stood for.

He poured her a cup. She drank it black, as if any dilution would make her less adult, but as he handed it to her, she reached for the box of individually paper-wrapped sugar cubes Karl had brought with him to the apartment and dropped two into her cup, just as her grandfather did. Aaron remembered as a child fetching the box for his father and was amazed to realize the cubes were still being manufactured. No matter how busy, Aaron had always done his best to cook his daughter fresh, healthy meals. She'd adopted vegetarianism with a vengeance, pinching her nose at the stink of meat and voicing offence at her mother's poor moral development. It was an alliance between them, a sign of mutual approval that Aaron had failed to discourage. He'd wanted to be a good father. No, that wasn't true. He'd wanted to be a great father. Unfortunately, he hadn't foreseen how, by siding with his daughter, that might make him a poor husband. He never could get the balance right. He'd wanted something different than his own upbringing, and in the process, it seemed, he'd ushered in the very thing he had wished to avoid.

"I'll only be gone three nights," he said, though, as with his departure, this was known by his daughter.

"You're flying thousands of miles just so you can talk

about global warming and the environment. Don't you think that's a bit hypocritical?"

Wary, Aaron stared down at his now empty plate. He would eat again on the plane, two meals before descending into Heathrow, and he would ask for orange juice with ice, a habit he indulged only while in the air. The plane, he'd already told himself, would leave with or without him, so staying home wouldn't solve anything. He could have purchased carbon offsets—they were offered to him by the airline—but quite frankly, that felt like one more way of getting money out of him, like charging extra for checked luggage, and besides, he wasn't a global warming activist. City hall had recently voted overwhelmingly to implement bike lanes in Toronto, and he was going to London not to give a speech or listen to one but to consult and learn what he could about the growing network being installed over there.

Several years back there'd been a push for congestion fees in the downtown core and Aaron had flown to London to see how their program was being administered, but after observing the number of Mercedes, Audis, Rolls-Royces and limos that blithely traversed central London, Aaron had reservations about imposing fees that only the rich could easily afford to pay.

Bike lanes seemed more democratic, healthy and properly coercive. Eliminating lines of cars in either direction affected all drivers equally, and the return of real estate to cyclists meant a better, greener city for all. Ordinarily he'd have expected Petra to agree, but as with vegetarianism, she'd shifted against him and for the same reason.

"You just want to force everyone to be on bikes, Dad."

It annoyed him, the way Petra painted him as some petty dictator.

"I want everyone to have a choice," he said.

"By making them do something else. This is Toronto, as in Canada. Who wants to ride a bike in January?"

In years past, he and Petra had pedalled through the city, as blithely indifferent to the sleet and cold as the luxury cars of central London were to the congestion fee. He could still see the autumn leaves thrown up in the wake of her training wheels, and, after he'd taken them off, the cutting line she sliced through a light layer of snow. Petra had never wanted to stop, even when the heavy snow came, and they would keep cycling, until her mother insisted it was time to store the bike for winter.

It wasn't snow and cold that had stopped them riding together. And bike lanes weren't going to rectify the situation. Driving cars had replaced her interest in riding bicycles. He and his ex-wife had farmed off the responsibility to a professional driving school. Hiring a trained instructor was in the best interest of his child and saved money on insurance, but try as he might to convince himself, Aaron knew he'd missed something essential.

The last time he'd been in the car with her while she was driving, he'd observed her new-found road skills as if they were a surprise, and he'd promised there and then that he would take her to her next driving test. Petra's graduated licence only allowed her to operate a vehicle with an accompanying adult. The next test would, if she passed, permit her to drive without a licensed chaperone. It would be a big step toward adulthood. But instead of honouring his promise, here he was preparing to leave for London.

He'd forgotten to put the date in his calendar, perhaps under a false assurance that he would remember it, and it was as if some malevolent force had determined that such a short trip should overlap with his daughter's test. Maybe he didn't want her to grow up, to become fully independent of him, at least not now, when he wasn't able to appreciate these finite moments. You were given only one chance to teach your child to ride a bike, or to drive a car, or, for that matter, to be a good father.

Aaron stood up from the table without clearing his plate, grabbed the two bed pillows off the couch and walked over to the closet. When he slept on the couch, he felt exposed.

"The nurse is going to be here in a few minutes," he said, opening the closet door and pushing the pillows onto the top shelf. There were more pillows in the closet, plus bedsheets and bath towels, face cloths, bottles of shampoo, even a snorkelling mask—all pressed and jumbled in a way that indicated erupting chaos. At the bottom were piles of shoes belonging to Aaron and Petra that they had essentially rejected. He would have to clean this up.

Aaron went back to the couch, collected his suitcase and dropped it by the front door.

"I'll wait for the nurse to get here. You can go," Petra said.

"I'll wait with you."

His daughter and father had taken a strange liking to each other, based in no small part, he felt it fair to say, on their antipathy toward him. Aaron could admit that he was jealous of their relationship, petty though that might be.

"You don't have to."

And I don't want to, thought Aaron. But of course he had to. He would wait, because that's what a good son did, a responsible son.

The buzzer went off, and Aaron let in the nurse, a woman from Eastern Europe who announced herself with the speedy formality of someone trained to insinuate herself quickly among strangers.

"Good morning, Mr. Kaufmann," she said, addressing not Aaron but Karl, who offered a shallow nod.

Aaron reached for his travel bags; it was late and he needed to get to the airport.

"I'll see you when I get back," he said to both.

He'd expected his father to show about as much interest in him as in the nurse, but the old man stood up from his chair. Unable to reciprocate, Aaron held onto his bag and failed to move toward him. Even his father's friendly gestures came as distant missiles, launched from so far away that Aaron didn't hear them coming. They were still awkward strangers, with no more understanding of each other than before they'd reluctantly begun sharing a roof. Several days can't make up for lost decades, thought Aaron, and it was risky to think otherwise. He would sort all this out when he got back. His father would soon be moving into a proper nursing home. He'd get his room back, and his daughter. They had problems, but what parent of a teenage child didn't?

"I'm sorry I'm missing your driving test," he said to Petra, who joined him at the front door.

"You think that's the problem, Dad?"

"I think it's why you're angry at me. And you have every right to be."

"Don't tell me what's right, Dad. Not when you're treating Grandpa like some dog you can just leave at the kennel."

"He's not in a kennel. He's in my apartment. He has a nurse. And he has you."

Aaron took a few steps back so that he was beyond the threshold of the apartment, beyond his father and daughter. Everything he did was wrong, was stupid, was hypocritical. She mocked him about the bike lanes, she ate meat and she spoke to him as if she were the wiser of the two. That he was a bad son confirmed, in her eyes, why he was a bad father. He'd made a promise to her; he was putting work over family. Yes, he'd messed up, but nothing like his own father, whom Petra stood up for. That too was a kind of betrayal, a decision to put one of them above the other.

For some reason, Grandpa's past was not an issue. Growing up, she'd spent so little time with her grandfather that she could make him into whatever she wished him to be.

"I've got to go," Aaron said.

"Off to save the world?" called out his father, just to be a bastard.

Off to get away from you, thought Aaron, but not before Petra had already shut the door on him.

* * *

THE DAMP ENGLISH air lacked the hint of winter harshness that was descending on Toronto. It was dark out. Flying eastward this morning, he'd sped away not only from his daughter and father but from the sun. Aaron kept the taxi window rolled down until they reached the highway leading into London.

Sealed inside, he phoned his daughter, who didn't pick up. He called the nurse, who said everything was fine, and would he like to speak to his father. Aaron said no and wrote a text to Petra, because it was the only way to communicate with her.

Your dad has arrived and says hello
xo

It sounded weak, even piteous, but he sent it anyway. Nothing he did or said would muster favour with her.

He'd booked into one of those hotels whose employees were as international as the clientele who stayed there. The woman at reception came from somewhere in Eastern Europe, and the man who offered to take his bags to the room came from somewhere farther east, Pakistan or India or Bangladesh. The British had voted to leave the European Union, and Aaron wondered what might happen to some of them, what might happen to London itself. Half the people living here came from somewhere else, and what was home would suddenly become a foreign place.

The room was stylishly bland, with a partial view over Hyde Park, which like the Atlantic Ocean he'd flown over just a few hours ago was a dark patch below. He readied himself for bed. Tomorrow he'd be touring various sites with local planners and politicians. A master plan for bike lanes was already in place, and construction of the first cycle super-highways had begun in south London, part of a growing network that would link central London with the outer boroughs. Soon the whole, great city of London would be connected, and Toronto too. He, Aaron, would be a part of this joining, and he felt good about that.

No, he wasn't going to save the world, as his father had remarked disparagingly this morning, but that wasn't Aaron's goal. As a senior policy adviser for the provincial government of Ontario, he was just trying to make the world a little bit better. He wasn't someone who could get elected, who knocked on doors and made promises that couldn't be kept. He worked behind a desk and wrote position papers that could, if necessary, be disowned if they proved unpopular among those who had opened their doors.

That was the way the game was played, and Aaron felt he played it well. He was here in London, wasn't he? As he drifted off to sleep, he imagined bike lanes threading through city streets, stitching up the world.

When Aaron woke up the next morning, he was surprised by the bright, almost Miditerranean light bursting through his window. The park below, so dark and mysterious the night before, was a brilliant sea of green. It flooded London like a high water mark of prosperity. Aaron dressed and went outside, forgoing breakfast at the hotel and picking up a coffee in one of the side streets. The man who served him was no more English than the woman who'd checked him in to his hotel last night. These people, citizens of Europe, would soon no longer be subjects of Great Britain. If he were a different sort of person, he'd have asked how they felt about it and what they intended to do. Did they feel they belonged here, or did they think of themselves as visitors? And what of Aaron, who held a Canadian passport with a fussy, overly complex emblem of lions, unicorns and, noticeable if one looked, a Union Jack. Aaron had no English heritage, but the country he was born in was a member of the Commonwealth and placed the Queen's face on its money. She'd come for a visit when Aaron was a child, and the entire school had been brought out to greet her. They'd stood in front of the school fence, along a road with squat brick houses on the other side, the sort of houses his father might have built, and the Queen had passed in her motorcade, waving listlessly.

His father, like the Queen, came from Europe. He'd landed in Canada after the war and become a small-time developer, part of the post-war passion for tearing down history, both natural and man-made, with ferocious abandon. Forests and farmland were felled and paved to make way for new suburbs. Old, venerable buildings in the city centre were ripped out like rotten teeth, replaced with something too shiny and straight. His father had no instinct for the past, no interest in it; he just happily bulldozed it down.

His father had once—and, so far as Aaron could recollect, only once—taken him to one of the construction sites, walking him across the chewed-up land that sprouted dead lumber instead of trees. Aaron would always wonder what his father had wanted to show him. The visit was not to instill pride in his father's achievements. His father was too serious for simple boastfulness and too purposeful in the way he'd smacked down the miniature hard hat on Aaron's head with his clenched hand. He must have wanted to show Aaron something but seemed too distracted to follow through, repeatedly leaving him alone while he consulted with men on the site. Perhaps that was the lesson—that a man was always alone? That he couldn't depend on anyone, even his father? Especially his father.

While standing there on his own, Aaron had discovered a bird floating in a pool of muddied water. He'd taken off the hard hat Karl had dropped on his head and used it to scoop the bird out, hoping to revive it.

"It's dead," Karl said when he returned, even as it twitched in one last effort at survival. Aaron wanted to take the bird home and mend it, but his father saw there was no hope. "It's just a bird," he said, and at that moment, Aaron felt his father had been responsible for its death.

England, and the Europe his father came from, was once again convulsing. Refugees were streaming across borders, and no one knew who belonged and who did not. Senior policy advisers weren't supposed to float romantic notions in front of their eyes, and certainly not in front of the eyes of the ministers they served.

* * *

LONDON'S STREET FURNITURE always impressed him, the way, for instance, the black median poles separating street from sidewalk were all perfectly erect and scuff-less. The park benches and barricades, the airport-grade signage and street lights didn't look as if they'd been purchased from the cheap discount stores of North American cities. Before Aaron knew it, he'd walked himself down to the river.

It was the heart of rush hour, the road choked with blocked cars and whizzing bicyclists, although fewer of them than he'd have expected for such a sunny day. It would have taken too long for him to return to the hotel, and so he followed the blue strip of dedicated bicycle lane toward Embankment and his morning meeting. He arrived a bit early, sat down on a bench and took in the Thames. It was said that salmon now spawned in the river. Embankment was more than a roadway running alongside the river. Beneath his feet ran one of the great sewer pipes of the world, built to clean up the filth and muck that had plagued the city for centuries. There'd be no more flooding from the Thames, no raw sewage splashing into the septic waters, causing cholera and chronic disease. Instead there'd be an elegant boulevard with gas lamps, monuments, balustrades, and now, bike lanes.

The group of city planners, political operatives and small contingent of media that he met took him through the routes planned for the city, the projected costs and decisions made on a financial and political level. They spoke of the extensive feasibility plans for traffic management, future ridership numbers, greenhouse gas reduction figures, and Aaron absorbed what he felt might be useful for his ambitions.

"You look a little stunned."

The woman who said this was a member of the media. She'd been following along with the sort of smile that in his mind made her dangerous. He'd done his best to avoid her.

"I must be a bit jet-lagged," he said. "I got up too early this morning."

"Good. I thought it was because you believed in all this shit."

"Pardon?"

"Do you believe in it?"

"Sorry, I don't think I should be talking to you."

"I'm off duty." The woman raised her hands to show they were devoid of notepad and phone recorder. "And even if I was on duty, it's just a small community paper."

That should have been the end of it, but he found himself walking beside her. "I'm going back to my hotel," he said, retracing his steps along Embankment, which, though it was long after rush hour, was still jammed with cars.

"These lanes have already caused massive gridlock," she said. "Pollution levels have skyrocketed. Police and ambulance can't get through. It's all one big vanity project set up by the former mayor. You know what we call the bicyclists? Lycramen. They don't commute, they race. Mainly fit young men, a few women, all holier than thou, morally superior arseholes."

"There are always going to be a few problems," said Aaron.

"So you are a believer. That must account for the stunned

look on your face. But that's okay. I like believers. Are you hungry?"

Aaron hadn't eaten breakfast and was starving but unsure of the situation. What was actually happening here? It occurred to him that she was having a bit of fun at his expense but also flirting with him.

"Where's your hotel?" she asked.

Aaron told her it wasn't far, and as they walked through Green Park and then down Piccadilly, he wondered at what point they'd stop for some food and why he felt their movements toward the hotel were unstoppable. There was a promise of flesh, and Aaron had a sudden urge to be with a woman; it was the urge of a bachelor, the first since he and Isobel had split up. But it was still vague, the woman before him unknown, the conversation about bicycle lanes unimaginable. Yet there it was, he thought, the tug toward a new life, even though the very thought of finding another person to share a life with seemed exhausting. All that work, all that learning, all that retelling of one's stories in order to convert a stranger into a spouse. But he was getting ahead of himself, far ahead.

Even as they passed through the lobby and stepped into the elevator, the thought of what they were possibly about to do seemed improbable. He decided they were going up to his room to order room service.

His room was still flooded with light, and Aaron wanted to close the curtains, though that would seem bold and obvious. But then, what was she doing here with him? And he with her?

Just then, the phone rang. He looked at the screen. *Home*, it said.

"Don't answer it," she said.

"I have to."

"Kids?"

Dad.

He let it ring, staring at the illuminated word, momentarily unclear how his father could be reaching him; it was as if the man possessed a rubber arm that had stretched around corners, down city streets, across oceans and then grabbed Aaron through the sunlit window. His head throbbed. He'd forgotten about Petra and the fact she hadn't texted him back.

"Hello?"

"Mr. Kaufmann?" It was the nurse.

"Yes," said Aaron.

"Mr. Kaufmann, your father has disappeared."

Aaron checked the time. It was half past eight in the morning.

"Is everything okay?" the woman in his hotel room asked, after he hung up the phone.

No, thought Aaron. It wasn't. Jet-lagged, he'd been thinking about wounds and birds and other things that strangely tore at him and that no bicycle lane was ever going to solve. But there was someone in the room with him who might be able to help, and so he picked up the remote and commanded the curtains to close. He'd give himself a few hours before catching the first flight for home.

2 KARL KAUFMANN LISTENED TO THE DIS-
cordant and extremely irritating pips emanating
from the crosswalk and wondered why the blind,
if they'd already managed to penetrate this far
into the heart of the city without any aural assistance,
would need it now, at this particular juncture, to guide
their movements across one small patch of asphalt. He
believed the pips were meant not for the blind but for the
sighted, who vandalized the air so they could loudly dem-
onstrate their compassion for those less fortunate than
themselves. It was like that nowadays, all public compassion and showy safety.

Karl looked down at his watch, its oversized numerals
compensating for his failing eyesight, and saw that it was
a little past quarter to three. He had somewhere to go, a
meeting of some sort, and though he wasn't exactly sure
why, he felt certain that he would be late if he didn't get on
his way.

And then he forgot where he was.

He stood there, not taking a single step forward or
backward, listening to the pips from the crosswalk, certain,
though he could not say why, that their repetitive message
was meant for him, and he told himself that he was lost,
that he did not recognize the street corner or the buildings

because he'd never been here before. But he wasn't sure if that was true, and, far worse, he wasn't clear where he'd come from or where it was that he needed to get back to, which meant that he wasn't lost at all, because for that to happen, you needed to be lost in something. There needed to be a point of comparison between what you knew and what you didn't. It was as if he were holding onto a map that was burning from the centre out, until there was nothing left but blazing fragments scorching the edges of his fingers.

He needed to escape, to find somewhere quiet, so that he could remember.

"Are you all right?"

Karl quickly answered "Yes" without looking at the man addressing him. He was fine, although he realized that he was staring down at the pavement, at his shoes, which were burgundy and a little too scuffed for his liking. Had he selected them himself?

"Do you want help crossing the street?"

"No."

"Where are you going?"

It was the sort of intrusive question that the strong can ask of the weak. Karl knew that the great advantage of health was the distance it allowed you to keep from other people.

"*Bitte, verlassen Sie mich allein.*" Karl discovered that he spoke German.

"Are you a tourist?"

No, he wasn't a tourist. That was another scrap of information he could hold onto, though he'd forgotten where he was.

"I'm from here," said Karl, and, because that was the truth, he walked away and kept on walking, until he turned a corner and found a patch of shade beside the doors of a commercial tower whose air-conditioned chill flowed over his body like a cool stream. It was warm out, but Karl was dressed for cooler weather. He was sweating but refused to take off his wool blazer. There was a row of trees planted along the sidewalk whose leaves were curled and turning, and the sky had a faded brightness about it, like a shirt left out in the sun too long, which informed Karl it was the beginning of autumn. His name was Karl Kaufmann, it was hot, this was home, he knew German but spoke English, and he didn't know where he was. He was scared.

But he'd been in situations much worse than this, of that he was sure, and he consoled himself, while enviously eyeing the purposeful strides of office workers advancing in and out of the air-conditioned building, that he'd always come through, as he would again this time. The important thing was to keep one's head clear, although the problem was that his head *was* clear, drained like a kitchen sink, with only a few pieces of food scraps to remind him of what he'd had for supper.

He decided to move on for fear that someone else might approach to offer help, so he walked along the street, emulating the quickened pace of those who knew where they were. The road was a long line of heated, venting metal, waiting for the lights to change. Maybe he had driven here and had parked the car. It had happened to him before, losing his car. And forgetting names. That had happened too.

One minute he'd be talking to some acquaintances, and the next minute he'd forget not just their names but who, exactly, they were. He'd carry on talking for a minute or two, crossing his arms, trying to recapture their identity, but if that failed, he'd let them speak, while he nodded with unearned sagacity until it came back to him, which, thankfully, it had always done.

There was a lot of construction: cranes, jackhammers. Farther up, a helicopter arrogantly staked out a patch of sky. Down below where Karl was, there were stores selling shoes and suits and kitchen appliances, in bright new shops that wouldn't look the same in six months time. And as Karl walked on, he began to suspect that he wasn't the only one who didn't know where he was, that everyone was like him, pretending. Every building along this road was either new or touched up, and all were ready to be torn down again and replaced, a ceaseless act of insolence that the living visited upon the dead, who no longer had a constituency, a voice, to croak in protest. Karl sensed his present circumstances were a symptom, a premonition, of what was to come: he could no longer remember what others had already chosen to forget.

Fair enough, thought Karl, as he ducked inside a store that sold furniture, but what he needed was a solution for what was happening to him right now. He was tired and needed to rest, so he walked himself over to a quiet corner of the store. He sat down on a chair, became enveloped in its buttery scent of new leather, and closed his eyes, trying to call up precise images of his home.

It was on the tip of his tongue, like a mislaid word, this place—his home—that he couldn't recognize; he felt a certain hatred for it, which was promising, because there was a measure of intimacy in hating something, and Karl wilfully attempted to bring the emotion into fuller existence. He was angry too, but the anger seemed more general, less precisely tied down to any one place, hovering like the helicopter he'd seen outside.

"May I help you?"

Karl opened his eyes. A young attractive woman stood over him. Actually, youth and attractiveness had become synonymous for Karl. He briefly wondered, before answering her, at the pointless and rather exhausting distinctions of beauty he'd once made when he too was young.

"I'm just resting here for a moment."

"You can't really do that." As cover for her embarrassment, she offered Karl a commercial smile. He would have to go.

"I will buy something," he said and noticed immediately how pitiable he sounded.

"There's a Starbucks next door, if you'd like to sit down and rest," she said.

Karl nodded, wishing that he could close his eyes for a few more minutes and be back home in his own living room, where no one would interfere with his decision to rest, because the chair would be his, and the light, at this time of the day, would be streaming through the back window, illuminating the newspaper, which he would be holding in his hands, and he could, if he wished, stand up and get himself a cold glass of water from the kitchen, or some cranberry juice watered down with an abundance of ice. His fridge made ice—he'd always thought it a small miracle— and sometimes, when he was sitting in his chair, in his living room, he heard the rattling deposit as another batch of cubes skidded across the tray.

And then Karl saw it, from his chair: the fireplace to his right, with its triptych protective grille, and the brass fire utensils—shovel, brush and poker. The potted plant. The couch that sat in front of the bay window. The hallway and staircase to his left. The kitchen with the double sink.

Karl lifted himself out of his chair and instinctively accepted the assistance of the young woman's outstretched arm. He felt pleasure being so close to her. She smelled like the furniture, new, unused and ready to be placed in the right setting, and it was only when they reached the exit and she'd let go of him that he once more mislaid his sense of direction.

The image of the living room was burned off by the afternoon light. Back out on the street, he tried to fasten onto it by repeating the details—fireplace, plant, couch, hallway—while staring straight ahead, seeing nothing before him but the details of his home. And then he heard the pips. The sound frightened him, and he turned away. He was heading in the opposite direction when a taxi pulled up in front of him, which surprised Karl, until he became conscious of the flagging motion of his arm. He climbed inside the car and offered an address before being asked, then leaned back and watched an unknown world slip past him.

The radio was on, not music, but baseball, a lethargic-sounding announcer calling the game, and Karl remembered the first time he'd been introduced to the sport as a young man, really still a boy; he recalled the tropical field, the Dominican boys throwing the ball to one another beneath a bright, hot sun, with only six mitts to be shared among the impoverished group. The mitts and bat had been donated to them by the Jewish charity in New York, but it was the Dominicans who'd been more interested in playing. Karl would sometimes join them, because he would take the centre field position, and he liked the way it felt to be part of a team and yet on his own, deep in the backfield, on the edge of the clearing, where the crack of ball against bat took a second to reach him through the humid air.

"Am I here?" he asked.

The cab driver looked at Karl through the rear-view mirror and wordlessly pointed to the house with the green door. Karl stepped out onto the curb.

"You haven't paid."

Karl blinked, and thought, Money, yes, he needed to pay him money, and patted down his pockets. Finding a wallet, he offered it with both hands through the open window in a sign of supplication and waited for the driver to take what was his. Then he proceeded toward the house.

He pushed the front door open and saw that he was home. There was the fireplace, the chair, the couch, everything that belonged to him.

He'd learned as a young man to dislike tracking dirt into the house, felt it was a sort of contamination between two distinct spheres and was happy to take off his shoes and leave behind the accumulated confusion he'd picked up outside. He walked, practically ran, to his waiting chair. God, he was tired. And thirsty. He leaned back in his seat. The house was air-conditioned. He'd had an argument about that with Claire, thought it was an unnecessary luxury, a weakness of some kind.

"So is heating" was Claire's response.

He wouldn't tell her what had happened—it had already begun to appear vaguely preposterous—but he was happy for the coolness. He wouldn't tell her about that either. They'd had a lot of quarrels back then, *arguments* he preferred to call them, though he knew they were much more than that. It was his fault. He'd made her unhappy, but it was all right now. Why argue against air-conditioning? Why fight at all, he wondered, searching for his newspaper. Usually it lay on the floor, beside his chair. He was trying to remember if he'd read it this morning, when he heard Claire's voice call out from upstairs.

"Hello? Is someone there?"

"It's me."

He heard her footsteps on the stairs, so distinctive the way they pressed down on the wooden boards as if each step were exploratory, in need of reassurance that the ground wouldn't give way.

"What are you doing here?" she asked when she saw him.

Karl thought he might have missed an appointment—perhaps it was the doctor's—because she looked at him with worry, if not outright alarm.

"I came home early."

Claire leaned forward just a bit, as if she hadn't quite heard him. Then she laughed, a quick nervous burst, before she placed a hand over her mouth.

Karl sensed danger, and if he'd had the newspaper beside him, he would have picked it up and obdurately started reading it. Unfortunately he had no cover, nothing to hide behind, and so he sat there with hands that throbbed on the armrests, and waited.

"Karl," she said, "you haven't lived in this house for almost forty years."

HE SAT IN the chair beside the fireplace, a glass of untouched juice beside him along with a newspaper that Claire had brought him. It was a thoroughly domestic setting, which heightened the oddity of the situation.

"You gave me quite a scare, Karl."

Karl rustled the newspaper, an impotent thunderclap to show his disapproval of Claire's disruption, and resumed reading, or rather he resumed the act of reading, his eyes scanning the print for Middle East wars and bombs and global financial chaos that offered him a measure of dark satisfaction, though he knew he could no longer follow the sequential order of pandemonium that was so neatly and rationally arranged before him. The mortar that bound each sentence and paragraph to the next had, like the synapses in his brain, become soft and loose. At this moment, what remained was the habit of reading, the remembrance of it, which he could, like the newspaper itself, hold up against them.

"I was upstairs putting fresh sheets on the bed, when you walked in."

Karl put down the newspaper and took in the news that he could understand: this woman, this house, and the life they'd had together. He glanced at her wedding finger and saw that it was bare. She'd placed clean sheets on the bed for her own comfort and no one else's.

"The house looks to be in good shape," he said. Karl couldn't be sure, but it appeared to him that hardly anything had changed since the day she'd asked him to leave. And what was true for the house was also true for Claire. She'd aged, of course, but still the pale blue eyes peered out of a roundish, if somewhat thinner, face than the one he remembered. No wonder he could walk through the front door and make himself at home. She hadn't done anything to smooth out the wrinkles or tuck back the unwanted parts of herself. He could recognize her as he could the house in all its familiarity, and it was a source of great comfort.

"How's the roof holding up?"

The roof was always leaking. He'd go up there and lay down roofing tile, but somehow the water always found its way into the house again, and he'd climb back up in frustration, searching for cracks and imperfections to seal up. Claire liked to say that their house was a strong man with a bald head, and he recalled the day, years ago, when he'd climbed to the top of the house to make some repairs and seen himself, in an endless duplication, standing on all the other peaked rooftops searching for leaks. It had been some sort of mirage conjured up from rippling heat and light. Or a hallucination. Whatever it was, Karl had turned his back on all his other selves and focused on the roof he knew himself to be standing on, to plug the hole the best he could, because it was the roof that belonged to him, and that was all that mattered.

"Is that why you came over, Karl? To ask after the roof?" She looked at him—studied him was more like it—tilting her head a few degrees as if a different angle might help adjust her thoughts. "I guess there are a few leaks, but the house is still standing, just like I am."

Her smile revealed a missing tooth, not in the front but just a little back, so that it took a large smile to notice. He suddenly felt sad that she hadn't seen the need to fill the gap, that she'd accepted it.

"That's good," he said.

"Are you hungry, Karl?"

"I don't think I've had any lunch," he said and immediately wished he'd been less equivocal, that he'd said, *I didn't have lunch*. "I was downtown," he added, because it was true, a fact that he could recall, but it came out as boosterish, as something a child might exclaim to his mother after an excursion.

"Did you drive here?"

"Yes," he answered.

"Where's your car?"

"The car is parked, Claire."

"Where is it parked?"

He didn't like these questions. They felt cruel and dangerous and forced him to lie. He wasn't as sharp as he once had been, as he needed to be. *Slippages* was what he called these strange mental lapses, when he seemed to misplace people and places. None of which was out of the ordinary, he told himself. Especially at his age. Most people were dead.

"So how come you decided to walk through my front door? You always used to warn me to keep it locked in case a stranger walked in, but I never thought the stranger would end up being you, Karl. Are you feeling okay?"

"Yes," he answered carefully. "I think so."

Now it was all coming back to him as if through layers of mist and fog—his apartment, which he reached by pushing the letters *PH*, the acronym for the penthouse that offered a secret measure of pride and thrilled him each time he stepped onto the elevator, the southward view of the city and the recently replaced sidewalk below, the concrete still white and virginal.

Noticing his confusion, Claire softened her tone. "Would you like something to eat? I can make a plate of salami, some cheese and pickles."

"You never liked salami."

"That's true," answered Claire, without explaining any further why she'd have some in the house.

"I think maybe just some coffee," said Karl.

"It's too late in the day for coffee, Karl. You know how you are when you have coffee in the afternoon. You can never get to sleep."

Karl, who felt as if he could sleep harder and longer than at any time in the past twenty years and who was even hoping he might be able to slip upstairs to take a nap on those fresh sheets, accepted Claire's suggestion of tea instead. After she walked into the kitchen, he realized that she hadn't asked how he took it, and for a fearful second, Karl wondered if he might not know himself, but she returned with tea that was sweet and milky just as he preferred it, and he discovered that everything about the present arrangement satisfied him.

"Thank you," he said.

"Be careful. It's hot."

Karl blew on the steam, took a few sips and then, just for a second, closed his eyes.

He had been seated in this very chair—or if not the exact chair then one just like it and in the same spot—when she'd accused him of transferring money every month to an account in the Dominican Republic. He hadn't expected her to find out. He'd always done all the banking. In those days, a wife needed her husband's signature to do practically anything when it came to banking, but then things changed—as they always did—and Claire was no longer dependent in the same way. She made her own deposits and withdrawals and eventually asked questions that she shouldn't have asked and that the bank should never have answered.

"Why are you sending money there?" Claire had demanded.

She'd sat on the couch opposite him.

"I send money to help the community."

"That you lived in during the war?"

"Yes, that's right."

"Who, specifically, are you helping?"

"It's a private matter," he said.

"No, it's not," Claire said bluntly.

"There are things you don't understand. That you don't need to understand." Surely, he thought, she could see that. Karl had spent the war surviving somehow, and then he'd come to Canada and worked hard and met Claire and married her. That was the only explanation worth offering, the only one, like the leaky roof, that mattered. All his other selves were not worth dwelling upon.

"Karl?" A hand touched his arm. It was Claire, waking him for dinner.

"You must have nodded off," she said, and Karl realized that he was not at home and that Claire was no longer his wife. "Come and have something to eat."

Karl took his seat at the table set with plates and cutlery and cloth napkins and began eating the food Claire had placed before him. He was so famished, he didn't notice the arrival of a man and teenage girl who had come through the front door without knocking. They stared at him, and he stared back, before realizing that it was his son and granddaughter. The son he'd had with Claire.

"Aaron's here to drive you back to your apartment after you've finished eating," said Claire.

His son didn't appear happy at the prospect, and it was strange, too, that he came with a suitcase, as if he were about to go somewhere. Or perhaps he'd come from somewhere else and had now arrived to collect Karl, as if he were an item his son had forgotten to pack away.

Nobody else seemed to want any food except Karl, so he ate alone, his son and granddaughter and ex-wife speaking among themselves, as if he didn't exist.

And at that moment, Karl thought they might be right.

"TAKE YOUR SHOES off," Karl commanded, unlacing his shoes and placing them on his shoe rack, something he was fairly certain he'd done when entering Claire's house.

"They're off," his son said, and Karl watched him petulantly slip one shoe off with the other, the way a teenager would do it. In contrast, his granddaughter actually used her hands, as if purposely declaring her maturity.

"You always ask me to do exactly the same thing at your place, Dad," said Petra.

Aaron just stood there by the door as if expecting something to happen.

Karl strode toward the row of floor-to-ceiling windows and pulled back the curtains to reveal the high-rise illumination of the city centre. He was pleased by the decision to live in a penthouse apartment, furnished in a Spartan style uncluttered with mementos or bulky objects difficult to dispose of. Stepping back, he noticed a pile of magazines fanned out across the coffee table but also, next to them, a vacuum attachment. It stood upright like a steam-ship funnel, as if purposely placed there.

Yes, it was a mistake to visit Claire, and the vacuum

attachment spoke to him of other problems, but now that he was in his real home, Karl felt as if things might be put back in their place. That included his son, who along with his granddaughter had not just dropped him off at his home but had gotten out of the car with him and carried on through the lobby like tenants. As they stepped into the elevator with him, Karl had pushed the *PH* button with a sense of infringement.

If he'd been thinking more clearly, he would have foreseen this eventuality and done something about it, said something. What he had said was "Thank you for escorting me home," singeing his words with enough sarcasm to let them know what he thought of the idea, but his son and granddaughter had ridden up with him anyway and then stomped through his apartment.

Making his way down the long hallway, Karl flipped on the light switch to his bathroom and caught his reflection in the full-length mirror: with his hand still on the wall, he looked like a thief come to rob his own home. Age had ruined him. Karl held no illusion on that matter, but on closer examination he was pleased to see that his features remained sharply focused, as if everything non-essential had been stripped away. He was like one of those monumental buildings Albert Speer had designed to age gracefully, like a Roman ruin, long after the disappearance of the Third Reich, and it gave Karl pleasure to think that he was here, still defiantly aging, while those other bastards were dead.

There were two sinks in the bathroom, and Karl sidled

over to the one on the left while looking over at the other sink and wondering whom it was for. He hadn't dated a woman for years. A bar of soap between the two sinks had dried and cracked from lack of use, and he suddenly noticed the sorry state of his bathroom. Floor tiles had been ripped up, revealing small ridge-lines of sealant that were no longer able to bond and seal. He spotted the telltale signs of water damage and stared at the bathtub. Workmen had been here and not yet finished the job.

He leaned over the sink and splashed cold water on his face. Feeling the rough stubble, Karl decided to shave before going to bed. It was not his routine to shave in the evening, but turning on the tap and waiting for the hot water to course its way through the copper pipes, he admitted to himself that it had been anything but a normal day. It had been a long day, a wrong day, Karl thought, the whole of it unaccountable to him.

Karl pulled the blade across his lathered jaw, using his free hand to tug the skin taut. On an impulse, a dare even, he looked again at the other sink, the one to his right. He'd had a number of relationships with women since the end of his marriage to Claire, and looking back, what he most appreciated was their brevity. The last woman he'd been with, Sophia, was sixteen years younger than Karl and a good cook, but she'd started to complain about his cigars. "They're not cigars, they're Davidoffs," he protested, after she'd once again admonished him for smoking in the apartment, especially in winter, when she couldn't open the windows. He'd burned something, maybe the striped blue and white couch, and she said, "I can't take care of you anymore."

"Who says you need to take care of me?"

The idea had shocked him. If there was one thing he knew, it was how to take care of himself—

"Dad?"

He'd forgotten about his son. But there he was, hovering at the bathroom's entrance.

Karl spoke to the mirror. "What is it?"

This son of his was in front of him, behind him, impossible to be rid of.

"Dad, we've got to go."

Karl was pleased they were leaving. As his son stood there waiting for him to finish shaving, it occurred to him that, truth be told, his son could do with a shave as well. He looked Semitic, which was odd, because his mother wasn't Jewish, and Karl, with his blue eyes and once blond hair, looked Austrian—*was* Austrian, Karl reminded himself. That was something they couldn't take away from him, something only he could voluntarily renounce, and lately he'd felt a perverse pleasure in not doing so.

"Dad, I'm exhausted. We've got to get going."

So get going, thought Karl. "Hand me that towel," he said, pointing to a pristine, sun yellow hand towel that in the mess of his bathroom looked like something from a museum exhibit of a lost domestic era.

At his son's beckoning, Karl followed him down the hallway while dabbing at his face with the towel and enjoying the sweet and sour smell of shaving cream. They stepped into his bedroom. The mirrored closet doors had been slid open, exposing a row of plastic and metal hangers, some with paper adverts of their local dry cleaner still on them.

While he'd been in the bathroom, his son and grand-daughter had been snooping around the apartment, entering his bedroom and opening closets and drawers. By what right did his son have to do such a monstrous thing? Who had given him permission?

With his granddaughter watching from the corner, his son pulled a suitcase out of the closet and dropped it on the bed. Karl noticed the sheets and blanket were tucked in and securely anchored beneath the mattress, but the pillowcases were missing.

"What are you doing?" he demanded.

"Packing."

"Why? Where are we going?"

"We just came here to get some more of your things," said his son. "Then we're going back to my place."

His son unzipped and opened the suitcase, baring a hungry emptiness that Karl feared would swallow him whole. He thought back to all the suitcases he'd seen lined up on the street, darkening in the soft drizzle that enveloped Vienna, while their owners, in panicked subservience, darkened alongside them. Karl was determined that he would not be one of those who lined up to disappear. Suitcases marked the ending of things.

"I am sleeping here," Karl said.

"You can't."

"I want to sleep here."

"I know you do, Dad. And believe me when I say that I wish you could, because I'll be sleeping on the couch tonight. Do you have any idea how long my day has been?"

Karl noticed that his granddaughter's reaction was to cross her arms, as if to protect herself from feeling any sympathy.

"Dad moved into the apartment after he got divorced," Petra said.

"That was two years ago," Aaron said.

Karl had only the vaguest sense of Aaron's ex-wife. She had a face that worried about things, and he remembered how she once told him that his son kept his distance and said it in a way that implied he might be the cause. He hadn't been to his son's new apartment, though after two years, perhaps "new" wasn't the right way to describe it.

"I need to get some more things," Karl said, because at a certain point begging to stay meant a further loss of precious dignity. Right now the only thing he wished he could lose was his family.

His granddaughter followed him down the hallway to the kitchen and opened the fridge door without asking his permission. "You know, you were the first person who ever made me eat a pickle."

"I'm not sure I could have ever made you do anything," he said.

"I still think they're gross." She peered at the brightly lit but empty shelves, opening the door wider, so he might take a look.

"There's no food in here."

"You're letting all the cold out."

"But there's nothing in here to be kept cold."

"More reason to close the fridge door."

"You told me they would grow hair on my chest," his granddaughter said, returning to the pickles.

Trude had hated pickles as well. He'd chop them up into small chunks and put them in his sister's ice cream, and sometimes she'd pretend to be angry, and sometimes she really would be angry and break into tears. He'd been punished more than once, his mother sending him away without dessert. Regardless of his behaviour, Trude always sneaked something sweet into his room.

"I only came here once, and there was some other place you lived. I visited you there too. That was before Mom and Dad split up. Do you remember?"

Yes, he did. She was about ten years old at the time, the same age his sister had been before he lost her.

Karl was irritated by her intransigence. He'd asked her to do something in his own apartment, and it was only right that she respect his wishes.

"My cigars are in there," he said, pointing not to the fridge but to the lower cabinet to the left of it.

Without further instruction, she closed the fridge and stooped down to open the cabinet door.

"They're in the far back," he said, because just like that, they'd come to an understanding.

His granddaughter thrust her arm and shoulder into the back of the cupboard, rattling the pots and pans stacked like Russian dolls. Karl had stashed them far away from Sophia's scornful eyes. He'd reluctantly promised to do away with the habit. The cigars he'd hidden meant he hadn't been faithful.

Petra pulled out the bundle and brought it to the tip of her nose. "They smell really cigary," she said.

"They shouldn't," said Karl. "But I guess they've been back there for too long. Tobacco should be properly stored to keep it fresh. That's why I never liked smoking cigarettes. They sit neglected on store shelves for months, even years."

"Which is why you hide cigars in the kitchen cabinet?"

Karl held out his hand. "Here, give them to me."

"Where are you going to put them?" she asked without releasing them. "Dad doesn't smoke." She raised an inquisitive eyebrow in the direction of the open cabinet door. "You'll have to hide them from him too. I'll just hold them. Dad won't suspect anything. I'll keep them out of sight until I can slip them to you, okay?"

"Okay. Yes."

She took another sniff of Karl's cigars as if to compare, but this time she appeared to take pleasure in their fragrance.

"I know Dad, and he's super freaked out right now."

"I'm just staying for the night," Karl insisted, but even then, he could see it was a lie. The allotment of cigars in his granddaughter's hand could not possibly be consumed in a single evening.

Petra looked disappointed by his self-deception.

They went back to his bedroom, where his son was busy packing up Karl's clothes into two suitcases that sat open-mouthed on top of the mattress. The drawers were open, the closets emptied. Petra, cigars hidden behind her back, stood by the doorway and eyed her father, as if she'd seen this all before.

Aaron zipped the suitcase closed. "Ready?" he asked Karl.

"Ready," Karl answered. But he wasn't. He'd never been ready to leave, but somehow he'd always been forced to.

3 KARL'S CLOTHES AND SUITCASE HAD BEEN unpacked and put away in a chest of drawers and a closet. There was a window in his room, rectangular, that could slide open from left to right or, using the other panel, from right to left. He'd been ordered not to open the window—a note to that effect was posted on the glass pane, citing high heating bills—though he suspected the reason for keeping it closed had more to do with his perceived safety. Outside was a small parkette with a wooden bench that he would have sat down on, if he'd been allowed to walk out the door himself. There was a note about that too, posted on the locked front door. He tried to force the door anyway but couldn't get out.

He walked into the kitchen. His son—and now, by extension, Karl—lived in a condo-sized two-bedroom, two-bath. The apartment was clean, bright and modern, with varnished hardwood and granite countertops. Pleasant enough, thought Karl, but there wasn't much else that was commendable about the place. It was a temporary home furnished and decorated with future vacancy in mind. He turned on the gas stove, heard the metallic click, click, click, caught a whiff of gas and watched the burner ignite into blue flame. It was one of the back burners. He wanted the one in front, so he started fiddling with the knobs—

"What do you want?" Aaron said, edging him away from the stove.

His son made a habit of startling him like this, of just appearing.

"I'd like to go home." The thought of being alone brought to mind the cracked bar of soap and its withering parchedness. And how had it come to pass that he was living here?

"You can't be on your own right now. Why did you turn the stove on?"

"I'd like some tea," he said.

"I have an electric kettle for that."

It was made of glass, so Karl could see there was already water inside, which he would have liked to change. When his son turned on the kettle, it emitted a blue light. Karl sat down at the table and waited for the tea to be prepared and served.

"I'd like some sugar," he said.

"There's a sugar bowl on the table."

"Not that sugar. My sugar."

"Sugar is sugar, Dad." With that insightful point made, his son fetched two cubes which Karl unwrapped, putting one into his cup and the other in his mouth, just as his own father had done, trapping its sweetness under his tongue. The trick was to use your tongue as a valve, allowing just the right amount of moisture to seep down into the basement of your mouth for two enjoyable cups. It took discipline to tease out the cube's sweetness without dissolving it whole, something his father had taught him through example. Karl might have been drinking tea, but it was the rich, bitter scent of his father's coffee that he smelled.

"Why aren't you at work?" Karl checked his watch. It told him that it was just past nine-thirty on a Tuesday morning.

"Because you're here."

"So you're going to stop working and just stay with me?"

"I never said anything about not working. I can work out of the house."

"It's not a house. It's an apartment. Where's your wife?"

"We're divorced, Dad, separated. Have been for over two years."

Such an ugly word, *separated*, like *serrated*, *snipped*, *snapped*. A tearing away not from what was yours but what was you. He and his son were like two pieces of the same puzzle that did not fit together, because they belonged to different parts of the picture. His son had always liked jigsaw puzzles, wanting to graduate beyond his age group to ever more complicated pictures of German castles, the Alps, sunlit meadows. He could never complete them and always ended up trying to force the hundreds of pieces together, as if through sheer will he could force a picture to emerge.

"And now you aren't working," Karl said.

"I *am* working."

Karl had never really understood the exact aspect of his son's occupation. Aaron worked at a think-tank, so it had something to do with *thinking*, though he wasn't a professor or a scientist. So far as he could surmise, his son was interested in bicycles.

"Are you doing it now?" asked Karl.

"Doing what?"

"Working."

His son answered by getting up from the table and going to take a shower.

Karl wanted to get some fresh air and the sense of a view, something beyond this apartment, so he went out to the balcony. He was prepared not just to ignore the cold and rain that puddled in the far corner but to embrace it. His son feared that the world was warming up and had told him, had actually said this to him, that global warming was the greatest danger facing humanity. He called it a "national security issue," but his son didn't know the first thing about danger, the real danger that came not from the sky but from the person seated right beside you.

"You'll catch cold." It was his son again, his hair wet from the shower.

It struck Karl as contemptible that his son was wrapped in bath towels during a workday. It wasn't so much that a man should work but that he should always be prepared.

"So will you," said Karl.

"Come back inside."

His son meant well, he supposed. He was trying, but Karl felt bullied and patronized. He clasped the handrailing as if he were about to be pulled back inside and stared down at the street.

"Careful, Dad. It's dangerous."

And it *was* dangerous but for reasons his son did not understand. He was on his family's seventh-floor balcony overlooking a wide and elegant street, Mariahilferstrasse, the entrance to every building sized for giants and greatness. He shut his eyes and hoped that when he reopened them, he would see modern bland towers of glass and concrete, but as he feared, when he looked out again, he saw that the street was decked out with immense banners stretching from streetlamp to streetlamp, bearing three signs in endless repetition: "We Thank Our Führer," "One Nation One Empire," "Sieg Heil."

Jews were ordered to vacate their apartments for the duration of Hitler's triumphant motorcade, and his family went to a friend's apartment, one that didn't overlook Mariahilferstrasse, yet they still huddled in one of the backrooms, afraid to approach even the windows that overlooked side streets. His mother had been assured that once Hitler came through Austria, a certain order would be installed. Even if it wasn't a comfortable order, they would manage.

If so, why cower in someone else's apartment? Karl had slipped away and returned to his apartment to watch the parade from the balcony. It was a sea of red banners and noise and great crowds, one row of SS guards surveying the street, the other holding back the ecstatic surging crowds. Every three or four yards there was a white pillar that the Hitlerjugend had adorned with gold swastikas. Like everyone else, Karl was waiting for Hitler, when he felt a strong hand on his shoulder dragging him back inside. It was his father, in a panic. He'd never seen his father scared by anything before then.

It wasn't long afterwards that Jews on their street

were forbidden not only from standing on their balconies but from looking through their windows. "We're no longer Austrians," his mother whispered, as if even in her own home she might be overheard.

Karl had no desire to live among this diminished and disinherited family hiding inside their apartments. He wished to be part of that vast unyielding crowd, not because he was a Nazi or even because he didn't want to be a Jew. During summer vacations in the mountains, Karl and his father dressed themselves in loden jackets, lederhosen, embroidered suspenders, high white socks and mountain boots, while Trude wore a flowered dirndl. She'd execute cartwheels across the alpine grass, when no one but Karl was watching, and Karl would make himself look stupid by crossing his eyes and telling her in a plodding country accent that she needed to milk the cows. "You don't even know what cows look like," she would tell him, and Karl would say, yes, of course he did, they looked just like his sister. Despite herself, Trude would start laughing again, and if, as usually happened, she fell to the ground, he would pull her back up and brush her off, so that no one would suspect what his little sister had been up to.

If they found it funny to dress like Austrian peasants, it was not because they were Jewish but because they came from Vienna. Once, when he and Trude had been walking along the river—his parents had impressed upon Karl a fear that little Trude might stumble into the water and be swept away, so he always walked on the river side—they'd come across a farmer who asked to look at Karl's hands, and he felt he had no choice but to present them to him. "Soft," the farmer said, pressing his nail into his uncallused palm, deep enough to make Karl wince. *Zimperlich* was the word he'd used, which also implied that he was prissy and nervous. Karl was humiliated, especially after the farmer asked for Trude's hands and examined her palms as he would some farm animal. Did the man expect his ten-year-old sister's hands to be hardened as well? The farmer dismissed them with barely concealed contempt. Unable to defend his sister or fight back, Karl sensed he'd proven the farmer's point. He was *zimperlich*.

Nothing about Karl or Trude signalled they were in any way different from any other child born and raised in Vienna. Photographs in the apartment drawing-room proved it: one was of Karl playing in Rathauspark at the age of two, dressed in a double-breasted coat with velvet collar, leggings with straps and a little cap over his curly blond hair. A similar photo of Trude, when she was two, showed them standing side by side, respectful little Austrians. Yet there'd been something in the farmer's attitude that suggested he saw in those soft city hands the very origins of the Kaufmann family.

Karl's grandfather had founded the leather glove factory that had sustained his family throughout two generations and that his father, Bernard, intended to pass on to his son, as his father had before him. Soon after Karl graduated from primary school, his father decided to show his son the workings of the family factory, the source of the family fortune. Karl had seen and smelled the hides, the flesh with fat and dung clinging to them before being stripped clean, salted and graded. And then, in the tannery, the stink of putrid chemicals softening the hides, turning flesh into leather. Fine leather, his father proclaimed. That's what his father had wanted him to see, to understand: it was an issue of quality. Only the very best would do for his clientele, the discerning man and woman who knew and appreciated such differences, though, Karl guessed, not the grisly processes involved in getting to the final product.

The idea that something ugly lurked behind every item of order and luxury—though it was not the lesson his father might have expected or wanted his son to take away with him—lingered with Karl. More than that, it lurked behind even the good, a lesson Karl's own son, who seemed on a perpetual search for some way to help the world heal itself, seemed never to fully grasp.

His father always returned from work at exactly half past six, when the dinner table was already set by the maid, with the silver cutlery, the china soup tureen, the linen serviettes, everything and everyone in their designated place. It wasn't overly formal; there was light and engaging banter, nothing serious, or frivolous either. After dinner, his father retired to his study, where he would catch up on his correspondence with friends and associates for a further hour. Bernard's moments of pleasure were carefully orchestrated. Then, and only then, did he come back out and light a cigarillo, seating himself at the small table in the drawing-room beside the window that overlooked their street. The window would be open if it was warm enough outside. This routine was so established that Karl, without having to be asked, opened the window minutes before his father exited his study.

After the "disturbance"—that's what his parents called it in front of their children, and, who knows, it might even have been what they called it themselves—his father took to sitting at all hours of the day and night smoking his cigarillos one after the other, abandoning a lifetime of careful discipline and control. Once cigarillos were no longer available, he switched to cheap cigarettes that stank of misfortune. His clothes grew ever shabbier, after the best of what he owned was sold along with the household furniture and linens. Soon there wasn't much left but a table and a chair, his father sitting on it with the windows and curtains closed, as if he couldn't accept what was happening outside yet still needed the illuminating light, however dim, of Vienna.

When his father did go out, he never left without his Carinthian Cross service medal pinned to his chest, as if that small piece of metal earned for running munitions through heavy fire in the Dolomites during the First World War would help him or his family survive this too. He'd worn it one day when visiting his bank, asking to see the manager, hoping his decoration would signify that he and his family were respectable, prosperous and accepted citizens of Austria. He looked the part, with the military posture he'd kept up all his life, his waxed moustache and impeccable clothing. They all knew Herr Kaufmann at the bank; he'd been an important and valued customer there for more than twenty years. The manager had refused to see him, and he had walked out of the bank humiliated.

His father took to writing cloying letters, sending copies to Field Marshal Hulgerth, asking him to respect the needs of a decorated war veteran. "I'm an ex-officer—nothing will happen to us. You can rely on that!" he'd shout at his family. To Karl, who'd always pictured his father as worldly, experienced and pragmatic, it seemed he had been broken in half.

"We all need to leave here," Karl told him, and it was the first time in his life that he'd found his voice when speaking to his father.

"Where would we go?"

Karl, caught off guard by his father's question, said, "America."

"America?" His father posed it as a question, as if his son might provide, however improbably, an answer. "How can we go there?"

Karl hadn't thought through his answer. He knew he was being simplistic. He also knew something needed to be done.

"How can we stay here?" he asked.

"At least we're together."

Karl joined him by the window, but unlike his father, he looked out over the city that was both menacing and promising. It was only out there, beyond the window, that help could be found. To stay here was to hide in a cave whose walls were about to collapse. His father was seated; Karl was standing, as if expressing the need to use his feet, to run. He suspected that part of the reason he and Trude hadn't been sent away was that his father could not bring himself to break apart the family.

"Then let's get away together," Karl said, and they were back to where they'd started, his father asking where they could go, and Karl not offering a proper answer, because he was only fifteen, and it wasn't up to him to find one.

Later that night, Karl overheard his parents whispering in a dark pocket of their apartment, trying to fathom the events that had overtaken them and for which, as it would turn out, they would never find an explanation. There was talk now of sending their children away, possibly to Belgium, where a branch of the family resided, or possibly to England. Unfortunately they had been too late in applying for residency permits, and now they'd run out of time and money, or so his father said.

His mother was completely unable to keep up with the daily disasters. She'd tell Karl to go to bed, because it was late and he had to go to school next morning. "But I'm not allowed to go to school anymore," he'd remind her. She was always tripping up that way, then reddening when her mistakes were pointed out to her. Hers was such a delicate response, thought Karl, like an organism whose defensive camouflage had been rendered useless against some vicious evolutionary terror.

"They've gone crazy," his mother would say, but what Karl thought was crazy was the behaviour of his own family, who'd observed the gathering storm clouds without preparing themselves for impending disaster.

"We should do something," Karl pleaded. "We need to

help Trude." Perhaps his mother might better be able to understand if he appealed to her fears for her youngest child.

"What can we do?"

Again the question was put to him, as if he might have an answer. And again, Karl could not offer one.

The moment his mother had to stitch the Star of David onto their clothing, Karl knew they were doomed. He watched her fingers, red and raw in his imagination but in all likelihood pink and nimble, meticulously work their way along the yellow edges, pinning the star to his coat, an action Karl found unbearably intimate. Their daily maid had gone, after the law had been passed prohibiting Aryans from working for Jews. She hadn't been with them for long, so there'd been no tears of regret or unexpected bursts of fury over years of servitude. Instead, a final payment was made, and she left, never to return.

"It's the law," his father said, when Karl questioned him, as if that were a perfectly adequate answer.

The law. Bernard Kaufmann had always upheld it, even when it turned against him, even when it contradicted the higher law of survival.

He was absurd, thought Karl. Did his father think that his Corinthian Cross would cancel the stigma of the Star of David? Though Karl had pleaded with his parents not to go out of their way to mark themselves with the yellow star, his father had told him it was too dangerous to go against the authorities.

When his father ran short of his prized cigarillos, it was because Karl had sold them. It was a testament to his father's decline that he failed to notice the loss of his property, and it confirmed in Karl's mind that what he was doing was, if not right, then certainly necessary.

With some of the money he got, Karl bought pastries for Trude, who always loved the Austrian ritual of *Gabelfrühstück*, the second breakfast. He'd sit and watch her eat, taking delight in her enjoyment, and then they'd play *Schnapsen*, smacking their hands down hard on the pile of cards as if to smother the agitated hiccuping sobs of their mother and the wet heavy sighs of their father in the adjoining room.

"What are we going to do?" Trude asked one day, dragging toward her a pile of cards he'd let her win.

"Escape," answered Karl.

"How?"

"I don't know."

"Promise you'll take me with you."

"I promise," he said.

He'd heard, while trading on the black market, that it was possible to cross the Swiss border, provided you had money or valuables to bribe the border guards. But there were reports of Jews being robbed, not just by bandits but by the guards themselves, who'd take the money and then deny the Jews safe passage. Even if you did manage to cross over, the Swiss authorities were known to send you back, and then you'd be beaten or taken away. Or maybe not. Some returning Jews had simply been allowed to go home, and they were the ones whose stories Karl heard. Nothing was predictable. Nothing made sense.

Yet surely there were tricks, digressions, methods to

ensure survival and escape. That's what he kept attempting to impress upon his father, and also on his mother, who under the kitchen light sewed what was left of their valuables inside the lining of her husband's jacket.

"We can cross over to Switzerland," Karl said to his father. "I've heard the border guards accept bribes." This was a better plan than America, and he expected a more positive response.

"We're not allowed near the border," said his father.

"We're not allowed many things," Karl answered. "But that doesn't mean we shouldn't do them."

"They won't even allow us on the trains."

"You mean they won't allow Jews."

His father looked at him as if he were deficient in mind. As a child, Karl had found the look withering, but now it only induced contempt.

"And what do you think we are?"

"We're what we want to be. So let's not be Jews. We don't have to wear the star."

"I won't allow this family to get into danger."

"You won't allow it? What do you think is happening right now? What is your plan?"

"When the time comes, we'll be safe," his father said.

"How?"

"Don't question me!"

Trude, frightened by her father's raised voice, began to cry. There was no room for secrets in the apartment, and his father, no longer able to understand the new order, could not extend a comforting arm and stop his daughter's tears.

She, too, and in her own way, had to stop respecting her father. Karl could not forgive him. His stupidity. His befuddling deficiency when it came to self-preservation. His own children's preservation.

As it was when they'd encountered the farmer, Karl couldn't offer Trude any help when it mattered. Would he be able to take her to Switzerland with him? Could he save her? Afterwards, in the apartment hallway, he told her that if their parents wouldn't leave, at least the two of them should, but Trude started sobbing again. The idea of leaving her mother and father, their familiar life, no matter how unfamiliar it had become, terrified her. She stifled her sobs, because she knew others in the apartment might hear her, and began to whisper. They'd all been reduced to whispers, thought Karl.

"Don't leave," she said. "Promise me you'll stay here with me."

Trude was probably too young to journey to the border, and once there, what would he do? What if he took her, and everything went wrong? Could he accept that responsibility?

Perhaps his father really did have a plan, but all Karl could properly calculate was what was best for him. He couldn't protect Trude; it wasn't his place to do so. Karl was only fifteen, a boy, he told himself.

"I promise," he said.

The time came when the glove factory was declared *Judenfrei*, and the new Aryan owners were given a contract to supply dress gloves for the German navy, part of a goodwill economic package the expanded Reich was offering its newest acquisition. As the Reich went out to strangle the world with the fine-gloved hands of Kaufmann & Sons, Karl realized he couldn't wait a moment longer.

Late one night, after everyone had gone to bed, Karl slipped past his sister's bedroom and tore open the lining of his father's coat, taking out a gold necklace and two gold and diamond rings.

"Are you leaving?" Trude's silent approach had shown more stealth than Karl's planned escape. She was in her nightgown, obviously unprepared to leave, as if she had always known that he would break his promise to her, that he was a liar.

"Yes," said Karl.

Trude looked at the haul of jewellery in her brother's hands.

"If you go now, I'll never see you again," she said.

"We'll all be together again. I promise."

As if afraid of the draft, she stayed away from the front door as he closed it behind him for the last time. She was probably still standing there, clutching at her nightgown, as he hurried through the dark drizzly streets to the same West Station where Hitler had entered the city, passing the Vienna Opera House, which now displayed a huge banner reading "Jewishness Is a Crime."

Karl had left behind his parents. Worse, he'd left behind his little sister.

Jewishness wasn't his crime. Survival was.

4 AARON AND PETRA STOOD ON EITHER SIDE of Karl, waiting for the lights to change so they could cross onto Yorkville Avenue and stroll past the shops and restaurants. They'd all been cooped up in the apartment watching an Attenborough nature show about the appalling lack of interest male mammals have for their young. Most fathers in nature appeared to be not only neglectful but often hostile, eating their children when they were hungry or just trampling over them when they got in the way. Aaron had turned off the television, declaring it was time for a walk, and on his insistence, they'd all bundled up.

Aaron had grasped the principles of survival long before listening to Attenborough or reading Darwin. The imperatives of natural selection had singled out his father, who'd done what he needed to do in order to survive. His father was born in Austria. He was a Jew. He'd fled and had saved himself. That much Aaron knew but little else. One did not ask a lion for an apology. If his father had been neglectful, then so be it. His father wasn't a predator but a victim, someone who'd been attacked and now needed always to be on his guard. If Karl had trampled over him, it was because he was still running away. From an early age, Aaron had been on guard not only for predators but for victims. They could be just as dangerous.

They crossed the street, he and Petra keeping a few steps back in some unspoken acknowledgement that Karl needed to regain a sense of autonomy and authority. Let him lead them rather than the other way around, but not too far ahead, because his father, withered down to his sinewy essentials, was astonishingly nimble for a man of his age. He might at any moment scuttle off, thought Aaron, and dash for a home he could no longer return to. They were both stuck here and with each other, Aaron no more at home than his father.

They walked by plate-glass windows behind which people ate and drank without the slightest awareness of the family passing so close to their tables, before Karl stopped outside the display window of an antique furniture store, his attention fixed on a polished brass candelabra which sparkled beneath the halogen lights.

"What's it doing here?" his father asked. He meant the menorah in front of him, polished and shiny beneath the lights.

Aaron could have explained this was a shop that sold antiques and that the items were for sale, but he sensed such a straightforward answer would not have assuaged the pain he heard in his father's voice. It was as if he were staring at some lost possession that had been taken from him.

"They're holding it for you, Grandpa. To keep it safe."

Petra took his arm and let him stare at the candelabra for a little longer before gently leading him away from the window. Then she dropped back and resumed her place beside Aaron.

"Grandpa was talking about his sister last night," she said.

"What sister?" Aaron asked.

"You didn't know Grandpa had a sister?"

"I don't think so."

"You mean you're not sure?"

"I guess not."

"Do you know how bizarre that sounds?"

The night before, Aaron had heard them speaking behind the closed door of Karl's bedroom as if concocting a conspiracy. Stupidly, he'd felt excluded like a child, as if they didn't want to play with him.

His father was like a thief, robbing him of who he was. Everything he might need to know was inside his father's head. And his father's head was failing, which may have been the best for both of them, because all Aaron wanted was for this time with his father to end, as cruel or insensitive as that may have sounded. He'd done his best to keep these desires hidden from Petra but without much success.

"I think I remind him of her," Petra said.

Aaron found this alarming. "There's a whole world scrambled inside your grandfather's head. It's making my head a bit scrambled as well."

"Your head has always been scrambled."

Petra did not say this in a kidding way, but he decided to take it as if she had. "That's very kind of you."

"Well, you didn't know about his sister, and you act like you don't really care."

"I don't."

His answer took Petra by surprise. She was trying

to force him into saying things he didn't feel, and it was important to draw a red line through her bullying. Why did she care so much? What was all this to her? She was trying to get under his skin. Karl was angry for being taken out of his apartment and had his own reasons for forging a relationship with Petra. But what was Karl's point in telling her about a lost sister? Why her? Why now? Karl had never provided any links to his past, which was Aaron's past too, of course. After Karl walked out when Aaron was eleven, his mother used to say the only time one should talk about the past was when it had a future. Since it was clear Karl was never coming back, they never talked about his leaving. Soon even his father became the past. There'd been nothing for Aaron to hold on to, no mementos and hardly any photographs. Karl had taken all of him with him.

"Grandad is getting cold," Aaron said, steering them toward the mall entrance on their right.

There'd been an outdoor rink encircled by two floors of shops and restaurants. His mother had often taken him there as a child. They would sit down at one of the inside patio tables and order hot chocolate. Aaron had come back many times throughout the years, watching young women skate past the windows with the happy self-absorption of those who knew they were admired.

One of those women had stepped off the rink, tiptoeing on the edge of her blades until collapsing on the seat next to his. He didn't know her, but he knew her friends, who'd waved at them, while they drank hot chocolate and talked until it turned dark and the skating rink lit up.

He'd married that young woman, and when Petra had turned into a good skater he'd brought her to the same spot, the laces of her white skates tied together and strung around her neck. He'd never been a good skater, and in years past the two of them would wobble along, until the day his daughter spun around him in an easy circle, having shaken off the clumsiness of childhood.

But the rink had been replaced by an enclosed food court, bright and ugly, with a piano in the middle of the atrium, the lid open like a burglarized house. There was no more outdoors, no more fairy lights, and the air, vigorously sucked clean of dust, smelled barren, as if the nutrients had been taken out. He'd dragged Petra through the mall as if maybe the rink had moved, in search of that magical place his mother had taken him to and where he'd met her mother. Petra must have sensed in him something more than anger, because she'd given him her hand, still so small Aaron needed to remind himself not to crush it.

At least they still served hot chocolate, Aaron thought, ordering three without asking either Petra or his father whether they wanted one. He'd worried that a part of Petra would always remain the little girl with skates around her neck, wondering why there was no place for her to use them, but as they sat down at the food court, she seemed oblivious.

"I'm going to look at the stores," she said.

As she walked across a floor she'd once skated on, Aaron realized it was he who still wore the skates around his neck.

"There used to be a skating rink here," Aaron said to

his father, because he couldn't let go of the idea. Staring at his daughter's hot chocolate cooling on the table, he told Karl that's what Mom used to buy him, and he also told him about the pretty women who'd skated beneath the open patch of sky, one of whom eventually became his wife. It seemed, under the glare of shop lights, as incomprehensible to Aaron as it evidently was to his father, who didn't appear to be listening. Where had his father been during those years, and why hadn't he ever brought him here to teach him how to skate? And why was he telling him a story that he should already have known? *This is where I met my wife. This is where I took your grandchild.*

"Petra is talking to a boy," his father said.

"What boy?"

"Behind the pillar."

A peal of laughter echoed through the food court. Petra's. The boy had made a joke. Aaron didn't like him.

She hadn't brought any friends over since Aaron had moved into the apartment. Understandable, he supposed, but it had been a long time since she'd spoken about anything of consequence when it came to her private life.

"Is that her boyfriend?" It rankled that he had to ask.

"She told me that there is someone she likes."

How did his father even feign interest? The man who had never listened to a single story of his and who in turn had never expected him to listen to one of his own was talking to his sixteen-year-old daughter about boys?

Petra and the boy suddenly came into view, his arm around her waist. It was obviously not the first time he'd done this. And the kid was large. Not fat, just big, in a way that suggested he was easily a year or two older than Petra.

"Go easy on her. She's had a hard time of it."

His father stood up and announced that he needed to use the toilet. He did not say "bathroom," because he'd never lost the clipped precision that came from acquiring English as a second language. As far as his father was concerned, he wasn't going to take a bath, so why say it? As he walked away, Karl looked out of place amid the reflective sheen of polished floors and gleaming storefronts, like some cobblestone that hadn't been tarred over. He was, in an intense way, a stranger to Canada.

Aaron, alone at the table, took another sip of his hot chocolate. His father had a sister. This was news to him. But what of it? His father was a dark star, some form of anti-matter from which no light could escape.

Feeling a sharp stab in his stomach, Aaron set his hot chocolate on the table and bent over in pain. This wasn't the first time he'd felt a stab in his gut, but the symptoms had been worsening since his father had moved into the apartment. Did he have an ulcer? Was it something worse? Whatever the problem was, his father wasn't making the ache in Aaron's stomach feel any better. It was as if Karl had taken residence inside his gut. A man can live through the Holocaust and still be an asshole. It certainly didn't make Karl a saint. In the meantime, it wasn't doing Aaron any good thinking about lost skating rinks.

Something touched his arm, and when he looked up, he

saw that it was Karl's hand. His first thought was that his father was reaching out to steady himself, but then it dawned on him that Karl was touching him out of concern.

"I think we should head out of here," Aaron said.

His father raised his right leg and brought the heel of his foot down on the marble floor as if trying to break into the lost ice below.

"Maybe," he said, "we can skate home."

5 Skating home. That's what he and his best friend, Erich Nussbaum, used to do in the purpling light of a winter's day, when the setting sun caught the icy surface of the river, turning it into a rainbow of colours. Nussbaum could skate much better than any of their friends, but he always made a show of flailing and falling on his behind, banging into snow piles at the side of the frozen river especially when there were pretty girls nearby. Karl supposed it was because he knew he was so good that he could afford to pretend not to be.

Nussbaum was modest about other things too. He lived in a much larger apartment, and unlike members of Karl's family who had ridden in on the collapsing borders of the Austro-Hungarian Empire, the Nussbaums' Austrian heritage stretched back many generations.

And then one day, they weren't allowed to skate anymore.

Karl sat around the table with his family discussing whether they were even permitted to own skates, let alone use them, as if the authorities might find it intolerable for Jews to have the slightest means of gliding past Aryans and possibly sliding away. Jews were meant to shuffle now, to be hobbled, said his father.

But not his friend. Not Nussbaum. When the day came for Jews to be rounded up and dragged away, Nussbaum went down to the river, strapped on his skates and, without once pretending to fall, sped along the ice in great long strides, never to be seen again.

At least that's how Karl remembered it, but he couldn't be sure if he had actually seen Nussbaum skate down the river or had conjured the whole thing up in the same way he supposed his son had conjured up the lost ice rink, as if for both of them there would always be a patch of ice hidden beneath their feet.

They hadn't skated home but had walked, and it wasn't his home or even *a* home, just a temporary space inhabited by him, his son and his granddaughter.

Karl looked at his watch without registering the time, so he looked at it again. It was past eight. His son was still sick, some pain in his gut that hadn't gone away, and he heard Petra from the other bedroom, a low rumble like constant wind as she spoke on the phone. She'd told him that kids didn't talk on the phone anymore—they texted each other. She said this as if he needed a lesson in modernity, when in fact, no one had talked on the phone when he was growing up. If you wanted to reach someone, you wrote a letter. Not that he'd written many. Letters needed to have an address, and the only one whose reply he could be sure about belonged to him.

Lying on the bed, thinking about Nussbaum: wasn't that like writing a letter and addressing it to himself? His granddaughter had told him they'd go back and collect the candelabra he'd seen displayed in the window, but he knew it would not be waiting for him, not now, not ever. There'd been a gold candelabra just like it at his family's home in Vienna, and it came with a story. Karl's great-grandfather, a dirt-poor peasant who lived in lower Silesia, had obtained it from a starving French soldier retreating from the Russian front, in exchange for a sack of potatoes.

He still had vivid memories of his great-grandfather's scars, the purpled hairless knots of skin running like a polluted river down his chest. It had happened when the boy's mother accidentally knocked over a scalding pot of coffee. Karl could barely remember anything else about his great-grandfather except those terrible scars and the gold candelabra he'd brought into the house, which had remained with them ever since. There'd been masses of starving soldiers willing to exchange their plunder for food, and with the profits, his great-grandfather had opened a store. So began the ascent of Kaufmann & Sons. Karl understood that such beginnings had been the basis for his family's eventual rise to respectability, a respectability that ended the day his father entered the bank, service medal pinned to his chest, and was denied his money.

It was the candelabra, passed down from one generation to the next, that illuminated the darkened corridors of their family's past. It had looked strangely out of place in the window, as if, like him, it should have been somewhere else. There must be an inner ear for location, thought Karl, just as there was for balance, something he was losing but that his own family never had.

Now Karl had a plan in place, or the beginning of one. He had left other families. He'd leave this one, too, because that was how he survived. The trick was to keep an open mind and wait until a way out offered itself. Then he'd make his move.

FROM THE WEST Station in Vienna, Karl had taken the train to Feldkirch and Hohenems, then crossed the river into Switzerland with only a small bag of possessions and no identification papers. He arrived at a small land crossing, having walked for several hours from the nearest train station. It was dark, and he feared bandits as much as the police. Everything and everyone was a thief, even the air that stole warmth from him.

He gave the border guard the gold necklace stolen from his parents, the delicate chain looking grotesquely out of place in the guard's raw, meaty hand.

The guard, pocketing his family's heirloom, stepped to one side. "Go on, then," he said.

The road was dark beyond the puddle of light at the border crossing. Karl had not planned past this moment and did not know what lay beyond the darkness. He'd envisioned almost everything but this matter-of-fact exchange. His greatest concern had been crossing the border. Now he hesitated in walking away from it.

"There's a camp for people like you," said the guard. "Just keep walking, and you'll find it. Do you have any food?"

"No," Karl answered.

"Too bad, then. It's a long way, but you're young and will make it."

Karl walked all that night and continued walking long after the sky brightened. People on the road were neither hostile nor welcoming, walking or driving past him with a purposeful lack of curiosity. He was something other than a visitor and brought the sort of news people weren't interested in hearing. He asked a few passersby about a camp, but they either didn't know or wouldn't tell him.

Finally a male voice said, "Follow me. I'm going there myself."

A tap on his shoulder instructed Karl to turn around. The man who stared back at him had wary eyes. He was a few years older than Karl and taller than him, but from the beginning, Karl never felt he was being looked down upon.

"It was good luck for you that you found a border guard with the proper combination of greed and sympathy," he said, after learning about Karl's crossing the night before.

Felix Ziegler was German, from Frankfurt, and like Karl had crossed the border alone. There was no mention of Felix's family, and as they walked to the camp, he asked nothing about Karl's.

"Remember, it's not the strong who'll save us," said Felix, "but the weak and the compromised. If you'd arrived an hour later or an hour before . . ." Felix took hold of Karl's shoulders and shoved him backwards. "It'd be back to Austria for you."

After another three hours of trudging, they passed through the barbed-wire gates of Diepoldsau, the Swiss refugee camp that he, Felix and about 150 men and women would now call home.

Karl and Felix along with the other men were accommodated in an empty embroidery factory and slept on straw sacks, while the women were housed in an old schoolroom that had long ago lost its schoolmaster.

"It's cold here, and there's not really enough food, but it's better than where we came from," Felix said.

The menu consisted primarily of potatoes and cheese and wasn't bad as far as such things went, but Karl noticed that Felix always ate with ravenous dedication, as if he weren't sure there'd be a next meal. Karl had never gone hungry before, even during the last months before he escaped Vienna. His family might not have had the best furniture to sit on, but there was always something to eat, and when Karl made money on the black market, there was even a treat of some kind for him and his sister.

Felix, on the other hand, must have known hunger before his escape. He talked about hot soup and steaming wieners with sauerkraut long after the weather warmed. Maybe this was because there wasn't much else to talk about inside the camp. People could be divided into two groups, those who wanted to talk about left-behind family and those who didn't, and it was clear from the start that he and Felix belonged to the latter. If Karl thought about it, that's what bound them together.

Not to say he didn't think about his parents and Trude, but mail between the two countries was mercifully slow. After sending a letter to say that he'd safely made it across the Swiss border, he'd received only two replies, the first from the family expressing relief, the other from his father articulating his outrage over the stolen valuables. Karl replied that they might try to get across the border themselves, but it was months before he received a reply, and then it was to say that the family were relocating to another apartment in Vienna, that they were all right, and that he was not to worry. No mention was made of coming across, either because his father did not wish to acknowledge the advice or because, as was just as likely, he'd never received the letter.

Besides, it was too late. With each passing month, the border was more tightly sealed, with news that officials high and low, for reasons of altruism or greed, were being fired for helping Jews.

It would have been impossible, but even if he had managed to get Trude across the border, she would not have been allowed to stay in Diepoldsau. There were only two children in the camp, a young girl and a boy who at age nine was a year younger than Trude. Their parents had been told by the Swiss authorities to return to Austria or give up the children to foster parents who could properly feed, house, clothe and educate them. The parents refused, and the Swiss, unsure how to proceed, let the matter go, though Karl had seen another family recently turned away from the front gates.

Trude, too, would have been refused entry. Then what would have Karl done? He was too old to be considered a child, too young to take care of his sister. What did he know of anything?

The two children in the camp were educated in ways

practical and impossible. A man not much older than Felix knew all of Faust by heart, and he recited it to the boy, who was urged to memorize entire passages and recite them back.

> *Wild dreams torment me as I lie. And though a god lives in my heart, though all my power waken at his word, though he can move my every inmost part—yet nothing in the outer world is stirred, thus by existence tortured and oppressed I crave for death, I long for rest.*

Karl, whose education had also been halted, listened in, wondering what, if anything, he could offer the boy. Felix, on the other hand, wasn't impressed.

"Faust should make up his mind. If he wants death, he'll get it soon enough in Germany. C'mon, we have our own things to worry about. Faust isn't going to help us."

It wasn't just the boy who was getting an education. He and Felix took lessons from other men in the camp who taught sewing and carpentry and other useful skills. They needed skills, things they could do with their hands, something that up until this moment in his life, Karl had never considered. He was to have taken over his father's company. But that was before the Nazis. It was a different world now. He slept on straw, with dozens of other men, with a warm enough blanket to keep out the cold but not much else to comfort him. It was a rough life, but many of the men, like Karl, were not rough at all. If they didn't talk of home, it was because they were as frightened by their circumstances as Karl was and sensed at the same time that they needed to be even stronger if they were to survive the years ahead. Survival required different skills, including learning how to steal from your parents and break promises to your sister.

Eventually the two children were taken away, the boy's head filled with Faust, the parents weeping by the front gates, where a banner put up by the refugees read, "Thanks to the Swiss People."

"What are we thanking them for?" asked Felix. "We sleep on straw sacks like animals, and except for taking the children, they won't let us leave here, for fear we'll contaminate their country."

Felix's chatter was beginning to get on Karl's nerves. We're safe, thought Karl, that's why we're thanking them. And again he wondered if Trude wouldn't have been better off taken away by the Swiss authorities and given to another family, rather than the one she had.

Occasionally they were assigned jobs outside the fence, and they passed through the gates just as the two children had, to spend their days digging ditches and then, when the summer came, repairing roads in the hot sun. They did it for better rations and the opportunity to remain strong and active.

ONE EVENING, WHEN the early darkness of returning winter was once again upon them, an American showed up at the camp. Noticing the men's work clothes, which, despite the cold, were dampened by sweat, he said, "I bet you'd like to put that hard labour toward making a better life for yourself."

Mr. Solomon Trone represented an organization called the Dominican Republic Settlement Association. He had come to explain to the camp that there'd been an international conference in Evian, France, to deal with the problem of Jewish refugees. Most countries, he'd informed them, had been unwilling to help—a fact that came as no surprise to the refugees—but there was an important exception. To the astonishment not only of those listening to Mr. Trone but also, Mr. Trone suggested, to everyone who'd attended the conference, the president of the Dominican Republic, Generalissimo Rafael Trujillo, was willing, even eager to take in Jews. He wanted strong, healthy men with agricultural experience to settle land in a country Karl had never heard of.

"This is our chance," Felix said later, while raking hot tar on roads that neither of them, he pointed out, would ever use.

"But I don't know anything about farming."

"No one does. We're all from Berlin, Vienna, Munich, what do we know of farming? My father spent eighteen years as an insurance agent, before they took his job away from him."

When Karl told him that his father had been the owner of a leather glove factory, he claimed it was perfect. "He worked with leather, so here's your story. Your father was a successful cattle dealer, and he taught you animal husbandry." Felix caught the look of doubt on Karl's face. "No?

Then what would you prefer to be? A refugee? You think that makes more sense than being a farmer?"

Karl was young and strong, and despite his initial hesitation, he did what needed to be done. He lied to Mr. Trone about his background and experience, adding two years to his age. He needed to lie in order to survive. Mr. Trone handed him a pen, and Karl signed a statement declaring, "I herewith confirm that I am going to permanently remain in the settlement of the Dominican Republic Settlement Association (DORSA) and under no condition for a temporary stay only." It was a strange statement, unclear to Karl but memorable for its mention of permanence, a condition Karl knew had been lost to him forever.

"Where is the Dominican Republic?" asked one of the other men accepted by Mr. Trone as a farmer. "I've never heard of it."

"Who is this Trujillo?" asked another. "And why is he taking in Jews?"

Karl had not been to school for over a year, and apart from some remembered passages from Goethe and what felt like a few other scraps—learned so long ago, it seemed—he couldn't recall much, and the gaps in his knowledge had begun to disturb him. He was relieved to know that he wasn't the only one who was lacking.

It was Felix who put an end to the speculation. "Who cares where it is? Or what it is. Or who runs it. All that matters is that there is a man who has opened the cage of Europe. We're all going to leave this place."

* * *

THEIR FIRST STEP on their journey to freedom was Lisbon, a city awash with refugees like them. The agency responsible for transporting them to their new life in the Dominican Republic put them up in a small hotel. Felix, who at twenty-one was five years older than Karl, had taken the one single bed in their room. Karl slept on one of the three cots. It was crowded, but they were grateful to have any sort of room at all. The agency had also given them a stipend to purchase clothes and food.

But before they left on the next step of their journey on the *Nea Hellas*, a ship that awaited them in the harbour, Felix decided that Karl was going to lose his virginity.

"Let's put our stipend to a more interesting use" was how he put it.

Though Karl was fairly certain the agency money was not meant to be spent on prostitutes, he was happy to go along with Felix's instructions.

"We can't have you travelling to the New World as a virgin," declared Felix. "You can take the clap with you as a souvenir."

The Polish woman in the brothel Felix found for them was pretty in a practical and practised way, and the whole event was over before he knew what to make of it. He'd felt more exhilarated afterwards, when Felix and the other men with whom they shared the hotel gave him congratulatory pats on the back, but after he slipped into his cot, no longer a child but a man, he thought he'd never felt lonelier. Everything he had done up until that point had been directed toward his own survival, but the night in the brothel was different. It had been an act of pleasure, and so in a sense, even before watching Lisbon and Europe disappear behind the wake of the *Nea Hellas*, he'd taken his last step from family and home.

The ship was headed for New York. Many on board were, like Karl, refugees leaving behind one world for another—men who'd fought in the Spanish civil war, French politicians, Polish army veterans—but there were also men on business and even, to Karl's surprise, a few tourists returning home. During the passage across the Atlantic, they were all designated as passengers, served by waiters who wore white gloves and called them *Sir*.

This sudden equality offered Karl the opportunity to discriminate. On a ship where uniformed men opened doors for him, Karl responded with a polite acceptance that demonstrated neither contempt nor undue deference. His acknowledgement of privilege and responsibility had come from his father, and the farther the ship sailed, the closer to his old self he became. Not everyone was capable of negotiating their way with the same ease and acceptance. Felix either talked too loudly or sank into a sullen silence, and Karl couldn't help observing that he, along with several other men from Diepoldsau, ate their food with a hint of gluttony—a habit of which Karl silently disapproved.

If you believed Jacob Weinberg, whom Karl had been seated next to for dinner service, this journey heralded new beginnings. Like Karl, Mr. Weinberg, his wife and two children were travelling to the Dominican Republic. With thinning hair and wire-rimmed glasses, Mr. Weinberg looked older than most of the other refugees. More surprisingly, he had a family. Karl had never envisioned parents and children making the trip, and it made him look back at his own family with bitterness. If only my father had had more foresight, we could have been the Weinbergs, he thought.

Perhaps because of his age or because he was a father, Mr. Weinberg seemed to know more than the others about what was happening and why.

"The British don't want us in Palestine. And we tried to go to America, but they don't want us either. Only President Trujillo has opened the door to Jews." Then he said something that truly surprised Karl. "God has interceded on our behalf, and we are going to work the land and remake ourselves."

Karl had never given God much thought; He just wasn't something talked about with any seriousness in his household. Except during the High Holidays, when his family attended synagogue, discussions of God weren't considered in good taste. That was for the poverty-stricken Jews of Leopoldstadt district, many of whom had come to Vienna from Russia and Romania. They dressed in outlandish clothes, smelled, and talked of God and His business seriously. His father always believed they brought with them the bad odour of anti-Semitism. "They're an embarrassment," he said. If the Austrians disliked the Jews, he'd heard his father say, it was because of them. They didn't fit in.

But Mr. Weinberg wasn't dressed outlandishly—in fact, because he'd managed to bring with him not only his family but many of his possessions from Germany, he was one of the better dressed passengers on the boat, and he didn't wear a long beard or a kippa. His fourteen-year-old daughter, Ilsa, was blond, like Karl, and spent her dinners offering Karl her shy smiles. It made him wonder why it should be God's business to bring her, her family and Karl halfway around the world to live in a strange new land together. If it was His business, then why not save Karl's family too? For that matter, why not just kill the Austrians who'd humbled his father and forced Karl to flee? Or Hitler? *That* would be a God Karl could believe in.

After the plates had been cleared from their table, Jacob Weinberg turned to Karl and asked, "Are you alone?"

Karl shook his head. "I share a cabin with four other men."

This wasn't what Mr. Weinberg was getting at.

"I mean do you have any relatives meeting you when we arrive?"

There was a code among the refugees not to pry into one another's past. Some couldn't stop talking, but the silence of those who wished to say little or nothing was respected. Karl, for instance, had never asked after Felix's past, and Felix had never asked after his.

"No," Karl answered.

"Come with me," Mr. Weinberg said, getting up from his seat.

Karl followed him into the ship's lounge with unforeseen gratitude. He didn't like it when anyone thought he was in need—one of the reasons he'd been uncomfortable about the other men knowing he was a virgin—because it made him feel weak, and weakness was something he'd seen in his father. It was dangerous. For Karl, pity slid straight into contempt. But Mr. Weinberg was his father's age, and he'd made it onto the boat. Karl felt neither pity nor contempt for him.

The large wooden door with a metal studded porthole was open, because the evening was warm, the sea calm. So far it had been a good crossing, thought Karl, who'd grown up with tales of great sea disasters, where ship-wrecked survivors found precarious sanctuary on islands much like the one he was heading for. Yet here was the smell of coffee and beer and pleasant comfort.

A group of refugees had already assembled along a rectangular table whose best seat was reserved for Mr. Weinberg. On the table was a large and detailed atlas.

"This is the Dominican Republic." Mr. Weinberg motioned Karl to come closer, so that he might better observe the green clump of land on the map that lay open before them. "It's a very large island. Notice that there's another country on the island called Haiti." Mr. Weinberg traced the rickety boundary line, which looked as if it had been drawn by the unsteady hand of a child, his finger moving north to south, then turning eastward along the Caribbean coast toward the capital. "This is Ciudad Trujillo," Mr. Weinberg said. "The City of Trujillo."

One of the men in the group expressed surprise that the president shared the same name as the city. Was it a popular name?

"The president renamed the city after himself," answered Mr. Weinberg.

This impressed the refugees sitting around the table,

including Karl. Mussolini hadn't renamed Rome after himself. Even Hitler wouldn't dare change the name of Berlin or Vienna.

"What sort of man names the capital city after himself?" someone at the table asked.

"A dictator," answered another.

"What does he want with us?"

The refugees were more than curious; they were becoming suspicious. Who was this man with the power to save their lives? And why should he do that? Weren't they all Jews? Nobody liked Jews. This was something Karl didn't need to think about; it was something he just knew. They could be poor and dirty or rich and clean, it didn't matter; it was an insight his father never possessed, for all of the obvious hatred that ended up surrounding him. Bernard Kaufmann thought of Jew hatred as some sort of administrative mistake, as if presenting the correct information to the acting authorities could rectify everything.

"He wants our labour," answered Mr. Weinberg.

"Why? Doesn't he have enough of it in his own country?"

"He wants us," reiterated Mr. Weinberg.

"What about those people?" A man pointed to Haiti on the other side of the shaky border line.

"I've been reading about all this. It's a poor but proud country." Mr. Weinberg turned to Karl as if they were all attending a Passover dinner; it was the youngest at the table who most needed to learn the important questions of the day.

"All the islands you see here in the Caribbean Sea, they

were like prisons. Each and every one held slaves. Millions of them, all working for men as cruel and uncaring as any pharaoh of Egypt. The slaves came from Africa, and some tried to become free, but only in Haiti did they succeed. They killed their French overlords and proclaimed themselves the first black republic in history."

Karl and the rest of them all stared at this strange land populated by free slaves, its blue and red flag embossed with an insignia of two cannons, a fan of spears and a lone palm tree.

"So they're black?" asked someone at the table.

"Yes," said Mr. Weinberg.

"Then what about the Dominicans?"

"They're Spanish."

"So they're not black?"

"They're brown, I think."

Mr. Weinberg shifted his finger back up to the north coast as if to move the conversation forward. "This is Puerto Plata, which in Spanish means 'port of silver.' It was from here the Spaniards transported their gold and silver and precious stones. It was here that Christopher Columbus first discovered the New World, it was here that European civilization first took hold, and it is here"—Mr. Weinberg stabbed at an empty, nameless patch of land just east of the silver port—"where we'll be settling."

Farming in the tropics had seemed an impossibility while surrounded by the snow-capped mountains of Switzerland, but it seemed even more so now that they were steaming across the Atlantic on their way toward the tip of

Mr. Weinberg's finger. Everyone had questions to ask: What could they grow on the land? Were there houses for them to live in, or would they need to build their own? Who was already there? And what about diseases? It was the tropics; everyone knew people died in the tropics.

"So blacks on one side, Spaniards on the other, and once again, we're in the middle."

The man who said this offered a cautious laugh, which was picked up by all except Mr. Weinberg, who most likely thought it was God who was in the middle of all things. In Karl's experience, it was men, not God, who had the power to destroy lives or save them. They were sailing toward one such man whose power was so far-reaching he could rename the capital city after himself. Knowing this made Karl feel exposed and wary, as if he were merely cheating authority, not defeating it. For all that he'd heard around the table, he still had no idea what had motivated this man or his country to take in Jews, but he suspected the answer might not be pleasant.

After the meeting ended, a Spaniard who had overheard their conversation leaned next to Karl at the railing. "The Dominican Republic, eh?" The man let out a morose whistle. "You'll die there for sure."

But Karl had not come this far, and done what he had done, just to die. And he wouldn't. That was the promise he made to himself as the boat glided past the Statue of Liberty's unexpectedly stern and gloomy face. America was the future, but not his. He and the other colonists—for that was what Mr. Weinberg and the others had started to call themselves—had been issued temporary visas for the United States only after they'd been able to prove they were travelling on to the Dominican Republic, that a country other than America was willing to take them in.

The boat docked at Ellis Island, where the officials wore ill-fitting uniforms and looked bored. Some had faces like pigs, fat and red, while others were long and narrow with sallow cheeks. Unlike the Swiss guards, these men could not be bribed or appealed to. They were doing their job, and their job was to keep them on Ellis Island and make sure none of them ever set foot on Manhattan, until another boat was ready to take them away.

And when would that be?

No one knew. Not even Jacob Weinberg, who was taken to another building, one for families, while Karl was moved to an enormous dormitory filled with single men. Again they were refugees, not passengers, barely tolerated and strictly controlled. In this atmosphere, Felix, whom Karl guilty admitted to himself he'd been avoiding during their boat journey, once more came into his own.

"They think we might be fifth columnists."

Karl looked at him questioningly.

"It means they think we might be German spies, so they won't let us go to New York, even for an hour. First we are Jews, now we're Nazis. We are everything to everyone except what we are."

They were outside when he said this, staring at the sky-line, and the high wall of brick and stones, the great tall buildings, seemed menacing even in the sunshine. Cars could be seen speeding along the far shoreline, oblivious to their existence.

"I was in New York," a woman said, joining them. Her name was Esther, and Karl recognized her from aboard the *Nea Hellas*. After complaining about the food and service, she'd taken to her cabin and disappeared. It was rumoured that she'd been a talented pianist and was bitter that the Nazis had put an end to her career. "And I've been to Boston and San Francisco and Philadelphia." She named a few more places that Karl recognized from the westerns he'd watched at the Stadtkino cinema back in Vienna, places like Albuquerque, New Orleans and Houston. It seemed incredible to Karl that he was here, in this same land.

"Are you travelling to the Dominican Republic?" she asked.

"Are you?" Karl asked, incredulous. He had no idea what it would be like, but he was certain there weren't going to be any cabin doors to hide behind.

"Yes."

"What do you think it will be like?" Karl asked her, because she seemed so well travelled.

"I don't think it will be anything like this," put in Felix.

"No, I suppose it won't," she said mournfully, staring at the New York skyline that lay just beyond their grasp, along with the road that could take them there.

Eleven days later, they were loaded onto guarded buses and taken along that very same road. Requests were made to drive through the city, if only to take a look, to be treated as a tourist, a visitor. Instead they were taken straight to a dock, where a cargo boat far smaller and less hospitable than the *Nea Hellas*, with thick rust stains running down its sides, was waiting to take them to Puerto Plata.

6 THE COLONOSCOPY WAS, AS THEY TERMED it, "precautionary"; they were searching for pre-cancerous polyps. But the only thing the monitor revealed, as the camera snaked its way up Aaron's intestine, was a glistening pathway of healthy tissue.

Afterwards, in the recovery room, he felt his stomach cramp, the body's price of having been made to reveal itself, and he pulled his knees closer to his chest in the hope of staunching the stabs of pain. He was in a room with other beds, other patients, all recovering beneath dimmed lights and thin blankets. He heard someone moan, and then, as if it were a birdcall, someone else moaned in response.

It had taken another attack after the mall for Aaron to see a doctor, who'd pressed her fingers into his belly, asked a few questions and then booked him for a colonoscopy.

"Is there something wrong?" he asked.

"That's what we're going to find out," the doctor told him.

His wife would have driven him to the hospital, if Aaron had still been married, because that's what people who were married did for each other. But Aaron was no longer married, and he couldn't ask Petra to take him. So he'd locked his father inside the apartment because he'd only be gone for a few hours, made his way alone to the hospital and then up to the fifth floor, where he checked in, disrobed and let himself be wheeled into the OR with a Demerol drip plugged into his forearm.

"You're free and clear," the doctor told him after the Demerol wore off, but Aaron knew that he was neither of these things and that what had beleaguered him was a secret polyp, nurtured in some other part of his body, that could be neither found nor excised.

"Why am I having this pain in my gut?" he asked.

"You probably have lactose intolerance."

"That's it?"

"You'd like something more? Your body no longer produces the enzyme capable of breaking down lactose, which is found in most dairy products. It's particularly common among the Chinese and Ashkenazi Jews."

"You said 'probably.' Is there a test?" asked Aaron.

"Sure. Go home and drink a glass of milk."

Or have some hot chocolate at the mall, thought Aaron.

The sky was startlingly intense as the hospital doors slid open and offered exit. If he didn't have a wife to drop him off at the hospital, he certainly didn't have one to pick him up. He'd signed the consent form that demanded he have a responsible adult accompany him home and called an Uber. He reached into his pocket for his sunglasses to cut the brightness but realized he hadn't brought them with him. Had it been overcast this morning? Aaron couldn't remember as he stepped into the taxi and slumped into the back seat, the greasy funk rising off the seat-cloth a welcome tonic after the medicinal air of the hospital. As they pulled away, it occurred to Aaron that he'd been tested not only for a missing enzyme in his body but also for proof of patrimony.

His father had always been at such pains to deny him his past, starting the day he'd brought home a census form from school. In a box marked "Religious Affiliation," Karl had written the word *NONE* in capital letters.

Aaron had fought him on it.

"I'm Jewish," he'd insisted.

"Your mother isn't Jewish."

"So?"

"That means you aren't Jewish either."

"Well, if I'm not Jewish, then what am I?"

"You're nothing."

His father had actually appeared proud, as if it were an achievement to make his son into nothing, but even now, with the Demerol still coursing through his veins, he felt the sting of it. To be nothing was to be anything. He supposed that was the point, though his father had never put it like that to him.

Aaron watched the tall and important buildings speed past him, blending into one another, as if he, Aaron, had the power to unify their purpose. He'd been busy all his life inside such buildings, and he didn't like the sensation of seeing things from the other side. He felt exposed as he got out of the cab and waited impatiently for the elevator to take him to his apartment. It was just past two. If he was lucky, Karl would be asleep.

But Aaron wasn't lucky. Opening the door, he found his father playing cards in the kitchen. With Petra.

"That's yours," his daughter said, picking up a small pile of cards and placing them face down on his side of the table.

Karl plucked a card from his hand and also placed it down. She did the same, and then he threw down another card, and they continued this way, back and forth in a competitive rhythm, until Petra shouted, "*Schnapsen!*" and brought her hand down over the pile, hesitating for just a second to give her grandfather a fighting chance.

"*Schnapsen!*" answered Karl. "It's yours."

His daughter claimed the pile. "It's a game Grandpa taught me," she said, without looking up.

Aaron had been staring at them. The game was one he'd played with his father long ago. He couldn't remember why they'd stopped.

"Everything okay?" he asked.

"Sure, considering you locked Grandpa in the apartment."

"I didn't lock him in," Aaron said. It was a weak answer. He'd done just that. "What are you doing here? You should be at school."

"Grandpa phoned me."

"He did?" Aaron turned to Karl. "Did you phone her?"

"I just said that he did," Petra answered.

"I didn't know where you were," Karl said.

"You were asleep when I left."

"I heard the door close," said Karl. "So I was awake."

"You were in your bedroom."

"That doesn't mean I was sleeping."

"I had to open the door with my key," Petra said. She

stood up from her chair and pulled it out, proffering it like a piece of evidence to a jury. "What's wrong with you? You can't lock him inside. He's not a dog."

Aaron wanted to lie down. He was just thinking about pulling the pillows out of the closet and resting on the couch, when the phone rang. It was Isobel.

"Hi," he said.

His ex-wife ignored his greeting. "Where's Petra?"

"She's here."

Aaron cupped the phone and whispered, "It's your mother," as he watched his daughter, his precious only child, mouth the words *You're fucked*.

"That's odd, Aaron, because she's supposed to be in school. I've been calling you, leaving messages."

"I was in the hospital," he said, playing for sympathy.

"The hospital? What for?"

"I had a colonoscopy today. They thought there might be a problem, something serious." Aaron offered a short pause in the hope it would elicit an expression of concern from her and the room. Then he said, "I have lactose intolerance."

"Is that some sort of joke?"

"No."

"You can't just pull our daughter out of school without telling me."

"I didn't pull her out. She just came over."

"Promise it won't happen again."

"I promise," he answered.

"How is Petra?" she asked, changing tone.

"Fine," he said, using one of their code words to indicate he wasn't free to talk openly. Divorce doesn't eliminate those little intimacies, thought Aaron. They continue to grow like fingernails on a dead body.

"She's dating someone."

"I know."

"I'm dating someone."

"That I didn't know."

"I thought Petra might have told you."

"No."

"I suppose she wouldn't. Anyway, I'm not sure how she's taking it, but she does seem to spend a lot of her spare time with your father."

"Is Mom pissed?" Petra asked, after he got off the phone.

"No."

"You were in the hospital because you have lactose intolerance?"

"I didn't know I had it. That's why I went."

"I have a few friends who are lactose intolerant. They can't eat ice cream, so they take a pill or something. That's why you locked Grandpa inside the apartment? Because you can't eat ice cream? That's pathetic, Dad."

His father still held a fistful of playing cards in his hand and was waiting to resume the game.

"Do you have trouble eating dairy products?" Aaron asked him.

"Trouble?" his father answered.

"It's a problem Jews suffer from."

"They do? I used to make cheese. And milk cows. That's

why you went to the hospital? Because you get stomach aches from cheese?"

Aaron detected contempt in his father's voice, as if his son had let him down with such a banal weakness.

"Yes, apparently. But they didn't know what the problem was," he reiterated.

"You milked cows?" Petra asked her grandfather, who nodded. "Did you know that, Dad?"

"No, I didn't."

"Maybe if you didn't lock your father inside the apartment, you'd know a lot more."

"Petra, can I have a word with you?" Aaron made his way to the balcony. Petra reluctantly joined him. He slid the door closed behind them.

"I want you to know how much I appreciate you taking care of Grandpa. He's old and has a lot of problems. Maybe this is a bit too much for you."

"Of course it's too much for me, Dad."

The honesty made Aaron laugh. "This is my fault. Grandpa's not going to be staying here much longer, so you won't have to go through this anymore."

"You mean so *you* won't have to go through this anymore."

"I can't take care of him, Petra."

"Sure. It's easier that way," she said. "Like getting a divorce."

"Getting a divorce isn't easy, Petra."

She'd burst into tears the day they'd told her. Aaron had rehearsed the scenario, talked with other divorced parents, even a therapist, but inevitably, it seemed, he and his ex-wife had fallen into the same predictable pattern all parents do when their marriage comes to an end. They'd told Petra that it wasn't her fault, that they would both continue to love her, that they would still be a family, just not one that lived under the same roof, which even then never made sense to him. With all the divorces that had preceded his own, Aaron was astonished there wasn't a wider range of options for expressing himself. Instead, all those breakups had produced the opposite effect, blunting and dulling the language until it all sounded wearyingly familiar.

"You'll always be our daughter," he'd said, taking her into his arms. He smelled the scent of childhood in her hair and wanted to find that special brush he'd used when she was a little girl, the one with the red rubber tips attached to the end of each bristle so that her scalp wouldn't be scratched as he ran the brush down her hair.

Since then, they'd hardly mentioned that day, or the divorce for that matter. Petra had stayed with her mother, and Aaron had moved into this apartment.

"Do you want to talk about it?"

"What, you and Mom getting a divorce?"

"Yes."

"Is that why we're out here on the balcony?"

"I just wanted to talk."

"About what?"

"About this."

"Okay. Why did you and Mom get a divorce? Did she catch you cheating with someone?"

"No."

"Did you catch her cheating with someone?"

"It wasn't anything like that."

"Then, what was it?"

"Sometimes things just end, Petra."

"That's great, Dad. Thanks for sharing."

"We weren't happy together."

"Why not?"

"If people had the answer to that question, they'd be a lot happier than they are."

"Did Mom tell you she has a new boyfriend?"

He sighed. "Just now, over the phone."

"I don't like him."

"You're not supposed to like him. I don't like him."

"You haven't met him."

"I don't need to."

"He tries."

"Well, there's that."

"Yes, there's that," she said accusatorially.

One minute they were allies, the next enemies. It was hard to keep up, and Aaron suspected it might not be the divorce they needed to talk about but everything that had happened and might happen afterwards. Her mother had met someone else. He would meet someone else. And there were other concerns: his father. Karl's insertion into the household had altered Petra's family equation.

"What are we doing for Thanksgiving?" Petra suddenly asked.

"Thanksgiving? I haven't thought about it."

"No surprise there. I'd like Grandma to come."

"I'm not sure she'll want to be here."

"I also want Mom to be here."

"We don't live together anymore, in case you haven't noticed."

"She just wants to hang out with her new boyfriend. I want Mom and Grandma here for Thanksgiving. I want my family around me," Petra said it as if family were a warm garment she could wrap around herself.

It must be a phase, thought Aaron, a moment in the wake of a divorce when a child wants to reconstitute the fragments, but he found something manipulative and possibly bullying in her request. That, too, was probably normal. She wanted all the adults to assemble on her behalf. He and his ex were civil toward each other, but there was no point pushing things. And before Karl had shown up unexpectedly at his mother's home, it had been years, actually decades, since they'd all broken bread together.

"It's not up to me," he told Petra.

Aaron retreated to the living room. He wasn't a good father. According to his daughter, he wasn't a good son either. For that reason, he sat on the couch, while his father and daughter resumed their card game. Petra threw out a card from her hand, then his father did the same, and the process repeated itself, back and forth, until Aaron closed his eyes and fell into a deep sleep.

7 IT WAS UNBEARABLY HOT AND THE SHIP stank of oil and paint, but the weather cooled as they made their way out to sea and became even cooler for the first two days of their journey southward. Then the heat returned and grew, staining the sky a mournful grey; it began to rain, forcing people inside. The sea roughened. Lying in their beds, the men in Karl's cabin started to vomit.

"What godforsaken place are they taking us to?"

"It's hot as hell."

"It is hell."

Karl rested on the upper bunk, rocked by waves and the shuddering propeller shaft. Nerves began to fray; even Mr. Weinberg, pale and exhausted through most of the voyage, looked defeated. It had been a long journey for all of them, and their capacity to imagine what awaited them was almost depleted by the time their boat glided into the tropical waters of Puerto Plata, its false, bright colours reminding him of the sickly vomit that had been spilled on the boat during the crossing. He couldn't explain the heat, and he felt it needed explaining. Much more astonishing were the improbable notes of the German national anthem wafting across the water.

To the strains of *"Deutschland, Deutschland über alles,"* the boat sailed past a square-walled fort that must have dated back to the Spaniards, with long abandoned sentry posts at each crumbled corner. A volcano-shaped mountain soared into clouds that had been created by its own height and dwarfed the town below, with its buildings of painted wood and tin-capped roofs. They weren't in New York anymore; they certainly weren't in Germany or Austria. He could see that plainly, but what he heard was all too familiar.

"Why are they playing that hateful song?"

It was Esther, wearing her best dress, stockings and black shoes, with a fashionable purse in hand, as if she were about to go shopping in Manhattan. She tentatively leaned over the wooden railing and looked down at the sea, as if it might be the source of her confusion and worry.

As more refugees joined them on deck and the ship docked against a concrete pier, the source of the music came into view. A raised platform on shore held a full band dressed in white uniforms. In the broiling sun, they played the anthem over and over again, while Dominican flags fluttered above them.

"I think they want to welcome us," Felix said.

"How is that possible?"

As with the other men, Karl wore a jacket and hat, but nobody, not even Esther, came close to what Felix was wearing. He had on a cream-coloured panama suit, his shirt buttoned up to his neck, a fedora rakishly tilted on his head.

To the continuing tune of *"Deutschland, Deutschland über alles,"* Karl followed Felix down the ship's gangplank. Maybe they *are* welcoming us, thought Karl. Over there, they were Jews; perhaps in this new land, they were considered Germans and Austrians. Wasn't that the point of getting away: to reclaim their birthright?

If so, it didn't make their first steps down the narrow gangplank any more steady. Dozens of men and women held onto the sides as if they might fall off.

"You must be admiring my suit," Felix said. "I bought it in Portugal off a man more desperate than myself. You'll find a lot of men like that in Lisbon. You paid for a prostitute, I bought a suit."

After disembarking from the boat, they entered a customs shed sheathed in corrugated steel. The anthem was less pronounced inside the building, but still it played, as the customs officers inspected their papers, putting people on edge. The officials were brown-skinned but not as dark as some of the Portuguese he'd seen in Lisbon, and they seemed to respond to Felix's theatrical style. A well-tailored officer inspected his papers through mirrored sunglasses at what appeared to be a respectful speed.

Still, there were queues for all of them, and despite the heat and humidity, few of the men thought of taking off their hats or jackets until they were safely on the other side of the processing line and assembled at the main exit of the customs shed, their suitcases and steamer trunks collected beside them.

They waited, for what no one knew exactly, but they were in someone else's country, and no one wished to complain. They turned their suitcases into seats and lit cigarettes, until they were summoned outside the shed in front of the platform Karl and the others had seen from the ship. Mercifully, the band had stopped playing. The musicians sat there hugging their instruments, seemingly exhausted. Finally a man walked onto the platform and strode to its centre. He stared at them with the confidence of a high official. He was handsome, with dark hair slicked back and a pinstriped suit that looked as if it had never been worn before today. He opened his mouth and shouted in Spanish.

"The General welcomes you to your new home. Here you will be in peace and quiet."

These translated words came from the left of the group, so everyone turned away from the man standing before them. Their translator wore khaki pants and a white short-sleeved shirt, and when he clapped, Karl saw how the sun had bleached the hair on his forearms a pale blond. The man continued to clap, until it became apparent that they were meant to join him. The man on the stage accepted the applause and attention with an embracing smile before continuing.

"In Palestine there is bloodshed, but here you will not have any kind of that. From this moment forward you are not foreigners but Dominican! And we want the brains and skill of the Jewish people. I myself am one-eighth Jewish." Hearing his translated words, the man on the platform repeatedly and boastfully pointed to himself.

This didn't sound right to Karl. Who at this time would want to claim Jewish blood? One-eighth Jewish meant seven-eighths *not* Jewish, an equation of survival. He looked around to see if this made any sense to the others, but after the translation they too seemed confused, if not suspicious.

What was the man up to? There was polite clapping as he continued his speech, eventually becoming so animated that he failed to pause for the translation that, when finally offered, didn't seem to justify the man's excitement. His words were repetitive and general: you are welcome here; you will be given citizenship; we will build a future together. Bulbs flashed; photographs were taken. A man whom Karl took to be a reporter scribbled down the words of the official. Standing in the debilitating sun, Karl lost interest. He waited for the speech to end, which eventually it did, but everyone continued to stand there, including the man on the stage, who now seemed as exhausted as the band.

Shuffling his feet and feeling ever thirstier, Karl fixed his eyes on an American limousine parked in the shade of a cluster of palm trees. Two men were busily cleaning the polished black metal while a third, in driver's cap and uniform, idly smoked a cigarette until the back door opened, catching the limousine driver off guard. Quickly throwing his cigarette down, the driver held the door open for a man who, sartorially superb but comical in his dress uniform mugged with medals and ribbons and epaulettes and gold braid, strode toward the stage. It seemed Generalissimo Rafael Trujillo himself had come to meet his new European refugees.

On cue, the band shot to attention and began to play, but it was a different anthem this time, the Dominican one, Karl assumed, one written for this man on stage, adding to his pomposity and stature. Even the flags cracked to attention. Then a row of pretty young women joined him on stage.

On orders of the dictator, Karl and the others formed a queue and one by one were led up to the podium, where the young women offered glasses of cold water. Up close, there was a fastidiousness to the General that Karl sensed was brutal. He was short, with a squat face that Karl was fairly certain had been covered in some sort of makeup designed to make his face look whiter than it was. He wore a moustache like Hitler's, though the General's was shorter and less bushy, a thick line connecting nostrils to upper lip.

Karl had spotted Hitler being driven through the streets of Vienna, but this was the first dictator he had seen up close. Dazed, he shook the soft hand of his new benefactor and then ambled to a table and accepted his new-found citizenship. They were no longer visitors. In Karl's hand was a piece of paper that claimed he was now a Dominican citizen, an act of national alchemy that was just short of magical.

Clutching his new identity papers, which were already stained by the sweat seeping from his fingertips, Karl was made to listen to a speech by Trujillo that he could not understand and that no one translated from Spanish. When the speech was over, the General speedily exited the platform and slipped back through the open door of his waiting limousine and, seconds later, was whisked away to the New World capital that he'd renamed after himself: the City of Trujillo.

The translator moved to occupy the spot left by the dictator.

"Shalom, everyone. My name is Joseph Stern. I'm from Sosua, a settlement of and for Jews located fifteen miles down the coast of this rich, fertile island. I know it has been a long journey for all of you and that you must have many questions, but first let us go to the bus and take you to your new home."

It may have been a long journey, but someone asked, "Why were they playing the German anthem?"

"They think we like it," said Stern.

"Didn't you tell them that we don't?"

"What to say and what not to say here is complicated" was how Stern left it.

Karl stepped onto a wooden bus painted in bright colours, as if the homes he'd seen from the boat had been put on wheels. There was no glass in the windows, and from his bench-seat, Karl watched the passing scenery without obstruction.

"Sugar cane," Joseph Stern called out, as they passed row upon row of plants undulating like green waves over the land, so tall that at times they blocked the view of the mountains and sea. Some had large seed stalks that made Karl think of the feather plumes the Viennese Horse Guards wore on their helmets. For all of its difference, the mountain ranges and brilliant greens reminded Karl of everything he'd loved and lost in Austria. He was even beginning to feel strangely at home, when he spotted some men in the fields, black men. They held machetes in their hands and wore soiled shirts and pants held up with rope belts. Maybe these were the Haitians that Mr. Weinberg had talked about. They stared at the bus with barely a glimmer of curiosity. And then the sugar cane ended, the flat, expansive fields giving way to humped hills while the bus slowly wound its way along a narrow pot-holed road that carried not a single other vehicle. They were being taken farther and farther away from anyone who could harm them. Karl was lost, and felt lost, but that was the point, because if he didn't know where he was, then neither did anyone else. No one in his family had ever seen anything like the world that now unfolded before him. He was truly alone.

The bus passed through a village that was nothing more than a few wooden houses with thatched roofs, where the adult villagers returned their waves with a little more curiosity than the men in the fields. The children ran after the vehicle, excitedly shouting at them, and the scene repeated itself through several more villages, until finally the bus turned left toward the sea and they arrived at their destination. Sosua.

The bus driver turned off the engine. It became very quiet, the metallic clicking of the bus radiator mingling with the swish of horse tails and clucking chickens. There were about a dozen buildings, some not fully built, scattered over a cleared field. They had stopped outside a small general store that Joseph Stern explained sold dry goods and fruits and vegetables, all grown by the colonists. Several horses were tied to a post, their heads slumped in rest.

"Most of us are still out in the fields," he said, adding proudly, "We have twenty-six thousand acres."

Karl had no idea what twenty-six thousand acres of land looked like, but it sounded a lot, and he suddenly became aware that when Joseph Stern said "we," it included himself

and all the other men, women and children who stepped off
the bus. No one ran or shouted. No one said much of anything. They just stood around, close to the bus, as if unsure
whether they were supposed to get back on it again. Rolling
up his sleeves and draping his jacket over his bare arm, Karl
was stunned to think that this strange, beautiful place was
now his home.

Four of the largest buildings in the cleared field were
housing barracks, and he was directed toward the one at
the far right. Inside, he discovered a total of sixty or so
beds lined up on either side of the wall. Beside each bed
were small shelves, many of them already filled with personal effects, books and a few photographs of mothers and
children and families. Claiming one of the spare beds, Karl
knew he didn't have anything to put on his empty shelves,
no books or photographs; all he had were two of his mother's rings that he'd stolen and not yet sold. Mosquito nets
fluttered in the breeze. After two long sea voyages without
any ill effect, he felt vaguely seasick.

News of the arrivals quickly spread through the colony,
and soon a crowd of men appeared wearing white, wide-
brimmed hats, their clothes stained by sweat and mud from
working in the fields. They surrounded Karl and the others,
clamouring for information. The colonists were bombarded
with questions. Where had they come from? What was happening in Europe? Names were exchanged, identities sought,
in the unlikely hope that someone might bring news of their
families back home.

Karl stepped back from the crowd, uncomfortable with

this need of news and home. Besides, he and the new arrivals had questions of their own. What was this place? someone asked. What were they expected to do? Grow food, came the answer. Tend cattle. Build homes. There were almost five hundred of them now. Many more were hoped for, they said. Children in shorts and canvas lace-up shoes ran between the barracks. And there were women. Some of them were beautiful, tanned and healthy, most of them not much older than Karl.

The Generalissimo had given them the land, said the colonists, it was theirs. The barracks, along with some of the other buildings, were from a long-abandoned plantation. They had no electricity, but they would have it soon, along with running water. That was another job for them to do. For now, each of the new colonists would be issued a hurricane lamp. And they would need work clothes. A cluster of men arrived on horseback and added their voices, saying that the newcomers would need to learn how to ride so that they could tend to the cattle in the hills. Felix, still dressed for the customs shed and Spanish colonnades, stared at them with incomprehension, as if to say that while he might have dug a few ditches in Switzerland for extra rations, he was not then and certainly not now—now that he was free—the sort of man who tended cows in the hills.

"Let's show them the beach!"

Karl followed a group past the general store to a path at the edge of the cleared field. There he saw Jacob Weinberg and Ilsa walk down a wide path that sloped toward the sea, until they arrived on the edge of a white sand beach.

"It's paradise," Mr. Weinberg said, gathering his family around him. He beckoned for Karl to join them, but he kept his distance.

"This way!" someone shouted. Karl heard the splashes of plunging bodies. "Don't be shy."

Karl didn't have any bathing trunks—it was the last thing he had imagined taking with him—but following the lead of several colonists beckoning him from the sea, he draped his shirt over a tree root, took off his shoes and, even though he was wearing his best trousers, edged his feet forward toward the blue waters that deepened and darkened farther from the shore.

He expected the water to be cold and braced himself; instead, a feeling of well-being spread through his body as he waded into the warm Caribbean Sea. Ilsa, who had never done anything more than smile shyly at him, joined him.

"It's been a long journey," she said.

"Yes, it has."

"And we've hardly ever spoken. You've been ignoring me," she teased, taking his hand beneath the water so that no one else would see. It was an act both daring and timid, and it reflected how everyone, including Karl, felt about their arrival.

Until that moment he'd hardly even noticed her. Despite all the days they'd spent together travelling from Lisbon, he'd only had eyes for the future he was sailing toward. It was Ilsa's father who had spread out the map of their new home and shown him where he was heading. His fourteen-year-old daughter was someone to be ignored or humoured during the dinner service. Karl had sat beside her a number of times, and he'd even danced with her, but always his gaze was directed toward her father and the other men, seated at a table, studying maps or talking politics, while the ship plowed its way to their new home. When he was with Ilsa, he always felt like one of the children left behind, and so concerned had he been about what people might think of him, and the future awaiting him, that he'd never even considered the possibility of this moment in the water, when the flickering sunlight on Ilsa's feet made it look as if she were dancing.

Ilsa had waded into the water wearing a collared, long-sleeve shirt, which she'd rolled up. It wasn't right for the beach, for this place. Without letting go of his hand, she sank down and dunked her hair beneath the water. He leaned down as well, so as not to sever the connection, and when she re-emerged, he noticed her breasts and the way her body curved and shimmered in ways that, like her dancing feet, seemed like an optical illusion.

"I like it here," she said.

In the distance, the volcano-shaped mountain that loomed over Puerto Plata was clear and sharp in the late-afternoon light. It seemed like years had already passed since Karl stepped off the boat into his new home.

8 "I'M NOT SIGNING ANY PAPERS," KARL SAID. His son slid the power of attorney document across the polished coffee table, turning it right side up, pen in hand in preparation for Karl's signature.

"I know it's difficult and believe me when I say I wish this wasn't happening, but it is and, unfortunately, we have to deal with it." His son spoke with the unctuous tone of a lawyer.

Karl stared hard enough and long enough at the legal document to ensure that his son was forced to examine it as well. It had coloured tabs jutting out the sides, little candy sweets for being a good boy. Karl had survived the murderous hands of dictators. He'd never allow some measly attorney to gain power over him.

"I won't sign this."

"Dad, it's precautionary."

"That's what they always say."

In need of fresh air and a view that extended beyond the walls of the apartment, Karl stood up and walked toward the sliding doors leading to the balcony.

"It's locked," said his son.

"Of course it is."

"It's raining."

"Yes, I can see that it's raining," Karl said and imagined

his son's condescending reply. *You might see that it's raining, but you don't understand that it's raining.* He pulled the handle; the door remained firmly in place.

"We can go out for a walk a little later, if you like," said Aaron.

"But I want to go out now. You're treating me like a dog."

"I don't see a collar round your neck, Dad."

Karl pulled the door handle again and in his frustration felt as if the entire world beyond the windowpane was locked, the trees and sky, even the grass, all of it set rigidly into position, motionless and inaccessible for those who, like Karl, no longer held a key.

How long was he expected to stay here, petulant and aggrieved like a child unable to control his own circumstances? He knew that his son kept the front door locked as well, for fear he'd wander off. Not too long ago, Aaron had gone off to the hospital, and Karl had paced the empty apartment in a panic over his need to escape, twisting and pulling the front door handle to no effect. It was illegal, locking a man inside a house, but he hadn't called the police. He didn't want them monitoring his predicament, putting things down in writing. It would work against him. Instead Karl had phoned his granddaughter, who came and slid the balcony door open and gave him the sense that someone gentle and kind was assisting him, easing his escape. She'd let him go outside to have a smoke, and that was when he began to calm down. They needed to look out for each other, Karl thought.

The street his son lived on, with its conglomeration of apartment buildings, appeared to be an anomaly. Some of them were fairly tall. He had no recollection of their construction, though he had to acknowledge that he must have been a witness to it. Buildings had been built, communities formed, the maple and oak saplings planted in trust that they would grow into the trees that now towered over him and his son.

He'd been one of the few refugees from Sosua to choose Canada over the United States, landing in Montreal and taking a train to Toronto. He'd travelled along a ribbon of steel that sliced through some of the most boring landscapes he'd ever set eyes upon. It was amazing how small the trees were in Canada, nothing more than twigs, except in the cities, where they grew to the height and stature he'd once imagined had covered the whole country. At first, he thought it was because of the weather, all that cold and darkness, and maybe the soil too, but later he found out that almost every tree in Canada had been felled and chopped to build the fleets of the British Navy, among other things, and what remained outside the train window was simply their orphaned offspring—an entire country reduced to a state of childhood.

Karl had felt liberated by all that stored-up history that had been plundered and hauled away; it seemed only fitting that everything old should be taken down. Felix had been right. This was a land that wouldn't make any grand demands on him, a place that was a kind of nothingness, an important, meaningful nothingness.

Of course there was anti-Semitism in his new home, but where in the world was that not the case? What group of people didn't exclude or reject other people? That came with the territory. If a country happened to like Jews, that only meant they'd found someone else to hate.

Karl had deliberately stayed away from typical Jewish occupations, especially the *shmatta* trade on Spadina Avenue, along with the congregation of synagogues and kosher restaurants and furriers that had sprung up along it. There were other people like him, Jews who had made it out, but for Karl, they weren't so much living in the city as lurking within it. It's why he stayed away from Jews altogether. "We shall never forget," they kept saying. All Karl wanted to do was not remember.

Always with Jews the future would be about the past, and that was not the sort of future Karl was looking for, which is why he'd tried to make sure that Aaron would never have anything to remember in the first place. Karl had blond hair, he was European, and, even if there was substantial anti-German sentiment, he was quick to point out that he was Swiss, which, considering the time he'd spent at Diepoldsau, was a worthy enough lie and not too far from the truth; like Switzerland, he was neutral. It was what he'd wanted for his son. History was an ugly birthmark that, like Trujillo's dark skin, could never be covered up with whitening powder. He'd wanted his son to have no history, no sides or convictions foisted upon him. What was the point of offering him a poisonous past? It had not done Karl, nor anyone who'd gotten close to him, any favours.

Using some of the trades he'd learned in Sosua, he entered the construction industry, which was booming after the war with returning vets and people like him, foreigners flooding into Canada looking for a new life in a new country.

It had taken time to piece it all together, to understand how the great abstract forces of history had reached down and grabbed him. He wanted the struggle to be over, but he couldn't even get onto the balcony. For that, too, he needed permission.

"I'd like a smoke," he said.

"Speaking of which, would you please stop smoking your cigars inside the apartment? The place stinks. How can you even be smoking at your age? If nothing else, it's a fire hazard."

"I promise to only set myself on fire."

They weren't cigars. They were Davidoffs, a fine elegant smoke, less caustic in taste and smell than a cigar. His son had never picked up his father's habits, which was a good thing, he supposed. Perhaps the only thing.

"You're not even wearing shoes, Dad."

Karl looked down at his feet before considering there was something compromising about the act; it was a bow of obedience.

"I know Petra is smoking," said Aaron accusingly.

Recently when Petra let him out on the balcony, she'd joined him, lighting a cigarette while he enjoyed his cigarillo. It was the only unsettling aspect of her rescue of him. He found it repellent the way she sucked smoke into her lungs. He'd always been suspicious of cigarettes. Felix had smoked a pack a day. He'd never found it an acceptable habit for women.

"I've told her it's not a good idea," Karl said.

"Well, it's not working. I think you're encouraging her."

"How can you say that?" Karl did not like the way his son was fostering blame. "The opposite is true. I want her to stop."

Karl could still recall with clarity his son's newborn howls, as if he'd been outraged by the sudden expulsion from his mother's womb. It had scared Karl off. The boy was still screaming even after they cleaned him up and dropped him into his mother's arms. And after he left the hospital. And after his first feeding as if, even then, his son had some allergic reaction to his mother's milk. He developed a rash from the disposable diapers and howled some more, until they covered his delicate bottom with cloth. There was a plastic container with a clip-on lid that contained his son's accumulated foulness. He had never gone near it, but he was aware of its presence, as if it were a vault containing incriminating documents.

"What am I doing here?" Karl asked. He wondered if there was a plan for the day, a course of action. Or were they supposed to just exist inside this apartment?

"I guess what we're doing is trying to figure out what we're going to do."

"I want to go home," said Karl.

"You can't live by yourself, Dad."

His son released a long intended-to-be-heard sigh while looking at the papers on the table. The signing pen was missing. Karl realized it was in his hand.

"None of this is your concern," he said, still staring out

the window. He could have retired to his own room, but it wasn't really his room, and he'd have felt even more trapped at the back of the apartment, behind another closed door. At least here he had a view.

"You're in my apartment. We're living together. You've made it my concern."

Nothing, Karl came to understand, stood alone and was of itself: in order to look out the window and understand what you saw, you needed to know what you'd seen. It was all a shuttling from one to the other, a constant and continual stitching together.

"I did not ask to come here. I do not want to be here."

"But you *are* here, whether you want to be here or not. We have to deal with the facts."

His son had taken him to a doctor, who'd administered a battery of tests—word and number games, mainly—that he'd been assured he could neither pass nor fail. *Just concentrate on the computer screen in front of you, Mr. Kaufmann, and try to answer as many questions as you can.* It was a lie, of course. It was *all* about passing or failing. And the fact that he was being tested meant he'd already failed.

His son, who'd waited for him outside, had been brought in afterwards to discuss the diagnosis, though no one had asked Karl's permission, and together Aaron and the doctor discussed the results, along with his recent history, focusing mainly on the visit he'd made to Claire's. Karl clearly saw that it reflected poorly upon him and that it signalled a fault of a particular kind.

"Does he have Alzheimer's?" his son had asked the doctor.

The doctor's response was pleasingly less than precise. There was no clear-cut, easy answer as to what was happening to him, he said. Karl knew otherwise.

It had been a stupid decision to return to his old house. Karl was like a domestic bird who, given its freedom, briefly flutters about the room before voluntarily returning to its cage. Why had he gone to Claire's? They thought it was because he was losing his memory, and so what if he was? It saved him the energy of suppressing it. Like sex, it was one less urge, one diminishing itch the aged could properly dispose of. If either his son or the doctor had gone through even a tenth of what he'd gone through, they might understand how easy it was to occasionally misplace the memories of common life.

As for misplacing things, his visit to Claire's did not strike him as all that great a transgression. If anyone had reason to visit the doctor's office, it was his son, and the diagnosis must surely be more serious than lactose intolerance.

One suggestion from the doctor: Karl should do crossword puzzles to keep his mind active. But Karl had no talent for word games. It seemed to him a waste of time, like golf, where you wandered around chasing a ball. He simply didn't see the point.

The real purpose of the visit was for his son to take control over him. Make him seem senile, weak. It would be the excuse he'd need to have Karl legally removed from his home. But so long as Karl had his mind, no one could sign his rights away. For all his troubles, the power still resided with him, though it wasn't clear for how long he'd be able to maintain his autonomy. When the doctor spoke about what was happening to him and what he could expect to have happen to him in the future, Karl saw that all was diminishment and foreclosure.

"So you want me to trust you with power of attorney?" asked Karl.

"You're going to have to make a decision," Aaron said. "We need to think about putting you in a facility that can take proper care of you."

"I don't want to live in a 'facility.'"

"The place we went to looked decent, Dad. I know it's not perfect, but what is?"

"I can't afford a place like that."

"You can if you sell your apartment. And I'll be paying for some of it."

"You won't be paying for any of it. I'm not going there."

After the doctor's appointment, his son had taken him to a nursing home, the thought of which caused Karl to feel nauseated as he conjured up the linoleum hallways, the cubicles off the hallways, the eating area with the television mounted on the wall and flowers placed on the tables, their petals flicking the air with faded colour. Yes, they'd visited the place. And no, he wasn't going to sell his apartment in order to pay $4,200 a month for the privilege of being locked inside, because that's what was really happening in there, wasn't it? It was just a prison you paid for.

There was an entire wing in the nursing home for people who couldn't remember themselves. Affixed to each door was a photograph of the occupants taken before they could have known what was in store for them, men and women caught in a smile, staring into the summer sun, a reminder as you passed their rooms that they had once been more than their sockless feet sticking out at the ends of their beds. Karl was horrified at the thought of a similar photo being placed on his door.

"All you have to do is let me out," he said, recalling the nurse who had taken them around. There was no jewellery or makeup to adorn her blowfish-round face that was vivid in its plainness.

In frustration, Karl retired to his chair and, resolute in his decision to ignore the legal papers, cast his eyes on the sheets and a folded blanket on the couch. When Petra stayed the night with them, his son slept on the couch. Karl would wake up early in the morning and find Aaron asleep in the living room, his body pressed against the back of the couch like a suckling pig in need of warmth and nourishment.

"Is Petra coming tonight?" Karl asked.

"Yes. I was just about to fix her room up."

Karl rose to his feet again. "I'll help," he said, surprising himself because he believed Petra was old enough to clean up after herself. It didn't do to treat children as children. They needed to grow up, and quickly. He had no patience for the romanticism of childhood, which had led to Americans, and most everyone else in the world, dressing like children, with sneakers and baggy pants and T-shirts with cartoon characters stencilled on the front. People dressed as if they were permanently readying themselves for bed and a bedtime story. There'd been a phase in his son's life when he had wanted his father's comfort, and Karl had sat with him on the bed and opened some books with pictures in them, but he'd always felt as if any excessive feeding of his son's imagination might lead to a kind of obesity. His son needed to remain lean and know the truth, because one day he might have to run away from it quickly.

Petra's room was a little less bare than the others; she had a desk and chair for her computer. There was a printer and shelves half full of books, binders and pictures, but the room suffered, as they all did, from a sense of temporariness.

Stripping off the old sheets, Aaron stood beside the bare mattress as if it were roped off and untouchable. Karl had never felt the desire to peer into his son's room when it was empty, nor did he recall ever having the need to crack open the door and hear his son's soft breathing when he slept.

"She's going to be all right," said Karl.

His son tucked in the corners of the fitted sheet and smoothed out the wrinkles with his hands.

"She's angry with me," Aaron confessed.

"And you're angry with me," Karl said.

A patch of sun from the window caught his son's forearm, lighting up his skin. Aaron looked at it as if he'd been shot.

"I thought of you when I told Petra about the divorce. You just left us. One day you were there, and the next you weren't. At least, that's how I remember it."

That's how Karl remembered it too, but he didn't say anything.

"I thought it would be different with Petra. I promised myself it would be different."

"It is," Karl said.

"You've been telling her things, Dad. Things about your past that I don't really know about."

Maybe that was the point about his son: from his own loins came an accusation, a pair of newborn eyes, ice-blue at first and unfocused but soon fixating on the man who'd made him, wanting answers, as if no lid could ever hide from his eyes Karl's own accumulated foulness. Why did it need to be a son? A daughter might have been better, thought Karl.

"I haven't said anything to her," he said.

"That's the way it's always been, and as far as I'm concerned, that's the way it always will be. But it's like your cigars. I think you're encouraging Petra. She's confused about a lot of things, and I'm not in her Best Dad book right now. Do we understand each other?"

Aaron began to stuff a duvet into its freshly laundered cover slip, eventually stuffing his own head inside in an attempt to reach the corners. He looked like a wounded animal burrowing for protection. Karl took the opportunity to return to the living room and leave his son be. The power of attorney documents sat on the coffee table, the cheerful rainbow tabs still reminding him of candy. Karl went into the kitchen, popped a sugar cube into his mouth and sucked on its soothing sweetness.

9 KARL WASN'T SUPPOSED TO OPEN THE WINdow in his room, and he wasn't allowed to step outside his son's home without an escort, another one of the "conditions" of his stay, as if he'd been offered any choice. Despite this restriction, after the doctor's visit he'd been given a cell phone with programmable numbers. All he had to do was push one of the buttons and it would immediately connect to either his son or granddaughter. Not that he had any intention of ever using the phone. They were treating him like a child. We are born helpless and we die helpless, thought Karl, and in between we torment those in the first and last categories.

Karl sat in front of a television, which was on though he wasn't watching it. He wore headphones not to enhance the sound but to muffle the world, which was the way he currently preferred it. The shows on TV just didn't catch his attention anymore; they cast out their colourful lures, bobbled them in front of him, and he stared back like a weary fish hidden in the weeds. He was probably staring at his son now in just the same way.

"Petra's in her bedroom, so ask her if you need anything while I'm out," Aaron said to him.

"I'll use my new phone to call her."

"There's hot coffee in the pot."

"Yes, thank you."

"And don't even think of smoking your cigars in the apartment, Dad."

His son was going out to his think-tank—a place where fish like his son could swim. Aaron had taken him there once, and he'd been unimpressed with the drabness and earnest faces of Aaron's fellow-fish. Bike lanes? Stricter traffic control? Cleaner environment? How paltry it all seemed against the tangled background of the Kaufmann men—great-grandfather, grandfather and Karl himself. As far as he was concerned, Aaron hadn't moved on from when he'd been a little boy crying over that dead bird.

"And don't let Petra smoke," Aaron added.

Karl nodded. Another feeble concern. Not that there was much he could do to stop her, and besides, he was grateful not to be locked inside the apartment again.

When his son finally left the apartment to enter that wider world, which Karl increasingly looked upon with the unease of a foreigner, he pulled off his headphones. He took pen and paper from the inside pocket of his jacket, smoothed out the folds and went over to the table, where he spent a few minutes drawing a map. Aaron might have taken away his apartment, his car and his keys, but Karl still had his wallet. Reaching into his other pocket, he pulled out cards with his name printed on them. There was his Visa card, his MasterCard and his debit card, which he lined up vertically beside his map, a cascade of reinforcing identity: *K. Kaufmann*. Three times confirmed. For extra measure, he took out the cash, a few crisp twenty- and fifty-dollar bills, and laid them out as well.

This his son as yet could not take away, though he would try again to gain legal control over his assets.

Meanwhile, Karl needed more money in his wallet and to know that, unlike his father, he could walk into the bank and stake his claim of independence and safety. The world was conspiring against him, converting rights into privileges. So, he would walk to the bank. In his mind's eye, he practised the route—he walked down the carpeted hallway, pushed the elevator button, waited, then stepped inside, pushed another button, rode the elevator down to the lobby and then strolled across the red-tiled floor to the front exit. And from there?

Slipping his cards back into his wallet, he once again put pen to paper, adding a path leading from the building to the sidewalk. Dragging the line downward for two blocks, he reached the main street and then turned left for three, possibly four blocks, until the main intersection. He knew there was a bank directly in front, but that wasn't his. There was a second bank on the other side, but that wasn't his either. He needed to keep going, keep going a bit farther past the lights, until he reached his bank. He'd driven past it a number of times while in the car with his son. It wasn't his branch, the one he'd used over the years, but he recognized the logo of a lion's paw perched in predatory ownership over the globe, as if it were carrion.

The map would be useful, prevent his getting lost.

Pleased by the bold straight lines of his composition, Karl plucked out a cigarillo he'd kept hidden in his eyeglasses case for just such an occasion, plus a book of matches he'd tucked under the sofa cushion. He lit the cigar, took a contented puff and swirled the captured smoke in his mouth just as his father had done, before leaning back and exhaling, the cigarillo clamped firmly between the fingers of his left hand.

Karl was a natural lefty. He'd been disciplined as a child to use his right hand, and it wasn't until many years later, in a sudden flash of insight, that he understood why—you wiped your ass with your left hand. Karl wondered if this was a natural phenomenon. Did all left hands instinctively reach for their bottoms, or was it learned, like driving on the left-hand side of the road, as the English did? His teachers believed it could be eliminated, that one could be trained to work from the right.

Later, after the Anschluss, when things turned serious, Karl fell to wondering whether all Jews were naturally left-handed. Was that why they were so reviled by the brutal, cigar-holding hands of the Austrians who had decided to stamp out the unsanitary ass-wiping Jews once and for all?

The peculiar direction of his thoughts was brought to a stop by his granddaughter.

"Grandpa! You're not supposed to smoke in the apartment."

He knew the young woman approaching him from the hallway wasn't his sister; he also knew that Trude would have looked like this, a woman of vitality, if she'd lived a few more years. Karl's sister had kept her hair in two long braids that reached below her shoulders; when she unfastened them to take a bath, her hair sprang and tumbled with the

same cheerful abandon as this girl, who was, Karl compre-
hended, his granddaughter. It was a gift, this similarity, and
a curse. She was here, and so he had, in some indirect way,
fulfilled his promise and saved Trude. But it wasn't magic,
he told himself, just genetic predestination. He couldn't
escape what they were and what they would become.

"Dad would be so pissed if he found out that I let you
smoke in the apartment. You should have heard him this
morning—'Make sure he doesn't light the stove. Don't let
him make any coffee; tell him there's already a full pot. Don't
let him smoke in the apartment'—I guess he's terrified
you're going to burn everything down."

"When is he coming back?"

"This afternoon."

Karl scrutinized his watch. It was early; there was
plenty of time.

"But you can't smoke in here, Grandpa."

As if proving her point, she slid open the balcony door.
Gusts of cold air swirled around, ruffling Karl's map. He
reached out his hand and pinned it to the table.

"What's that?" she asked.

"What's *that*?" Karl answered, pointing at the cigarette
that had found its way between his granddaughter's lips.

"Don't tell Dad."

"Doesn't he know?"

"He sort of knows, but he pretends not to know. It's like
that with him. Let's move outside to the balcony, Grandpa.
There's a chair you can sit on."

Karl was surprised by how upset he was, watching her

light the cigarette and inhale the poisonous mist of adulthood into her lungs. It reminded him of a fairy tale his mother had read to him from *Der Verschwender*, of evils spells cast and battled against.

Taking his seat, they spent a few moments quietly indulging their respective desires. Petra leaned her head back when she exhaled, just as his father had done.

"You are left-handed," Karl remarked.

"I guess so. Dad says I got it from him."

"Your grandfather was left-handed," he said.

"*Is* left-handed. You're not dead yet."

It took a moment for Karl to understand. "I meant my father."

"My great-grandfather."

"Yes."

It was such a long line of history, thought Karl, almost incomprehensible. "I'm left-handed too. Or I was. It wasn't considered acceptable, when I was your age."

Petra considered this for a moment and then took a puff of her cigarette, the smoke constricting her vocal cords. "Dad says you never talk about the past, because of what happened. He says there isn't anyone left."

Petra was wrong. There was him and there was her, and she looked like his sister.

"You need to put on something warm," she said.

Karl bundled himself against the cold.

"Dad always goes on about family, about how important it is and how it's the only thing that matters, but if he really wanted a family, why did he leave Mom and move here?"

It took a moment for Karl to realize that she was actually asking him, that she expected an answer.

"I don't know," he finally said.

"Mom says his thing about family is because he didn't have one. Which I guess makes sense. Mom also says that I shouldn't bother Dad. *Irritate* is the word she uses. Because he's dealing with you. He wants to get rid of you," she said. "He says there isn't enough room."

His granddaughter expelled smoke from her cigarette as if, thought Karl, she wished to pollute the world.

Karl tossed his cigar over the balcony.

"You shouldn't do that," she said, looking pleased that he had.

"*You* shouldn't be smoking."

"I guess there are lots of things I shouldn't be doing. But I do them anyway."

Petra leaned over and pulled one of her socks down. "See this?" She raised her leg, and Karl saw a red heart tattooed on her ankle. "Dad didn't know about this for two months, and he went ballistic when he found out. I wonder what he'll do when he finds out I have a pierced belly button."

Karl worried that she'd show him that as well, but thankfully she refrained.

"Some things are best left hidden," he said.

He knew about secrets. They had this in common, he and his granddaughter, and they could share it.

"The family motto," she said.

Karl nodded his acceptance. Then he remembered what he had to do.

He wouldn't be able or even allowed to do it alone.

"Let's go for a walk," he said.

"I'm sorry, Mr. Kaufmann, but you can't take that much out."

"Is it the amount?" he asked. That may have raised some concerns. Perhaps he should have asked for less than twenty thousand dollars, but it was his money, wasn't it?

"No, it's the account," the woman behind the counter explained.

"So how much can I withdraw?"

The teller wrote the amount on a piece of paper and slipped it through the bars. She had a very precise, neat penmanship of the kind one didn't see too often nowadays—his financial ruin was clear and all too legible.

"You mean to tell me I have no money?"

"You have three thousand, eight hundred and twenty-six dollars."

The teller swivelled her computer screen a few degrees to let him take a look. What Karl saw was a blinking cursor and a series of columns that seemed too active and dense for the impoverishment they were meant to proclaim.

"I want to withdraw all my money," Karl said, trying to keep his rising voice in check. Where was it, the money that he had worked hard for and accumulated over the years? The money he'd entrusted to the banks, because everyone knew that Canadian banks were reliable and trustworthy.

"Would you like to close the account?"

Karl stared down at his shoes, two black puddles staining the floor. His father had stood in just the same puddles all those years ago when they'd visited the bank together. Why had Bernard brought his son? Perhaps his father felt the sight of his child might elicit a flicker of sympathy in the bank manager? Had he been looking to bolster his claim of being a good citizen of Austria? Or had he up until that moment simply been oblivious to his fate? No explanation seemed entirely plausible, but then what part of Karl's past did?

"I'd like to speak to the manager."

"For what purpose?" asked the teller.

"For the purpose of finding out where all my money went," he almost shouted.

The teller secured her till and stepped away from the counter. "I'll get one of the branch managers."

When had it become the case that a small bank had more than one manager? Everyone was a manager nowadays, and everyone felt helpless.

"Mr. Kaufmann, how can I help you today?"

Spotting the manager's approach, Karl reached up to take off his hat, only to realize he hadn't worn a hat for many years and was grasping at nothing but air. Besides, the manager was impossibly young.

"I am having difficulty withdrawing my money."

"What sort of difficulty?"

"I don't seem to have any."

"Would you like to take a seat in my office, Mr. Kaufmann?"

"I don't want to go to your office," Karl said. Even when

it was done out of friendliness, he still sensed the manipula-
tion of being directed to places he did not wish to go. "What
I want is my money."

Karl stared at this impossibly young man who was
beginning to seem familiar, but he put that down to the fact
that the young all looked the same to him now, in the way
old people all looked the same to the young.

"We discussed this when you were here a few weeks ago."

"I was here a few weeks ago?" asked Karl.

"Yes, you wanted to make sure money was being sent to
an overseas account."

And so Karl was reminded.

He'd already talked to this impossibly young man about
the loss of funds. How, after all the years of caution, had
he let his guard down so badly? The monthly transfer to
the Dominican Republic had always been conducted in the
neutral silence of his bank, with nothing but the soft clack-
ing of counting machines and the scribble of signatures to
accompany his betrayal. It had all been done, and yet nothing had been done. Then he'd started to run out of money,
or he had lost money during the housing slump. As he got
older, Karl had done more investing than building, at one
point owning six homes and a small apartment building in
Toronto. He borrowed money and then was wiped out when
real estate prices fell by fifty percent. He lost money with
his investments and never really recovered. He had messed
the whole thing up, but he'd muddled through.

He remembered now. It was the shock of learning about
the bank account from this young man that had sent him

out to the intersection with loud pips for blind people. That's what the doctor had missed in his diagnosis. Karl had wandered through the city before jumping into a taxi and going to Claire's house, which had led him back to his son, which had led him here.

"Do you wish to withdraw funds from another account?"

Yes, the other account.

"How much do I have?" Karl asked.

This time it was the branch manager who wrote down the figure: $9,603.43.

"Is money still being sent to the Dominican Republic?"

"Yes, you were very clear on this point. Funds for Mrs. Kaufmann and her son are, as instructed, transferred each month."

Karl nodded.

"As you know, the money left in your account won't be sufficient to last the year."

Karl would be breaking the one promise he'd kept in his life. The longer things remained as they were, the worse they would become.

The manager excused himself, and the teller he'd originally spoken with asked him for his preferred denominations. He watched her count out close to three thousand dollars, one bill after another, a thorough notation of his freedom. He was about to reach out for his money when he felt a tug on his arm. It was his granddaughter who'd accompanied him to the bank. He'd given her the map, and they'd walked together as if they were on a hunt for hidden treasure, which was not far from the truth.

"Grandpa?" she asked, looking at the pile of money. "What are you doing?"

He kept forgetting her and she kept appearing.

"Everything is in order," he said, inadvertently echoing the words spoken by his father after the disastrous day at the bank. *Alles ist in ordnung*. He hoped he didn't sound as hollow.

"Don't forget your map," said his granddaughter.

Karl folded up his map and stuffed it into his shirt pocket.

"Come on, Grandpa. We need to go home before Dad gets back," she said, this time less gently. Karl was in no mood to return—the whole purpose of his journey had been to escape—but suddenly he felt exhausted. He looked at the steady young hand resting over his own, which was spotted and wrinkled, and the images all rushed back—his left-handedness, the white-gloved waiters on the *Nea Hellas*, Ilsa's soft hand in his. His wife and child, who could no longer rely upon his support.

Yes, they needed to get back.

AFTER HE SAT down in the living room, Petra brought him a coffee, dark and strong. She'd even placed the sugar cube on the edge of the saucer with the wrapping still on, just the way he liked it. Even with his clumsy arthritic fingers, he preferred to unveil the white block of sweetness himself.

"This is very good," said Karl, taking a sip. His son served weak, watery coffee that tasted of chlorine and bitterness.

The coffee before him testified that a good cup could be made from the ingredients at hand.

"What happened at the bank?" she asked.

It had been wrong to make her bring him there, but what else could he have done? Whenever he was alone in the apartment, his son locked him in. The only way of getting to the bank was with Petra.

"I was getting money."

"I know what a bank is for. Why do you need so much money?"

"You always need money."

"Why are you sending money to the Dominican Republic?"

"How many questions do you have?"

"Just a minute." Petra went to grab a device with a screen on it. "This is the country, right?" She placed the screen between them, so that they could both see the map of the Dominican Republic.

Karl plucked the wrapped cube of sugar from the saucer with his thumb and forefinger and held it up to his eyes, as if it were a single atom ready to explode with all the misery and sweetness of the world.

"Yes," he said. "That's the place."

"Dad once mentioned something about you living there."

"It was a long time ago."

"Where, exactly?"

Karl placed the sugar cube over the town of Puerto Plata. "That place is where my boat arrived."

"You took a boat?"

"Yes. That's how people travelled in those days."

Petra's nod held a hint of impatience. They weren't talking about a time fully in the past. He'd just been caught sending money to the place.

"Is that where you lived?"

"No, it was a smaller town down the coast."

"What was it called?"

"Sosua," said Karl. The name hadn't tripped off his tongue for possibly fifty years. But he thought about it every day.

"Is it still there?"

"Of course it's still there," he said, but over the years he'd wondered. Was it? Had it ever been there?

"Show me," she said, handing him the screen.

As with the sugar cube, which he dropped into his coffee, everything of importance could be grasped and compressed between thumb and forefinger, the whole world expanding and contracting on the screen with a mere flick of his fingers. Following his granddaughter's encouragement, they sped across the north road that he'd first taken all those years ago, past the sugar cane fields, humped hills and small villages, until, just like that, they reached Sosua.

"There," he said.

Karl touched the screen with his aged finger. Sosua came closer. He touched again and swooped through some light cloud cover. He saw rooftops. Homes. Roads. The beach. If he kept touching the screen, he'd catch the top of his son's head as he walked down the street, as if Karl were some failed God looking at his creation.

He turned the screen back to her.

With the dexterity and delicacy of her slim fingers, they leaped into the town. Pictures popped up of hotels and restaurants and people sunning themselves on the beach. It was a place for holidays. Even if it had all remained the same—and how could that be if people went there for vacation?—he still wouldn't be able to show her what it was like. He barely understood the place when he'd lived there.

"And that's where you send the money?"

"Yes," Karl admitted. That's where he sent the money.

"The guy at the bank said something about Mrs. Kaufmann and her son? Are you sending money to Grandma and Dad? I don't get it."

He didn't get it either. How could he begin to explain what had happened to him? He was the same age as Petra when he left his own family in Vienna. His granddaughter would never recognize the young man who had disembarked in Puerto Plata in 1938.

"I met a woman and had a child with her. A son."

"You have another family?"

Karl had never felt he'd had even one family, let alone two, but meeting the shocked eyes of his granddaughter, he had to concede that his feelings lacked validity.

"Yes," he said. "I have another family."

"You've been sending money to them?"

"Every month."

"For how long?"

"Over fifty years."

"Does Dad know?"

"I'm not sure."

"No wonder this family is so fucked up," his grand-daughter whispered as if in awe.

Karl took a sip of his coffee. It was already cold.

"When was the last time you saw them?" she asked.

"I haven't seen them since I left the Dominican Republic."

"Before you even met Grandma?"

An inconceivably long time for a girl of her age, thought Karl. His first-born would have grown up, married and had children of his own. He would have grey hair. It was possible even Karl's grandchildren had grey hair.

"Does Grandma know?"

"Yes."

"Is that why you aren't together?"

"There are many reasons, I suppose."

"But that's one of them."

"Yes, that's one of them."

"So you've been sending money to this other family, and now there's not enough money, right? That's what was happening in the bank?"

"I lost a lot of money."

"You should go back to Sosua," Petra said.

"It's impossible."

"Dad should take you."

"This has nothing to do with your father."

"I think it does. It has something to do with all of us."

"It's very far away," he said.

"How long would it take to get there?"

By plane, no more than five hours, perhaps less. People

flew down to the Caribbean for short vacations all the time. He'd known people who had taken the week off and returned with suntans and mosquito bites. How was it possible that a place so far away could be reached so quickly? For Karl, it was no more possible than entering a time machine and travelling to the past. It seemed unimaginable that at this very moment—at any given moment—both worlds existed simultaneously.

You can't go back to people you've left behind, thought Karl.

10 THEY TOOK WALKS TOGETHER, ILSA reaching for his hand whenever they wandered into a forested area that was damp and dark and loudly silent. But it was on an empty stretch of beach, the caramel-coloured sand pockmarked with coconut rinds, driftwood and broken coral, that he first kissed her. He'd never touched her lips before, and he closed his eyes in fear and then relief when she didn't push him away. Her hand was still and remained so, after he reopened his eyes and saw three boys and their father staring at them from the shoreline.

No matter where he and Ilsa went, every inch of land was inhabited by natives. Karl wasn't sure why this should surprise him, but it did, always. Yet Dominicans didn't count, at least in that way, and on their walks, Ilsa stayed close beside him, something she didn't always do when they were in town.

After six months in Sosua, he'd ventured only as far as his feet could take him. His home and sanctuary was nothing more than a small intrusion in a country that to Karl appeared enormous, because it included the ocean that surrounded and separated him from Europe. There were hills behind the town, and beyond the hills lay mountains that should have made him feel as if he were back home in

Austria but instead made him feel remote and lost, because he knew of no path that led to them. Very few Jews had reason to leave the colony, and no one could legally remove themselves and settle in the city, by order of the dictator himself, Rafael Trujillo. They were meant to stay here, in this isolated but safe place, and wait.

When it came to Ilsa, Karl was impatient. Her body was the only geography he really wanted to explore, but as with the mountains looming in the far distance, he didn't know the proper path. He did know that her fingers, which she allowed Karl to fondle, had adapted themselves well to milking the engorged teats of dairy cows. Her father, like some of the other intact families in Sosua, had been given ten cows to tend by the Jewish agency responsible for their survival and Karl had visited their homestead, two kilometres east of Sosua, to help out a few times.

Jacob, previously an accountant from Frankfurt, stood before the cows as if the first step to becoming a dairy farmer were to adopt a dignified posture in front of his animals. It was different with Ilsa.

"Don't be afraid," she told Karl. "They want to be milked, because if they're not their udders swell, and it hurts them."

She'd shown him how it was done, yanking at them with just the right balance of aggression and concern. When Karl rubbed his fingers along her naked, warm skin, he became light-headed.

Despite his encounter with the prostitute in Lisbon, Karl was unfamiliar with breasts, either cow or human, and although he dismissed the notion that women's breasts also needed to be milked, he couldn't disregard it with a hundred percent certainty. The idea of milking Ilsa's much smaller but still noticeable breasts stuck with him, and he wondered if she might be using the cows to train him. Perhaps only when he showed a certain dexterity would he be allowed to touch hers.

One day while kissing her, Karl placed a hand directly over her breast. They were on one of those long stretches of beach, away from the prying eyes of the colonists. She let it remain there for a fraction of a moment before removing it. She held on to his hand to ensure that it would remain at a distance, but neither of them said a word about it.

He asked her about school. Did she like going?

It wasn't the right question to ask on the beach. It changed things between them.

"Dr. Bruck cut open a cane frog today and made us look inside. He said there isn't really that much difference between us and a frog, at least on the inside. But if that's true, then why is it right to cut up a frog and not a human being?"

"I suppose because a frog doesn't have a soul?" Karl hated the way his answer came out as a question, as if she were the teacher and he the clueless student.

"But it must feel pain."

"Wasn't it already dead?"

This wasn't what Karl wanted to talk about, not after just touching Ilsa's breast. Why would she never kiss him when they were in town? Karl hadn't given her a thought on the ship sailing here, but now he wanted nothing more than for her to be with him, and for others to recognize that fact. So what was this nonsense about frogs? *Why not cut them up and eat them?* he wanted to shout at her, but she'd think him stupid, uneducated.

Karl hadn't been to school since Vienna. Diepoldsau was not made for children, and Karl had not been forced to attend school in Sosua because of his in-between age and the fact he had no parents to concern themselves with him. Every morning when Karl was out digging ditches or mending fences, he'd watch the children brought into town on the donkey-drawn school bus. Ilsa usually walked to school or rode in on her family's horse, but one day when he spotted her in the school bus with the other children, he took off his straw hat and waved after her. The children waved back at him and he felt, for the first time, terribly old.

"Why does Dr. Bruck have the right to cut up an animal?"

He knew about Dr. Bruck, a distinguished surgeon before the Nazis kicked him out of Germany. Now he taught the children of Sosua.

"Because he is helping you learn," said Karl.

"So it is right to kill another living thing, if it serves a purpose?" Ilsa didn't seem to think so, or at the very least didn't believe the purpose was worth the life of one frog. "And who says what is important to learn and what is not?"

Since Karl was no longer going to school, he felt he couldn't measure what was right and what was wrong. He was at a distinct disadvantage and wished he'd never asked about her education, because it only seemed to highlight his lack of one. Had he been in school, he might have had the chance to sit beside Ilsa every day and think about those questions. What were all these words about, anyway? If Karl had learned one thing, it was that right and wrong didn't seem to stop anybody doing anything to anyone.

"Besides," said Ilsa, "it was very hot in the classroom."

"It was hotter digging ditches today," Karl said, a little more roughly than he intended.

"Well, now you can cool off in the sea." Ilsa, bored with the conversation, dropped his hand and rushed for the water.

She'd hardly known how to swim when they first arrived in Sosua, and she still reverted to the occasional dog paddle, arms and legs kicking in a furious attempt to keep her head above water, but since then she'd learned the front crawl, and now he watched her cut through the water with hardly a splash. He thought back to his last, strangely peaceful summer at Kritzendorf on the Danube, his mother and father and sister enjoying their days, lazing on the river beach, fishing and swimming. It was the last time he'd swum with his family.

"Are you coming?" Ilsa called out.

Karl answered by diving into the water and swimming after her, pleased that he was wanted.

KARL'S ARRIVAL IN Sosua coincided with a sexual awakening that sprouted with the same sort of lush and unmanageable ease as the tropical landscape.

Ilsa, like other girls in Sosua close to his age, was already developing in an atmosphere of sun and safety that seemed to compensate for the broken bonds of family and home. Yet Karl didn't know what to do. He'd been so intent on his awkward embarrassment that night in Lisbon that he felt even more naive than before he'd slept with a prostitute. Compared to what he'd experienced, he knew his time with Ilsa was farcically innocent. He wanted more but didn't know how to go about finding it, and he wasn't alone in his problem.

There weren't enough women in Sosua. For every three Jewish men, there was just one Jewish woman, very few of whom were single. Fifty-one Jews, including Karl, had disembarked from the boat from New York. Of those, thirteen were married couples, some with children, twenty were bachelors and only four were single women. They hadn't brought enough of them in. That was how the men—the single men who, like Karl, lived in dormitories and quietly masturbated beneath sheets washed, pressed and folded by women—described the situation, as if women were one more item of which the colony was in short supply, along with fuel, rope, treated lumber, newspaper ink, various categories of machinery and machinery parts, copper wire, fencing and sulpha.

Those other supplies could eventually, hopefully, be found, but the women hadn't been planned for, and no more could be brought in. The colony had been cut off from Europe soon after Karl's arrival. His boat had been one of the last to make it with Jews on board, and they were now a total of 650, some 450 of them men, building and shaping the new community of Sosua.

"What's the difference between being a virgin and living in Sosua? Nothing." That was the sort of joke they made in the men's barracks. From what Karl could gather, he was the youngest—though he couldn't have been the only one who'd lied to get himself there. Most of the men appeared stronger and hairier.

Even if he wasn't technically the youngest, he was treated as the youngster in the group.

"The poor kid must be going crazy," they'd say.

That's what it was like when you were young. People spoke about you as if you weren't there.

"We're all going crazy! At least he doesn't even know what he's missing."

"Hey, Karl, you know what you're missing?"

"Not if he lives in Sosua."

They laughed, and so did Karl, but he wasn't sure if it was at his expense. That he wasn't sure made him feel childish. No one mentioned Ilsa, which was a relief, because he didn't want them to know how he felt about her. But they knew something, and knew why he didn't want to hear it, and he never had the courage to say directly what was on his mind. That too made him feel young.

"You'll have to marry yourself, Karl."

"That's what we all do every night."

So it went, Karl laughing but never trying to make jokes himself, because he worried they'd reveal something desperate about himself.

The trick was to do what they'd been sent here to do. The idea was to create a community of Jewish farmers, and for that you needed men who could hack their way through the landscape, rip up the soil and withstand the heat, privations that came with constructing a sanctuary in the tropics. It was no place for women. But then, Europe was no place for Jews. Some of the women had made the crossing because they were married, others because they were daughters, or because their strength was in their will to survive. And others simply because, in the end, they were lucky.

Karl dug trenches to siphon stagnant water, and unspooled wire fencing to pen in the rising number of farm animals acquired and born into the colony. It was hot, dirty work, but he preferred it to the earlier job he'd been given in the leather shop. That was where saddles and shoes were repaired, and it was hot and smelly. It reminded him too much of his father's business, and he was glad to be assigned to outdoor work.

No matter his job, Karl was paid, as was most everyone else in the community, a dollar a day with money supplied by American Jews. It was a living wage, the bare minimum expected for Europeans, as they apparently self-classified themselves. It afforded Karl certain luxuries like fruit and candies, and sometimes even chocolate that he bought from the community-run *colmado*, which had expanded its goods to include everything from canned fish and meat, to rubber boots, rope, sugar, coffee and bananas.

Their community was created on the former site of a banana plantation, so it seemed strange to Karl that he needed to buy this fruit at the shop. The dormitory where he slept, along with several other structures scattered across the cleared fields, had been built by United Fruit Company, a big American organization Karl had heard about after his arrival. They'd cleared and harvested the land and then, when it was no longer profitable, had abandoned it, leaving behind ragged banana stalks that grew too high. The drooping fruit was pecked by birds, infested by insects and devastated by a host of diseases before it could ever ripen.

There'd been discussions about reviving the plantation, but along with coffee and sugar, there was an ample supply of bananas in the Dominican Republic, and the government hadn't brought Jews all this distance to work on a plantation. From the day of his arrival, when Karl was taken along the road leading to Sosua, he'd seen the Dominicans—and many Haitians too—working in the fields, hundreds of them weeding the rows of sugar cane, while men with lighter skin sat on horseback, their horses' tails flicking away flies and heat.

As was pointed out to Karl from the moment of his arrival in Puerto Plata, he and the other colonists were Europeans, Germans most of them, and what they were meant to plant was the seed of European success. Karl learned that from the newspaper accounts of their arrival and the expectations of visiting officials, all of whom assumed the Jews were imbued with exceptional talent. That's why they'd been refused travel permits to settle elsewhere in the country, especially its capital, Ciudad Trujillo. They would help the people of the Dominican Republic but not compete against them.

None of them had any idea how to grow bananas or sugar or, farther up in the mountains where the air was cooler, coffee. They didn't know how to grow any crop anywhere, let alone in the tropics. They tried tomatoes and sweet potatoes, but all that green growth was a trick of the eye, a false fruitfulness, and one of the outdoor jobs Karl had been given was weeding their failure back into the ground. As with the banana stalks, much of what they planted rotted before ripening. They grew enough for themselves, but it was not enough, nor of sufficient quality, to market.

Everything looked so promising, as if you had only to drop a seed in the soil and pluck the fruit, but scarcity lurked behind seeming abundance. And this always brought the conversation back to women.

Some of the men managed to slink off with Jewish women who were already married, because in that air of heat and liberation, the women could no longer be contained by the constraints of home and family, even as they were attempting to build just that in their new community. Or so it was said by men in Karl's barracks. He heard eagerness in their voices but also betrayal.

Enemies formed. In the dining hall, clusters of men sat at specific tables. A group of Belgians who had arrived together a year before Karl kept to themselves, and Karl found that his fellow Viennese looked down on their less-refined German compatriots from Stuttgart and Hamburg.

Of course, it didn't matter where the women came from or, more dangerously, if they were married. But none of this concerned Karl directly. His age and interest in Ilsa protected him, though, as with his job assignments, he didn't like being overlooked or not being taken seriously.

Still, because of the community's concerns, a rabbi was brought in from New York. His first counsel was to build a synagogue, directing the excess passions afflicting the community toward its construction. Karl wanted to help, but other men who'd been in the colony longer and who were older got the work. An existing path was widened, some houses were built alongside it, and even before the pews arrived on a boat from America, the colonists, including Karl, had assembled beneath the synagogue's wooden roof to discuss their problem.

Hadn't they come to build a new home for themselves? asked the rabbi. Their presence here was an act of defiance, proof that our people would carry on and prosper.

But how could they do that, when there weren't enough Jewish women? Men wanted families, companions, someone to share their burdens and their future. What were they supposed to do?

The answer, said the rabbi, came from the very land that gave them sanctuary. They could marry Dominican women. Why shouldn't they marry those who lived on the land that had given them this sanctuary? God would surely understand. There were difficult and exceptional moments in Jewish history, when one needed to break from tradition in order to uphold it. This was such a time. Life must go on.

What if we have children? someone asked the rabbi.

If boys should be born from these unions, then they will be circumcised, replied the rabbi, and they will come to this synagogue, and they will be Jews.

* * *

KARL WAS WALKING down to the beach imagining the thriving colony he'd establish with Ilsa, when he practically tripped over Felix's lounging body. His friend lay on the sand like a tree root. Felix didn't even give Karl time to lay down his towel before voicing an opinion.

"What a bunch of hypocrites. Most of them haven't stepped foot in a synagogue in years, and here they are building one, so that they can have a rabbi tell them it's okay to screw Dominicans. Suddenly they all need to become Jews."

Because Karl had been daydreaming about Ilsa, the outburst felt abrupt and personal. Karl needed to defend himself.

"But they are Jews," he said. He might not want to get married or have children right away, but unlike Felix, he'd gone to the synagogue with the rest of them looking for answers.

"We used to be Germans, Austrians, Belgians. It was Hitler who made us Jews. Now we have a rabbi telling us how to be *good* Jews, as if we're the ones who have done something wrong."

"I'm not sure they think they've done anything wrong."

"And there's your problem," said Felix.

Felix hadn't waited for permission to take up with Dominican women; he'd done so within weeks of his arrival. Karl didn't think he treated them very well. "They're illiterate," Felix had said, as if that explained it. Karl could see for himself that some of the women Felix had taken up with were beautiful, and there were others that Karl, if he was interested, could have been with, but his heart only wanted

Ilsa, not because she was Jewish but because she came from a world that he understood and that might, one day, understand him. He fantasized about it, about how well she would know him; with a glance, she could tell what he was thinking and react in just the right way. There were times when he felt this happening, but it was awkward too, like the way she had held his hand when he wanted to touch her breast. She must have understood him then. Back in Europe they'd lived hundreds of miles apart and in two different countries, but over here they came from the same place, and that made this new life more manageable.

Felix didn't care to be understood. He'd already found his way of managing. He spent most of his time on the beach, lounging beneath the shade of a sea grape tree. He was usually alone, though there were always other men like him strewn along the mile-long stretch of sand, collecting their daily dollar without working, or hardly working, because what was the Jewish agency in charge of them going to do? asked Felix. Let them starve?

There might be houses to build, land to clear, drainage ditches to dig, crops and chickens to grow, fences to erect and mend, but for some the allure of the beach or bed was too much, and they shirked their duties whenever they could. It was as if the burst of energy they'd used to escape Europe had depleted them. The Dominican government should come down to this beach, thought Karl, if they ever feared Jews would desert the settlement and compete with the local population.

"This isn't home and I'm not even sure we're guests of

this place," said Felix, patting the sand beside him. "Sit down."

Karl dropped his towel but remained standing.

"Sure, do what you wish. That's my motto."

Staring at the horizon, Karl spied a funnel of smoke far off to sea, smearing the clear, blue sky, and he imagined Felix's mouth as another sort of funnel, spewing dirt into the air. They were no longer behind the wire of Diepoldsau, no longer refugees. They were colonists relaxing on a sandy beach. For all of its problems, Sosua was a paradise compared to where they'd been. Why couldn't Felix accept this place?

There was someone in the water, much closer to shore. She was the reason he'd come down to the beach. Felix saw Ilsa too, standing on the small rocky reef, her knees cresting the water's glassy surface.

"I know it's about women," he said. "But you don't need a purpose to sleep with them either." And as Karl made his way to the water, Felix called out, "Just be careful of the sharks."

Offal from slaughtered farm animals was dumped over a cliff not far from the beach, an unexpected bounty for sharks. Danger lurked in all sorts of places, often unseen, but when Karl found his footing beside Ilsa on the reef, he looked down and spotted through the clear clean water not sharks but striped sergeant majors, which darted around his ankles. Large waves often broke on the reefs along the coastline making it impossible to stand in the water, but today all was calm.

The vista from the reef was wide enough to put him and everyone else in their place. Rocky outcrops on either side of the beach reached out like embracing arms, sheltering them from the open ocean. The beaches were one of the reasons Sosua had been selected for settlement. Before the paved road from Puerto Plata was built, supplies had been brought safely to shore by boat; even now, when hard rains made the road impassable, the beaches offered a vital link with the outside world.

Behind the beach was a strip of trees that provided shade, and beyond the shade rose hills that a little farther inland and beyond their range of sight flattened into farmable land slowly being claimed by the community.

Karl stood with Ilsa under the sun, the ocean all around. Let others gather at the synagogue and worry about the future. Out here, he could see everything, including Ilsa's hand dipped beneath the water's surface, as if it were one more exotic and beautiful fish swimming toward him.

11 AARON NEEDED TO BUY THINGS FOR his father, and with Karl and Petra in tow, he joined families and bits of families— mothers, children, sisters, husbands, wives— diligently following the IKEA floor arrows past assembled dining rooms, bedrooms and kitchens promising the familial comfort he'd so recently rejected. Or had he been ejected?

The divorce was mutual, in that he and Isobel had mutually decided they no longer liked each other, but it wasn't clear who'd left whom. He was the one who'd left the house, but that wasn't necessarily the same as leaving *her*. Was it? Either way, the result was catastrophic.

Likely there were other shoppers at IKEA also contemplating domestic failure. Petra pointed out a middle-aged woman staring at a fake TV set as if she were watching a riveting show in the privacy of her well-furnished living room.

"Look, Dad," she said. "That's what Mom is like every night."

Clearly Petra was not thrilled about the divorce. She blamed each of her parents equally but also exclusively, depending on whom she was staying with at the time.

"Keep an eye out for anything you might want," he said.

In previous journeys down these trafficked lanes, he'd bought a bed for Petra, along with a side table, duvet and pillows, thinking it was best to populate her room with the necessities and let her work on the details herself. But the act of filling a household never seemed to end, and now, with the arrival of his father, it was expanding. Aaron's neck was feeling substantially damaged from his nights on the couch, so he was searching for some proper pillows for himself, as well as such perennial basics like plates, forks, and specialty lightbulbs found only at IKEA.

"I don't think I'll find it here."

"Find what here?" Aaron asked.

"What I want."

Petra, like him, was keeping an eye on the odd community of families in search of better furniture.

"Besides," she said, "we need to make sure Granddad doesn't wander off."

"I guess you have better things to do on the weekend," said Aaron.

"Not really," she said. "Do you?"

"Not really."

This was to be expected. He was a divorced man taking care of his daughter and father. But she was sixteen. Why didn't *she* have anything better to do with *her* weekend?

"What about that guy you met at the mall?"

"What about him?" she asked.

"Have you seen him?"

"I see him every day at school."

"I mean outside of school," Aaron said, aware of how adept his daughter was at evasion. He realized he sounded accusatory and decided to change tack.

"Dad, do you want to take a rest for a moment?" he asked.

Karl, out in front, didn't answer, but Aaron would have sworn that instead he picked up the pace. He was a stubborn old bastard, Aaron thought. And not very likeable.

The hot dogs were just on the other side of the checkout counters, and after paying for their purchases, Aaron, Petra and Karl joined the line of hungry shoppers. It had taken only a few trips to IKEA for Petra and him to develop a routine: they'd shop, and then she'd eat, ordering two hot dogs, a drink and a box of Danishes. Aaron ordered a tea. The food here was poisonous, he thought, but there were worse routines in the world.

This time Petra surprised him. She wasn't beside him; neither was his father. Instead the two had ventured over to the Swedish food section, where they were picking up crackers, cheese, smoked salmon and other items far healthier than the hot dogs his daughter usually ate.

The surprises kept coming after they returned home, because Petra, who'd never shown any interest in the kitchen before her grandfather arrived, prepared some food for them all. It was as if she'd decided that as the sole female in the household, it was her role.

Aaron watched her bring out a plate of cheese and crackers, along with the pepper grinder. Not a pepper shaker, mind you, but a grinder, because Karl insisted pepper needed to be fresh. Karl's arthritis meant he found it difficult to twist the grinder, so it was Petra who hovered over the sliced cheddar cheese, waiting for her grandfather's odd culinary command.

It wasn't forthcoming.

"Grandpa?" She held up the grinder to show him.

Karl sat in a heavy wingback armchair, one of the few pieces of furniture brought over from his apartment. Today's excursion had induced a vacancy of expression on his face, a dreadful oblivion from which his granddaughter was trying to rescue him. His father had good days and bad—good *moments* and bad. Blank periods like this, when his father sat in his chair staring into space as if he'd abandoned himself, were frightening, and they reminded Aaron yet again that he needed to keep looking for a place that could look after him. His father couldn't go home. And he couldn't stay here.

"Do you want some pepper?" Petra shook the grinder in front of Karl, as if it were a rattle.

"No," his father finally answered, without looking at her or the food.

"Okay, but you *always* like it with pepper."

Not this time, apparently.

Aaron watched from the couch with perhaps the same blank expression as his father. His newly purchased pillows were stacked on the other end, along with some sheets, and on the coffee table was an empty water glass, a pair of reading glasses and the book he was reading, *The Organic Diet*. Aaron didn't like sleeping on the couch. It didn't help matters that his father had fallen into the habit of getting up in the night, sitting in that armchair and staring at him while he slept. Aaron, sensing a presence, would open his eyes, and there would be his father, looking at him as if trying to figure out who he was. Aaron would declare himself—"Dad, it's me"—but there were times when he was certain his father knew exactly who he was, and that that was the problem.

The expression in Karl's eyes was disquieting—it reminded Aaron of a pet fish he'd once bought for Petra. It quickly became her favourite, and she named it Goggles because of its comically outsized eyeballs, which swivelled upwards and conveyed a state of perpetual anxiety. Something deeply unsettling about his father's expression reminded Aaron of Goggles' eyes—that longing for freedom from the confining contours of its world and yet, at the same time, the need for someone to take care of its daily needs.

"Go back to bed," he'd tell his father, and then Aaron would read from his book, fall back to sleep and dream he was a piece of organic fruit: easily bruised and with a short shelf life.

Unable to shake her grandfather out of his daze with the cheese, Petra tried another approach. "Tell me a story about Dad," she said. "Something I don't already know."

The question appeared to work. Karl stitched his eyebrows together, his forehead folding along the deeply incised vertical lines until the edges of each bushy strand made contact, a positive and negative charge ready to ignite thought. Aaron leaned forward. Aaron and his father didn't talk in stories; there was never any banter or family mythmaking, no *You'll never believe what happened to me today!* So whatever his father was about to say would likely be something he hadn't heard before. Forgetting about his lactose intolerance, Aaron reached for the cheese plate and popped a few slices into his mouth.

His father spoke. "He was a good boy."

It was the sort of vague, abstract and ultimately meaningless description he should have expected from a father who himself was vague, abstract and ultimately meaningless.

Even Petra sounded disappointed. "In what *way* was he good?" she asked.

But the tightness in Karl's forehead had already eased, and the sparking contact between his eyebrows was severed, along with whatever memory he had been replaying in his mind.

"Why don't you let Grandpa rest?" Aaron said.

Petra turned and looked at him as if this were the first time she'd noticed he was in the room; it was clear she wasn't trying to get a rise out of just her grandfather.

"How come we hardly visited Grandpa when I was growing up?"

"We visited," said Aaron, through a mouth full of cheese and crackers.

"When?"

"You want dates?"

"I just don't have a lot of memories of him when I was growing up."

"You're still growing up," Aaron reminded her.

"I meant when I was a kid."

"You probably don't remember the times we visited, because you were so young."

Petra looked rightly skeptical.

Aaron recalled the time he'd brought over a framed photo of Petra as a baby, taken while she was in the bathtub. Instead of propping it up, Karl had laid it flat on the table, where it stayed for the entire visit, Petra's glowing smile directed toward the ceiling.

"Why don't you ask Grandpa how many times *he* came to visit *us*? He's right here."

Karl stirred in his chair. "I'd like a cigar now."

"You know you can't smoke in the apartment, Dad. You'll have to go out on the balcony."

"But it's cold out."

"So wear a jacket."

"It's not pleasant," his father protested with unexpected delicacy.

"Neither is cigar smoke in the apartment. And it's not anything I want to expose Petra to."

"I don't mind," Petra said.

"Well, I do."

Aaron knew his father hid a stash of cigars in his room but couldn't bring himself to take them away, even after he'd returned last week to an apartment that reeked of smoke. Petra had been looking after her grandfather, but he hadn't said anything to her, just tried to show with slumped shoulders that he was disappointed, though this parental attempt to induce guilt didn't seem to have much effect on his daughter. He knew that she smoked cigarettes, another life-altering habit she'd formed after the divorce. Everything she did seemed designed to hurt him. The two of them probably smoked together, so he wasn't surprised now when she offered to help.

"I'll take him to the park."

Petra fetched her grandfather's coat, and when he rose,

he allowed her to place it over his shoulders, the sort of simple act that had eluded Aaron all his life. Aaron suggested gloves and scarf but was ignored.

After the front door closed behind them, he grabbed a pillow and tossed it behind his head, but he didn't feel like napping. Within minutes he felt a gnawing pain in his gut, which he unsuccessfully attempted to ignore. He got up and took the cheese plate to the kitchen and turned on the dishwasher in the hope its hum would soothe him, but there was something off-key about it, a whisper of a sound that exaggerated the unsettling quietness.

After the decision was made to leave his house, he had spent less than a day looking for a new place before settling on this apartment. When things fall apart, it's best to fit yourself into a mould, thought Aaron, and these four square walls with stainless steel appliances would do for now. He just hadn't planned on his father being there.

During Aaron's early years, there had been empty fields around his parents' house, but developers soon filled in the spaces with tract housing, brown and squat, each with a newly planted tree out front, a futile replacement for the imposing maples they'd knocked down. Then they'd widened the nearby highway. At night, he would hear the dull roar of it, the distant waterfall of tar and rubber. There'd been a mad race to transform the land, to make it as unrecognizable as possible, everything changing, nobody knowing what was there before and nobody caring.

Aaron spent a lot of his childhood watching television shows where aliens made frequent visits to earth, invading homes and bodies, often undetected. He'd find himself shouting at the television to relieve the unbearable tension caused by such a dark and dangerous secret. "He's an alien!" he would warn the townspeople, but it never made a difference, and besides, there was, in their unmentionable secret, something about the aliens that reminded him of his father.

Karl had once given Aaron an expensive leather-bound diary, the kind that looked like a published book but had endless blank pages to fill. "Your Story" was embossed in gold letters on the cover. Perhaps his father, unable to speak about his own past, hoped it might be different for his son. Aaron, intimidated by its title, had never written a word in it.

With both of them gone for a smoke, Aaron took a shower. The bathroom had the high functionality of a hotel room, everything impersonal and in its place, so that even a tube of toothpaste and a couple of razors made the sink counter look chaotic.

The room quickly fogged up with steam from the hot shower. Wiping the condensation from the bathroom mirror with the heel of his hand, Aaron stared at himself in the small circle of reflection. With dark hair that easily tangled and almond-shaped eyes, he'd never looked anything like his father, whose swept-back wavy blond hair, blue eyes and Aryan good looks had surely contributed to his survival. But what else had Karl done to survive? Aaron imagined that one had to do evil to survive evil, that it was the best and the finest who had perished. It could very well be that his father had been a shit all his life and for him to blame the Holocaust was false. But maybe that was just trying to make sense of what remained, at its core, inexplicable. Bad people lived; so did good people. There was no rhyme or reason to it.

He opened the bathroom window and leaned out, baring himself to the biting wind of late afternoon and stared down at the sight of daughter and father huddled in the small parkette below, Petra's blue puff jacket ballooned and partially unzipped, her body oblivious to the cold. He was horrified to see her smoking a cigarette. His fears were confirmed.

His father was also smoking, and though Aaron couldn't smell the pungent odour of his cigar, the smoke crept through the now open window of Aaron's memories. Then as now, his father took contented puffs, tasting the smoke as one would a fine wine, then blowing it up toward the sky.

Looking down at his father's wisps of white hair combed back over a freckled scalp, he felt as if he were decomposing like the fall leaves scattered about his father's feet. Aaron had never smoked and was careful where he placed his feet on the wet bathroom floor. He ate organic and was wary of potential danger, a gift from his father, whose absence in his life was contradicted by an almost obsessive concern for Aaron's safety. "Be careful," he'd say, when his young son stepped outside the house; sometimes he'd grab his coat and accompany him to a friend's house or the corner store, the two of them keeping step along the sidewalk, saying little to each other, as if they were soldiers on patrol, alert to danger. "Keep an eye out" was another of his favoured warnings.

164 | DAVID LAYTON

But an eye out for what? Aaron already knew there were people who wished children harm and that he shouldn't talk to strangers, but he never sensed that was what Karl was getting at; it was something far more menacing.

Aaron had kept his eyes open as instructed until the day his father left the house and Aaron discovered that he'd been blind to the real threat: abandonment. His father had never returned to the house or to him, eventually becoming the very stranger he'd been warned about.

Leaning out of the bathroom window, Aaron felt lonely and apart and wanted to call out, *Hey, Dad, it's me. Tell me what happened. Tell me the story.* It was probably the only thing worth talking about, the only real thing that would explain what they were both doing here and why he should feel so furiously strained.

Instead he hovered over them like the grey clouds above, damp and silent, until a sharp pain in the gut, a result of his carelessness, forced him to pull back into the room, doubled over in agony.

12 JACOB HAD INVITED HIM FOR DIN-
ner, and Karl was happy to be walking
on the road leading out of town, the sun
already sinking behind him. Now that the
heat of the day had subsided, he spotted several cows in the
emerald green fields, the air so still he thought he could hear
the sea's rhythmic attack and its retreat from the shoreline
more than a mile away. No matter how big the Dominican
Republic, with its ten-thousand-foot mountain and wide,
rich valleys, Karl could never forget it was surrounded by
sea in every direction.

In Austria the sun could speedily dip behind a mountain,
and during the winter months, it would sometimes hardly
appear at all. In the tropics, though it darkened quickly, Karl
always felt the sun, even when it was hidden behind thick
clouds. At night, the brightness of the moon and the constant warmth of the air spoke of its presence.

The road Karl walked along traversed the north coast
of the country, beginning at the Haitian border, onward
toward Puerto Plata, past the sugar cane fields he'd seen
from the bus, and then for a few short miles, Sosua and the
newly developed homesteads. Small tracks laid down by
Dominican feet led off from the main road, and Karl would
occasionally spot Dominicans walking to or from a home

well hidden behind thick tropical greenery. Perhaps they felt safer that way. These people were friendly but often seemed baffled by Karl's appearance, as if he were some fruit growing in the wrong season. These were not the Dominicans who had come to work for the colonists. These people lived too close to the soil to wander away from it. They were terribly poor, in rough clothes and bare feet, even worse off in some instances than the black Haitians who worked the sugar cane fields.

Walking past the impressive homestead belonging to the Sichels with its large front porch and *jalousie* windows, he noted that the Jewish colonists thought otherwise. They weren't afraid to be seen at the side of the road. The General had given them citizenship, and land too, which the Sichels were busily clearing for cows and crops. They were all favoured by the General.

The road continued through ever more primitive and remote villages and towns until finally reaching the town of Samana, located on a peninsula similarly named that jutted out like a fat index finger into the Caribbean Sea.

Less than a hundred years ago, a foundering ship full of American slaves who were being transported from one plantation to another had washed ashore, as if that index finger had beckoned them to safety. They'd found freedom in their new home of Samana, and it was said they still spoke an old-fashioned and courteous English from their time of American captivity. Karl wondered if it would be the same for the colonists, if in a hundred years his descendants would be cut off from the world, rumoured to have escaped a catastrophe and speaking an old-fashioned, antiquated German. The island was full of displaced people, thought Karl, and he was one of them. Like the American slaves, he had been shipwrecked and had come to this lost shore to find a home.

Jewish colonists, families mainly, were moving out of town, building homes, digging wells, clearing and seeding land and raising cattle. Dairy farming had become popular among the colonists. Every day a van—one of only two owned by the community—picked up fresh milk from the homesteads and brought it to town, where it was pasteurized and shipped to Puerto Plata and farther inland to the second-largest city in the country, Santiago. A few women had banded together to create the Sosua Fibre and Crafts store, where they embroidered Tyrolean flowers on sisal fibre belts that were then exported to the United States, Cuba and even faraway Argentina.

The recently incorporated Sosua Cheese Co-Operative was now producing various cheeses, ranging from Dutch to Danish but also lately adding a new mild-tasting, yellow-tinged cheese called "Sosuan." Karl had been involved with its earliest production, helping to press the mass of salted curds with his fists, so that it occupied the mould evenly. The perfected cheese had been invented just after the United States entered the war, and it was Jacob, along with other dairy farmers, who'd uncovered the white linen cloth, tasted a few slices of their new cheese and proclaimed with religious solemnity that "This cheese is the very first product made in the Hebrew Colony of Sosua."

Meals in town were taken communally, but cheese wasn't always on the menu, because what was made needed to be sold. It wasn't particularly missed by the children, who had quickly adapted to the Dominican diet of rice, beans and *plántanos*, whereas many of the older refugees still ate and cooked foods from home—meat and potatoes and fat that coagulated on the plate. Mrs. Baum, one of the first settlers in Sosua, had even started making apple strudel to sell out of her home. Felix had tasted it and thought it was delicious, but he stubbornly refused to buy any more, saying he didn't want to eat any food associated with the people who'd tried to kill him.

Karl never felt the need to pick sides but, like Felix, tended to stay away from Mrs. Baum's apple strudel, for a different reason: the taste transported him back to memories of his sister, who loved strudel, especially when the pastry was sprinkled with sugar. Trude loved anything sweet, which didn't seem to stop her having the whitest teeth. Sugar was rationed before Karl had left her behind in Vienna, and he sometimes imagined bringing back with him a few stalks of the sugar cane that grew like wheat, vast fields of sweetness ready to be plucked and sprinkled over another batch of apple strudel.

Not that he would be able to get back there any time soon. The British were in North Africa and still had a long way to go if they were to reach Berlin. The war news was typed up and posted to a mango tree in town, not far from the *colmado*, and over the course of time, the ink would bleed onto the bark, as if the great events beyond their shores were being washed away. He felt that way about his memories, as if they, like the news, had bled out but left a ghostly imprint. If the war ended in victory, would he simply reverse the journey? Would he take a boat, then a train back to Vienna and walk back to his apartment as if none of this had happened? He could not imagine it, and so he tried not to imagine anything at all to do with his family. He had a new one now, or something like it, anyway.

The spirit of communal eating in some ways accorded with the presence of a kibbutznik who'd been brought in from faraway Palestine to teach the colonists how to grow food and sustain themselves as a group. Beyond the kibbutznik's inexperience with tropical conditions—in Palestine he'd learned how to conserve water whereas in the Dominican the trick was finding methods to drain it away—his singular failure lay in his inability to marshal any true communal, socialist spirit among them. He didn't last. Shortly after arriving, he packed his bags and made his way home via New York and Cairo to join the bigger fight.

The truth was no one in Sosua wanted to share land; the communal barracks were only temporary arrangements, born of necessity rather than ideology. What people wanted, including Mr. Weinberg, were separate homes and plots of land they could claim as their own.

"We need to stand on our own two feet," Mr. Weinberg told Karl. "We Jews have always been dependent, looking for someone to solve our problems, to protect us, even to feed us. Now we will become farmers and feed ourselves."

But in Jacob Weinberg's haste to be settled and get on

with things, mistakes had been made. Though the house
he built was raised off the ground to avoid dampness and
insects, it was angled to the east, which allowed the wind
to blow rain through the window slats. Sometimes, Ilsa
told him, she would wake up during the night thinking her
sheets were damp from sweat, before becoming conscious of
the storm outside.

"One learns from one's mistakes," said Jacob Weinberg.

Things would get better. Improve. This was only one
of the platitudes that sustained the Weinberg family and
which Karl preferred over Felix's dark and, he felt, increasingly stupid mutterings.

As Karl approached the house, Ilsa, spotting him from a
window, came out to join him on the road.

"I didn't see you on the beach this afternoon," she said.
"I was worried that you weren't going to come tonight."

"Did you miss me?"

"Yes, of course."

Karl told her he had been working, but in truth he'd
avoided her so that he could walk the road alone. Sometimes
it was better to think about walking beside her than actually
doing so. He could talk to her more freely when he was
alone, and he could also ignore her when the need arose and
concentrate on other things, or nothing at all. He liked to
lose himself on the road, to forget who he was.

The question was who he wanted to become. Ilsa seemed
to be a part of his future self, but she didn't let him advance
toward it, keeping her distance. She let him kiss her and
hold her hand in the water, but that was really all she allowed.

Ilsa was young, but so was Karl. She seemed at times far more confident. Of course she missed him, she'd said, but in what way, and if so, why not let him get closer to her?

Together they walked to the front door, where Mr. Weinberg put out his hand, and Karl felt the grip of a proud man.

"It's good to see you, Karl."

"I brought these from the *colmado*." Karl handed over several lemons.

"Good boy, you remembered. Come, let me show you something," said Mr. Weinberg.

Ilsa took the lemons inside, while he and Mr. Weinberg walked around the house, past the well he'd helped dig seven months ago, toward one of the two modest sheds. Inside was a wooden paddle similar to one the Sosua Cheese Co-Operative used to churn milk. Beside the wooden paddle stood a series of glass jars.

"I'm skimming off the whey, pouring the cream into the jars and shaking it until I make butter." Mr. Weinberg held out his hand as if to ward off an objection. "I know I don't have any milk to spare, but why should the co-operative make all the cheese and butter? Maybe I can do something a little different."

"I'm sure you can," said Karl.

Mr. Weinberg stared at Karl, as if his words held deep significance. "Yes, why not! Here," he said, pulling off a layer of cloth from a wedge of cheese and cutting a thin slice. "Taste."

Karl tried it. "It's good."

"No, it's not."

"I think it needs a little more salt in the curd. And you need to paddle the milk more, let it thicken until your arms feel like they'll fall off."

Mr. Weinberg nodded. "When are you going to come and join us?" he asked. "We could do with your help, Karl."

Men like Karl, who were single and under twenty-one, were being encouraged by the town administration to move in with settled families and help out on the farms. He'd been asked on several occasions by Mr. Weinberg to live on his homestead, but so far Karl had refused the offer.

When they returned to the house, Ilsa handed him a glass of cold water flavoured with the lemons he'd brought from town.

"Soon we'll have our own," she said.

Karl took a seat on the porch and stared in the direction of two small lemon trees planted close by the country road that had led him here. On the other side was a bush, its upper reaches flamed by the setting sun.

"And oranges," said her father.

"And bananas," added Mrs. Weinberg, joining them on the porch. "We should have some of those soon too."

She was a quiet woman; she had never said much, here or when they'd first met on the ship. Karl had alternately thought her shy or stern but came to realize she was neither. Rather, she was infused with a deep moral conviction that was in its own way stronger than her husband's. She believed in this project, in this place, and in her Jewish family.

"Like the avocados?" Ilsa's words provoked weary laughter from her parents.

"Next year in Jerusalem," said Mr. Weinberg, his joke for failing crops and other natural setbacks.

They all clinked their glasses and repeated in unison, "Next year in Jerusalem."

"You see that we need you," Mr. Weinberg said to Karl. He turned to his family. "I asked him again to move in with us, but so far he says nothing."

"I'm thinking about it," said Karl.

"It's good to think. But sometimes you need to act. And Ilsa would like the company."

Karl turned away, furious at himself for blushing. Ilsa was one of his strongest motives for moving to the homestead. But she went to school and Karl would be alone during the day. He feared the isolation of living away from town. But then, there would be evenings like this, when they'd be close.

"Where would I sleep?" joked Karl. Their home was small, with only two bedrooms. "Perhaps at the Sichels'? They seem to have enough space."

Mr. Weinberg frowned at the mention of his neighbours' house. Karl knew he disapproved of the way they hired Dominican labourers to help out on the farm. Local labourers had built the Sichel house, which was why it was bigger and sturdier than Jacob Weinberg's, and why, too, it was properly situated to take full advantage of the breeze.

"We can build an extra room ourselves. Or maybe your own cabin, for privacy. I can get some extra lumber if you move out here," he said. "You don't want to stay in town forever, do you?"

"Maybe not forever," Karl admitted.

Mr. Weinberg was a socialist. He, along with the communists—Karl did not fully understand the difference between the two—worried that the Jewish refugees might one day lord it over the Dominicans, paying for labour they should do themselves. The Dominican Republic did not want Jewish merchants, and these sentiments seemed to be shared by Jacob Weinberg and others, who in some ways disapproved of the town they had helped to develop. Sosua encouraged activities and occupations that belonged to their past. He could tell there were those who suspected that their former problems might one day visit them here, that their only chance to change their future was to change themselves, to become something other than who they'd been.

Did Karl want to change? Lurking behind Jacob Weinberg's invitation was a question as much as an offer.

"And we might even build your own outhouse," said Jacob. "Think what privacy that will be after living in the men's barracks."

The toilets were a favourite topic of complaint in the community. They were kept as clean as possible, but they were infested with spiders, all of them gigantic, some deadly. Karl didn't know what the women's toilets were like, but the men's could be revolting on hot days after a recent rain, when the sun shone directly above the zinc roof.

"So, your own room, a private outhouse with no spiders, and good, honest work. What more could a man ask for?"

* * *

KARL MADE HIS decision three weeks later. With a towel slung over his shoulder, he was on his way to take a shower in preparation to attend a musical put on by the colonists, when he spotted several military vehicles driving down the town road and stopping outside the *colmado*. The soldiers remained inside the vehicles as if to allow the dust to settle, and all that could be heard was the low rumble of engines that had not been turned off.

Karl and a few of the colonists made their way over to see what was happening. The military had never before stopped in their small colony. A few Dominican dignitaries had visited from time to time, but that had all been organized and announced long before they arrived, and the community had been given time to prepare a special meal, to lay out tablecloths and offer speeches of gratitude and friendship. These vehicles had arrived without announcement, or none that Karl had heard about.

"What's going on?" Karl asked those nearest him.

"I have no idea." The man who answered had arrived on the last boat to make it out of Europe. His name was Francis. He came from Belgium, was at least ten years older than Karl and, by and large, kept to himself.

Karl had learned that upwards of a hundred thousand Jews had been offered sanctuary in the Dominican Republic, but after the outbreak of war, only 650 of them had made it over. They were it. As his mother might have said, they weren't exactly *das beste vom besten*, the cream of the crop.

It wasn't a standoff, but with the colonists waiting and the engines rumbling, it felt like one. Eventually the doors opened and uniformed men jumped out on either side of their vehicles, then walked toward the *colmado*, assembling where the news of the war was posted.

Karl had learned enough Spanish that he no longer needed Joseph Stern's translation, after he showed up and began negotiating with the soldiers. The men in uniform were requisitioning two of Sosua's valuable trucks, which they claimed were needed for the war effort. Stern was accompanied by a committee member belonging to DORSA, whose money supported the colony. Based in New York, DORSA had paid passage to Diepoldsau for Mr. Solomon Trone, who'd selected him and Felix for relocation. American money had paid for their passage across the Atlantic, had even paid for Karl to lose his virginity. And it had paid for the trucks. As proof, the man from the settlement agency presented a sheaf of papers that Karl was close enough to see had a series of stamps, swirling signatures and embossed emblems meant to impress anybody except the soldiers, who proffered their own documents.

Four soldiers from the end of the military convoy were ordered to join the men up front, and all of them walked over to the two trucks to be confiscated. A few of the colonists helped take out milk canisters and other hardware from the back of the trucks, which the soldiers allowed before jumping into the vehicles and starting up the engines. Then they drove off, a reminder to Karl and all the Jews that they lived at the mercy and goodwill of a dictator.

On his way to the musical shortly afterwards, Karl

wondered if it wasn't a better idea to hide, the way the impoverished Dominicans seemed to do, living off the main road and out of sight.

The performance took place at the makeshift cinema, where a Russian trader living in Santiago delivered battered film canisters every two weeks and returned with cheese and anything else he could sell back in town. On stage, the men and women of Sosua wore homemade lederhosen and feathered hats. They sang Austrian folk songs while dancing around a white picket fence festooned with ivy and meant to remind the theatre-goers of the tamer greenery of home. Was that, too, a form of hiding? They wanted to look just like Austrians, even in this place. It made Karl think of his summer vacations in the mountains, when he and his family would dress up in traditional clothes, and the time, seemingly so long ago, when a farmer had examined the palms of his hands and those of his sister as well. They'd been too soft for his liking, and there'd been something else that the farmer hadn't liked about them either. Karl now knew what it was.

After the musical ended, Felix found it comical to hitch up his pants and pirouette in the street. The confiscation of the trucks had made them all come a little unhinged.

"Who'd imagine that we'd sing and dance to the music of our enemies?" said Felix. His mocking tone, as it so often did, felt like an attack on all of them, including Karl.

"We have the right to miss our home. Or should they be able to take that away from us as well?" Karl was surprised by his anger. He wasn't defending only himself but, he felt, the colonists too, including and especially Ilsa, who had stood up and clapped after the performance.

"They've already taken it away. Look where we are." Felix extended his arms up to the sky. They hadn't walked very far but already they were enveloped in a starry darkness. "We're Jews who grow bananas."

"We don't grow bananas. And if you did any work around here, you'd know this. What do you suggest we do?"

"We wait." Felix shrugged. "Maybe after the war we go to America, maybe Canada. But we shouldn't be here. Everyone wants to pretend this place is paradise."

"No one ever worked this hard in paradise," said Karl, thinking of Jacob Weinberg, his neighbours and everyone else who was putting time and sweat into creating a precarious home for themselves. Like the trucks, it could all be taken away with a few pieces of paper and florid signatures.

"There's blood here," said Felix.

"What are you talking about?"

"You know what I'm talking about. Everyone here does."

"I don't."

"Remember that first day when we got off the boat? There was that official who told us he was part Jewish."

"Yes. I thought it was strange. He seemed proud of it."

"Well, that's not the strange part. When Trujillo arrived, he went on in Spanish, and Stern, who'd been translating, kept his mouth shut. Did you ever wonder what he was saying?"

"No."

"He was talking about the Haitians, how they were

black and reproducing at a rate that the Dominicans couldn't defend against. We're the answer."

"I'm not sure I understand what the question is."

"A white migration. That's what he was saying."

"How do you know?"

"Well, now that we don't need Stern to translate for us anymore, the answers aren't hard to come by." Felix pulled a creased newspaper clipping from his pocket. It was from *La Información*. "'The Haitians, a black race,'" Felix read out, "'are immensely more prolific than our race, a race of white and mestizo people. How can the Dominican Republic defend itself against this huge danger? The answer has been said a thousand times, by bringing a white migration.'"

"We're the white migration," said Felix. "We were saved by a black dictator, because we are white. Our glorious saviour, Dictator Trujillo, who wears makeup to make himself look whiter, brought in Jews, brought in *us*, to whiten the population. We're meant to breed with the Dominican women, like prime cattle."

"That's ridiculous."

"It may be. So are the Nazis, but they're dangerous too. They thought we were dirty Jews, the Americans in New York thought we might be Nazi spies, but now we're simply white. At least things are improving."

"If we're so favoured, then why did our trucks get confiscated?"

"That's just the price of doing business, and a small price, if you ask me. Do you know that the man who saved

us sends an American limousine out to the countryside looking for young, pretty virgins? Mothers push their daughters
in front of the windows, so that they will be picked and
saved from poverty."

"Did you read that in the papers too?"

"Here's something else you won't read in the local
papers. We're here because others died."

"Who died?"

"The Haitians. They're the Jews of the Dominican
Republic. They cross the border to find work, just like us.
But they're not white, and the Dominicans don't like them.
A few years before we got here, they were slaughtered by
the thousands. Men, women, children even."

Karl knew about the Haitians, had watched them
mainly from the road as they toiled away in the sugar cane
fields. He'd heard rumours about the tensions between
the Dominicans and the Haitians, and a few deaths here
and there years ago, but nothing specific and nothing that
would make it the business of the colonists. Nothing about
a massacre.

"Whatever you're talking about has nothing to do with us."

"Of course it does! And we know it. How else to explain
the need we have to justify ourselves, to show them we're
good people. To show *us* we're good people. Don't you see?
We've disregarded the dead. We are as guilty at Trujillo. In
all the time we've known each other, we haven't said a single
thing about our families. Not one word about what we did
to escape. It's probably why you want to spend all your time
with the Weinbergs. A second chance?"

"Leave them out of this."

"Or is it Ilsa that has you so interested?"

Felix was taller, but Karl was stronger; he'd developed a core of muscle that was his reward for hard work. A quick snap of his arm dropped Felix to the ground. It happened so quickly, they both stared at each other in surprise. For all the time Felix spent on the beach, he was as white as snow and seemed to glow against the dark, unpaved street. Karl had wanted to hit Felix for a long time. His friend had always been on edge, but lately he seemed to be worse than usual.

"You wouldn't be here, if it wasn't for me!" Felix's voice cracked childishly.

Karl, walking away, heard him call out, "She won't be with you. Not in the way you want her to be."

That was the moment he decided to move in with the Weinbergs.

13

AARON WOKE UP ON THE COUCH, HIS body overheated beneath the sheets, and peeled away the thin blanket. He kept the temperature in the apartment high for his father, who needed a warmth his own body could no longer supply. It was his father, and not the heat, who woke him up.

"Morning, Dad." *Father, Dad, Daddy, Pops, Papa*—the words surfaced on Aaron's lips like submarines, armed and malignant.

His father wore padded headphones and stared at the TV. Hands on the armrest, wearing a jacket, his prominent brow disdainfully bounced back his son's greeting along with the inane images emanating from the television screen. Aaron raised an arm off the sheet and wiggled his fingers in greeting but stopped when he recognized his actions were devoid of friendliness.

It was disquieting to see his father in front of a television so early in the morning, and Aaron wondered if there might be something deliberate in his actions, his way of showing just how low he'd sunk since moving into the apartment. In some perfect world, a father would be grateful for his son's sacrifices, but this wasn't a perfect world, certainly not for his father, so there was no point expecting Karl to behave differently.

He'd had a lawyer draw up power of attorney papers, which his father steadfastly refused to sign. The only option was to declare his father mentally incompetent. He'd taken Karl to the doctor for a diagnosis, a first step in finding out what was wrong with him and what might be done about it, but also for building up a medical file Aaron could use to gain legal control over his father's affairs. Regrettably, the dividing line between normal incompetence and mental incapacity was narrow and not easily defined. The lawyer explained it this way: "A man with three children can leave all his money to an animal shelter. You might not agree with his decision, but the law isn't looking for what is reasonable or just. The state only becomes involved when a citizen is a threat to others or themselves."

The lawyer had asked various questions pertaining to Aaron's relationship with his father. How often had he seen him over the years? Did they get together for special occasions or religious services?

"Not really" was Aaron's answer.

"Would it be fair to say that you are estranged from your father?"

"In what way do you mean 'estranged'?" Aaron asked, because there seemed to be something legal and therefore precise about the word. He felt he needed to be judicious.

"In the way of not seeing him that often."

Aaron accepted this might be the case.

"So under the circumstances, your father's wish not to give you power of attorney might be construed as a mark of clear judgment."

It was a trap, but a good one, the sort of thing he expected from a competent lawyer.

"We're spending Thanksgiving together," Aaron said in his defence.

The lawyer hadn't seemed all that impressed.

They'd never spent Thanksgiving together before, or he couldn't remember ever having done so, which amounted to the same thing. It wasn't a holiday his father had taken seriously.

"What time is it?" Aaron asked his father now.

A weak light filtered through the curtains, indicating it was early morning and probably overcast. Aaron rose from the couch and pulled back the curtains. The sun streaming through the window startled him.

"Jesus," he said, shielding his eyes.

"We've been waiting for you to get up," Karl said, without pulling off the headset.

"It's ten past nine," Petra answered from the kitchen, which meant it wasn't early at all.

He heard the hot sizzle of bacon hit the frying pan. "Smells good," said Aaron, even though he'd never adjusted to the smoky stench of fried pig.

For most of Aaron's working life, he'd been the first to rise. He'd taken pride in pulling back the warm covers, while others were still asleep, planting his feet upon the floorboards as if claiming new land.

Aaron went into the kitchen, leaving his jacketed father bathed in magnanimous light.

"Do you want an omelette or sunny-side?" Petra asked.

"What are you having?"

"I've already eaten."

"What did you eat?"

"I had some toast," she said, losing interest. She'd asked him a question, and he'd responded, as parents often did, with questions of his own.

"I made some coffee," Petra said.

The sight of her pouring him a cup intimated some future domestic activity that made him wonder how long he'd have her for. He felt time slipping out of his grasp, whole chunks of it disappearing from view. There were times when you needed to take stock of your profits and losses, and Aaron decided that this Thanksgiving was one such time. As with his father—perhaps because of his father—the day had never meant much to Aaron, and the celebration might easily have passed him by if not for his daughter.

"I'm sorry Mom couldn't come today," he said.

"No you're not."

"Well, your grandmother is coming."

"I have everyone I need," said Petra.

Aaron was surprised that such a small, awkward gathering could be enough for her. Surprised and a little saddened, too, that he couldn't offer her anything more substantial.

After breakfast, he showered and then went into Petra's room—*his* room when she wasn't visiting—and pulled out a pair of jeans and a shirt from his part of the closet. She didn't have a lot of clothes in the room, but he'd given her most of the space. There was a large gap between his garments and hers, as if to underscore their distance in other ways.

When he returned to the kitchen, she and her grand-father were playing cards. While he prepared the turkey, the air was punctuated with repeated shouts of *Schnapsen!*, until, forty or so minutes after the bird went in the oven, the apartment took on a warm holiday glow.

He might even have a slice of meat today, especially as Petra seemed so enthusiastic to be sharing Thanksgiving with her family. After learning of his lactose intolerance, Aaron had wanted to avoid becoming one of those precious foodies, overly delicate about what went into his stomach, so he began relaxing his food standards, enjoying fish and the occasional piece of chicken. He didn't think of it as a concession to his daughter's changed habits but secretly hoped she'd see it that way.

Aaron spread a white tablecloth he'd bought for the occasion and set the table with napkins and cutlery and, for a final festive note, two candles, which he lit moments before his mother arrived.

She'd brought a pumpkin pie. "Hello, Karl. It's good to see you again," she said before putting it down.

"It's always good to see you, Claire. Especially when I know where I am."

No one had expected humour, and their laughter caught them all by surprise. Aaron suspected his father had mustered his energy all morning long to deliver the line.

"I can see our son is taking good care of you."

"He's cooking a turkey" was all Karl said.

"It smells delicious," she said, this time to Aaron.

His mother smiled, and he spotted the missing tooth.

Because it was located toward the back, the gap was notice-able only when she showed signs of happiness.

"Would you like something to drink?" The question came from Petra. "White?" she asked. "We have red wine too, and whisky or vodka, if you want something stronger."

Aaron did not appreciate her ability to grade alcohol content. She must be drinking now, had probably even got-ten drunk a few times. He thought about the boy in the mall and hoped she wasn't doing drugs. They were all doing drugs, weren't they?

His mother accepted a glass of white wine. Aaron accepted the vodka. His father took a shot of whisky, and Petra drank a glass of Diet Coke he feared might be laced with something stronger. He'd never seen signs of impair-ment, which was a good thing, unless it merely indicated she was clever enough to hold her liquor when around adults. It was all a dim perception, his daughter's life conducted on the far margins of what Aaron could see or hear or touch.

It was like that with his parents as well. Even when they were right in front of him, when he could hear and see and touch them, they might as well live a thousand miles away. His mother, wearing what she would consider her second-best outfit, remained standing with her glass of wine, as if it were intermission at a play she was attending, while his father sat like a second-hand piece of furniture.

Aaron took a sip of his vodka and tonic and coughed. Petra had poured half the bottle into his glass.

"You look freaked out," she whispered.

"I'm fine," he said.

"No, you're not."

"I hope everyone's hungry," Aaron said to the room.

No one replied. His mother pointed out again how well he was taking care of his father.

"How's the house?" Karl asked her.

"As it was when you last saw it."

"Good."

Aaron escaped to the kitchen. He took the turkey out of the oven and let it settle, feeling as if he needed to do the same. Diluting his drink, Aaron took another sip, a large one to cancel out the effects of the dilution, and stood beside the turkey as if to appraise its death.

"Let's eat," Aaron said finally.

While he brought out the food, Petra rounded up his mother and father and placed them not at the head of the table but at the sides, as if to enshrine them as guests.

"Well, this is a feast." His mother smiled again, and again Aaron saw the gap between her teeth.

He felt sorry for her and then, quickly, selfishly, Aaron felt sorry for himself. His mother had failed to maintain a posture of hope and had long ago given up on any new relationship. Aaron knew how difficult it was to find another person to share a life. Did *he* really want to live with someone else? If he did, how would he find someone? Maybe he should go on a dating website or sign up with a matchmaker agency.

He was ashamed to admit that during his marriage, he'd spent almost every holiday with Isobel's family, always happy to sit back and relax and let another family do the work. While they'd been at the table, drinking and eating, his mother, he supposed, had sat alone. He couldn't blame that one on Karl.

It was his daughter, he acknowledged, who had brought them all together today. With Petra here, he had felt he could invite his mother. It would have been awkward without her, too intimate with just himself and Karl.

As a child, Petra's favourite toy had been an elephant she'd named Sweetgum. On Sweetgum's birthday, she threw him a party. She'd been selective with the guest list, attuned as she was to the inner and outer circle of doll friends and the intricate relationships among them. She'd sat there with Sweetgum at her small plastic table, feeding him imaginary cake, with only two other doll guests in attendance. "He doesn't have many friends," she said. "No one likes him."

Except Petra. She liked him. It was her decision to befriend and isolate. But when Aaron had a harder look at Sweetgum, whom he'd taken to be just another stuffed animal with the customary expression of dumb happiness on its face, he saw the problem. Sweetgum's eyes didn't sparkle with affection but were opaque and inward-looking, and his trunk was raised not in cheerful greeting but lowered like a shield. Sweetgum looked old and withdrawn and exhibited few of the attributes associated with cuddly toys. He looked, in fact, a little like Aaron's father.

"Do you want to say something before we eat?" he asked Petra. Because this ceremony was unfamiliar to him, he'd decided to defer to his daughter.

Taking her role seriously, she said, "Here's to family."

Petra raised what he saw was a glass of wine, but that was okay; it was her toast, her assemblage. She had every right to celebrate.

"To family," they cheered back.

"To everyone else who couldn't be here."

"To all the family," said Aaron, because it was important to acknowledge that he and his ex-wife had once been family and for Petra would always be family.

Petra looked at Karl, who'd been the first to raise a glass to his lips, but his eyes were focused on the candles Aaron had lit, the flickering light softening the steely grey of his eyes.

"We thank God for what we are about to receive," said Petra, which really was taking things a bit too far.

His father, who'd never uttered a religious sentiment in his life, answered with "*L'chaim*."

It might have been the tryptophan from the small amount of turkey meat Aaron had eaten or the alcohol, but he felt a pleasant fatigue as his mother brought out the pumpkin pie and sliced it at the table. They talked a bit more, in the stilted language of a fractured family until, placing the rest of the pie in the fridge, his mother decided it was time to go home.

"I'm driving," Petra said, after they'd walked out of the apartment, and he'd slid a key into the car door lock.

"Sorry, old habit," he said.

Petra drove, her grandmother beside her up front, Aaron in the back seat. They'd left Karl behind, all of them claiming he looked tired, when in fact, no one had wished to test today's pleasantries within the limited space of a motor vehicle.

Karl could get out of the apartment, if he so wanted, but the real problem, thought Aaron, was that he'd still be there when they returned.

They passed a church close to his mother's house, and it was Petra, driving with a practised confidence, who pointed it out. His mother played the trombone, an instrument Aaron had always regarded as mildly eccentric. She'd joined a seniors band a few years before he left for university, and the members still got together to practise everything from Schubert to Abraham Goodman in the church basement. Occasionally, they were brought upstairs to perform for community events. They also played in parks, where people who came to listen brought striped lounge chairs of the sort you found in England.

Those older folks were all dying off, and new members were hard to find, or so his mother was telling Petra. The church sat there squat and solid but neglected, which was not unlike his mother's condition.

"You're driving very well," she told Petra, who beamed with pride that she'd reached an age where she could take responsibility for adults.

Aaron guiltily remembered the promise he'd failed to keep about taking his daughter to her final driving test.

When they arrived, Aaron escorted his mother to the house, the same one he'd grown up in and couldn't, at the time, wait to get away from. He still carried a key, and perhaps because he'd just been admonished for trying to lock in his father, he pulled it out and opened the door for her.

"I had a very nice time today," she said.

"Me too, Mom," Aaron answered, and as he turned and walked away, the thought came to him that after his father left her, Aaron had essentially followed him out the door. He had not been a good son.

"I think Grandma's lonely," Petra said, after he slid into the passenger seat and closed the door.

"What gives you that idea?"

"What doesn't?"

Petra pressed down on the accelerator, and as they drew away from the house, he saw the upstairs bedroom light turn on. Somewhere in that patch of light stood his mother.

"She really enjoyed herself today," he said, echoing his mother's words to him but adding none of his own.

"Did she ever meet anyone after Grandpa?"

"Funny you should ask. I was just thinking about this guy called Lenny. He was in the band years ago." They passed the church again, and Aaron pointed to it for no good reason.

"And?"

"And nothing much. This was years after I'd already left, and you know your grandma— she keeps things pretty close to the chest."

"So maybe she's got tons of boyfriends."

"I doubt it."

"Yeah, me too. I need to take her shopping."

"And we need to take her to the dentist—"

"Do you have a girlfriend?" Petra asked suddenly.

"What?"

"Are you dating anyone?"

"No. Are you?"

"I was sort of seeing someone."

"That guy I met in the mall?"

"You didn't meet him but, yeah, that guy."

"So what happened?"

"The thing is, Dad, we're all sort of lonely, right?"

"Is that the thing? Are you feeling lonely?"

"I went to the bank with Grandpa," she said.

Aaron was having trouble keeping up with his daughter's abrupt changes.

"What bank?" he asked.

"His bank. We went for a walk, and he took me there."

"That's entirely inappropriate. He shouldn't be taking you to a place like that."

"It's not like he took me to a strip club. Anyway, the point is, I found out about a few things."

"Grandpa's financial issues have nothing to do with you. He's going to be fine."

"It's not about the money."

"Well, it is, actually."

"Okay, then it's about who he's been sending money to." Petra pulled the car over to the curb. They were not yet home, and this sudden standstill on a residential side street made him feel trapped.

"Grandpa should never have brought you into this. Whatever *this* is. I told you, there's a world scrambled up in Grandpa's head and—"

"Don't you know who he's been sending money to? I think Grandma knows. We all know. Even you."

"Let's go home."

"You mean let's drive to your apartment."

"*Our* apartment."

"And what about Grandpa? Where does he live?"

"He will soon be living at some very expensive assisted-living facility that I'll probably be paying for."

"He doesn't belong there."

"I've never known where your grandfather belongs."

"I do," said Petra.

This time she hit the accelerator and sped off with a force that snapped his head back.

14

ILSA WAS PACKING HER BAGS, EXCITED to be going on her first major trip since they'd arrived in Puerto Plata.

"I've hardly had a chance to wear good clothes," she said, admiring in her closet several dresses she'd brought with her on the ship but had outgrown. "But Daddy says we can buy new clothes when we're there. Can you believe it? New clothes! Bought in a proper shop."

"That sounds exciting," Karl said, without any excitement.

"Isn't it?"

Ilsa was far too taken with her trip to hear what Karl really meant. And why should she? thought Karl. The sound of his voice, even with the wind behind him, wouldn't carry much farther than the road, never mind the capital city, a full day's journey away by bus.

"I wish you were coming," she said. "We could see everything together."

"I will see it when you come back and tell me all about it," said Karl.

Mr. Weinberg, worried about being away from his farm, had sat Karl down and recited what things needed to be done while they were away. "I'm leaving you in charge," he said, but Karl didn't feel in charge. He wanted to be invited to their trip to the capital.

"I haven't even gone, and already I'm sad about coming back," Ilsa said.

"I'll be here waiting."

"Yes, of course you will."

"And we'll go for a swim."

They hardly ever went swimming together anymore. The town was too far away, and while there was a beach near the homestead, he was too busy on the farm, tending cattle and planting crops, erecting fences and clearing new land, for him to disappear in the late afternoon.

"Did you know that they have swimming pools in the city?"

Karl had never given the subject any thought. What did it matter? he wondered. They had the sea.

"And there are stores, real stores selling clothes and pastries and books. I won't have to smell a single cow for the entire time I'm away."

But *I* will, thought Karl, helping with the baggage. He'd come out to work on the farm and be close to Ilsa, but all she wanted to do was head for the city.

It was an overcast morning, with rain threatening to fall, but the family, wearing some of their better clothes for the journey, didn't seem to notice or mind. They waited for the single milk truck that hadn't been taken by the government to give them a lift into town. There would be no milk for the truck to collect this morning, at least from the Weinbergs' homestead.

"It will be good to put my mind on other things than tending cows," said Mr. Weinberg, echoing his daughter.

The purpose of the trip was to attend a conference organized by the Americans about the fate of Jewish civilization after the war. Jacob had been invited and had explained the reasons why in some detail, but for some reason Karl had been unable to retain the information. From the moment Jacob Weinberg unfurled the map onboard the ship and showed him where and what they were sailing toward, Karl had relied on him to offer a broader, more complete picture of things—his very survival depended on understanding what lay beyond the border—but now he felt hostile toward any notion of a world outside Sosua. He didn't want to think about the end of the war, and just as urgently, he didn't want others to think about it either.

"Don't get lonely," Ilsa whispered in his ear, as the truck came into sight.

"I won't," Karl answered.

The family waved at him as they motored down the road, and he waved back as if happy to see them go.

While they were gone, he slept in Ilsa's bed. He was ashamed at doing this and worried that he'd replace her scent with his own and that she'd find out, but he couldn't help himself. Their rooms were side by side, separated by the thinnest of walls, which had been erected for his arrival to the homestead. There were nights when he'd press his hand against the wall, willing her to do the same. Now that he was lying on her bed looking at the wall from the other side, he pressed his hand against it in the hope that his other self, the one in the other room on the other bed, would feel better.

"I love you," he whispered to the Karl who was listening on the other side.

The Karl on the receiving end was silent, unable to answer. He felt a deep strangeness at being so alone and wondered if he was being overtaken with fever. If so, what would happen to him? He'd been abandoned.

Karl kept the hurricane lamp on during the night, though it cast flickering shadows that made him feel dizzy. Still, it was better than the total darkness of a moonless night. The Weinbergs had left during the darkest part of the month, and Karl considered if this was not some sort of test to see if he was capable and worthy.

He'd worked hard ever since arriving on the homestead. Jacob, as he now called him, for all his will, was not a strong man, or not strong enough for the labour required for raising crops and cattle. Besides, Jacob was never fully satisfied with being a simple farmer. He wanted always to talk about politics and economics and other subjects that made him forget where he was and what he was doing. Karl listened, because his education had stopped after leaving Vienna, or at least the formal kind Ilsa was receiving at the school in Sosua. Karl feared that the longer he spent on the homestead, the less he'd want to know about the world that lay beyond his grasp. At first they had cleared the land, opened it up to the sky, but that only made the boundaries around the field more pronounced and powerful. Success meant at the same time a closing in. It troubled Karl that his interest was ever more focused on what was directly before him— the pasture, the cows, the crops, the freshwater well, the fruit trees, the fenceline—but the wider world seemed to him a disruptive place that, among other things, threatened to take Ilsa away from him.

When she was there, they slept almost beside each other, the wooden wall an impenetrable dividing line. Karl accepted the need for patience and silence. They woke up at the same time but never together, and Ilsa would ready herself for school, while Karl dressed for the fields. Then they'd sit and eat breakfast together, at first fresh eggs, until the chickens they'd acquired succumbed to disease and infertility, and then beans and rice and salted codfish. Then Ilsa would mount her horse and begin the journey into town. He would see her late in the afternoon, unless she went for a swim with friends at the town beach. Now that they were so close, she never took his hand except for brief and unexpected moments. "I always feel safe with you," she'd tell him, and then, just like that, she'd pull herself aside and act as if nothing had happened. It confused Karl, but if it was patience that was needed, he would offer it. For now, he would lie alone on Ilsa's bed and wait for sleep to overtake him.

"I see you've found the perfect place."

It was just like Felix to catch him like this. He hadn't heard the sound of an engine or the approach of horse's hooves.

"What are you doing here?" He didn't get off the bed.

"I heard the Weinbergs went to the city," said Felix. "I thought you might like to come back to Sosua."

"I'm busy."

"I can see that." Felix briefly rested his eyes on the hair-brush that lay beside the bed Karl had slept on but mercifully chose not to say anything.

"They've started serving cold Pepsi-Cola at the shop. We could play a game of chess, if you came."

They hadn't talked since their fight outside the theatre, nor had he played a game of chess with him since Diepoldsau. But it turned out that Felix, who hardly ventured anywhere beyond the beach, had walked all the way out here, which constituted something of a miracle if not an outright apology.

Peeling away Ilsa's sheets, Karl got out of the bed, pulled on his pants and led his friend to the outside porch. It was early morning, everything newly begun and so fresh that the world seemed edible. A rooster crowed, and he saw despite the coolness in the air that Felix was sweating profusely.

"How are you?" Karl asked.

"I had a touch of malaria recently."

"I'm sorry."

"It happens to the best of us." Felix grinned crookedly as if to ensure there'd never be any possibility of him being the best of anything. "It's actually rather pleasant. Not the malaria, of course, but time spent convalescing in the mountains."

There'd been several waves of malarial infections since Karl's arrival in Sosua. Some of the earliest work Karl had done when joining the colony was digging drainage ditches to prevent the mosquito larvae from hatching. Any stagnant body of water was a potential hazard. Though a great deal was being done to battle the disease, it hadn't been eradicated, and those infected were taken away from the coast. He'd heard it was agreeable up in the mountains, a cooling reminder of their past homes.

"They have pine trees up there," said Felix. "It actually gets cold at night, and you sleep with a blanket. Can you imagine?"

Karl couldn't, not really.

"I was even told it snows at the top of Mount Trujillo, but don't believe it. Dominicans like to exaggerate, though how can you really blame them, when their leader names the tallest mountain after himself?"

"And the capital city," said Karl.

"Where the Weinbergs have gone," added Felix, understanding where Karl's interest lay.

"I wonder what it's like."

"Well, may I recommend getting a dash of malaria, then maybe they'll confuse the city for the mountain, and you can find out for yourself."

"I think there must be an easier way."

"Don't think, do," Felix said, mimicking Jacob. "Though, look where that's led us."

Felix remained on the farm and during the next few days did practically nothing to help with Karl's chores, though in his defence, he'd had another attack of malarial fever. He spent most of his time out on the porch with a blanket around his knees. At night he slept in Karl's bed, which allowed Karl to sleep in Ilsa's without the sense of strangeness that had attacked him on those first nights.

"You must find it difficult to sleep here," Felix said through the thin wall separating the two bedrooms.

"What do you mean?"

"Ilsa. She's an attractive girl."

To claim he hadn't noticed would only make him sound foolish, but Karl didn't want to admit outright to anything either, so he remained silent.

"She must be the reason why you are here."

"I like being here," Karl said.

"It's so . . . rural."

"Sosua isn't exactly Vienna."

"Or Cuidad Trujillo," Felix pointed out. "So what's the plan?"

"Plan?'

"You can't just lie in her bed and masturbate every night."

"Who says I need to masturbate?"

"Karl, I've known you since Diepoldsau. I was with you in Lisbon, when you lost your virginity. I know that nothing has happened. Personally, I prefer Dominican women, and normally I would urge you to do the same but I know you won't think of anyone else but Ilsa. So my question again is, what's the plan?"

"I don't have one," Karl admitted.

"I can see that."

With that admission came many more about how Karl felt ignorant and how he felt he was being tested and how Ilsa kept telling him to wait, to be patient. He confessed to Felix that he worried Jacob Weinberg didn't believe he was good enough for his daughter. It all came out, more than Karl ever intended or had even realized he felt. Felix listened from the other side, and after Karl was finished, he knocked on the wall to announce himself.

"Passover is in two months," he said.

"Yes, I suppose." Karl didn't actually have any idea when it was.

"And Weinberg, being a socialist and a Zionist, is also a confused refugee like all of us."

"So?"

"So he's religious. He believes in God."

"I suppose he does."

"Don't be obtuse, Karl. He believes in God and the Jews, and that means Passover is very important to him."

Karl was familiar with the rituals of Passover from his own family, which had been conducted with a casual allegiance, interrupted with animated talk at the table between the visiting business associates his father had always invited. An air of prosperous ease accompanied the eating of bitter herbs; one did not wish to suffer or attach oneself to the effusive sentiments of the poorer Jews of Leopoldstadt district, their piety alien and embarrassing to his own family.

As the youngest, Karl's sister had been required to ask aloud "Why is this night different from all other nights?" For Karl the answer was that on this night he and his sister would go in search of the matzoh, hidden earlier that evening by his father. His reward was often a new coin for his collection of Austro-Hungarian currency, the bearded and stern profile of Emperor Franz Joseph offering, in Karl's imagination, a portrait of Moses.

Karl was no longer a child interested in collecting coins or going in search of the matzoh. Thinking of Ilsa, he knew it was something more exciting and serious that he was after.

"What are you suggesting?" he asked.

Felix sang his answer. Karl had never heard Felix sing before and had not known that he had a beautiful voice. The words were Hebrew, a language he didn't know Felix was familiar with.

"You're full of surprises!" Karl called out, but his voice was lost in the rising intensity of the song, which grew louder and faster, Felix banging against the wall to keep beat, until Karl feared the house might collapse.

When he finished, he asked, "Do you recognize it?"

"No," said Karl.

"You must be familiar with the basic songs at Passover, though I'm sure your Viennese family were too sophisticated to sing them. But this song is important, and I will teach it to you. Now repeat after me: '*Mimitzrayim gei'altanu umibeis avadim pedisanu.*'"

Karl stumbled over the Hebrew. "What does it mean?" he asked.

"*From Egypt You redeemed us, from the house of slavery You delivered us.*" Felix laughed. "This is something Jacob Weinberg ought to like. You'll see. I'll teach you how to sing the song. You'll impress everyone, and then you'll stop having to masturbate."

* * *

ILSA SHOWED HIM a postcard she'd brought back with her. It was a picture of a broad palm-lined thoroughfare stretching toward the capital building, where Trujillo's government assembled. The picture seemed to mesmerize Ilsa, offering proof of how sophisticated, how *kultiviert* the city was. Telling him about her week away, she described the broad avenues, and the hotels where people sat in evening dress and drank cocktails, everything made of stone and concrete, the roads paved and smooth. There was shopping, she said. Shopping struck him as grown up, as something his mother would do and somehow against the interests and purpose of Sosua, which he suddenly felt needed defending.

"What would you want to buy?" Even before finishing the question, he knew it to be a stupid one.

"There's lots of things," she said. "We bought books."

Why hadn't they brought *him* any books? The answer was obvious—because there was no need for him to improve himself. Instead, they'd brought him a work shirt made from American cotton, as if he'd won a prize for spending the week watering and feeding the livestock.

Karl heard the condescension in Ilsa's voice and rubbed his callused fingers over the shirt he'd been given, feeling a roughness that didn't come from the cotton fabric.

"And it's not just about buying things, Karl. It's a city, a real city with cars and shops and proper houses."

Shortly after their return, Karl helped to build his own

bunkhouse, a world separate from the family he shared a table with.

"You should have a place of your own," Jacob counselled. "A man your age needs his privacy."

Karl heard the worry in Jacob's voice. The way he masked it with false concern for Karl's comfort and well-being made him furious. The family hadn't appeared so worried about Karl's privacy before going away to the city. This wasn't about his privacy but theirs. Maybe Jacob found out Karl had slept in Ilsa's bed, or noticed the way he looked at his daughter, which was really a way of trying to *not* look at his daughter. But Karl couldn't help himself, and why should he? Ilsa was a woman, there was no denying the fact, especially after her return from Ciudad Trujillo. She'd brought back with her bras that she excitedly showed him when they shared a few minutes alone in her room, and Karl thought about the time he'd touched her breasts and wondered if this was some kind of invitation.

After the bunkhouse was built, Jacob strung a separate clothesline for Karl, and the sight of his flapping sheets straining to touch Ilsa's bras drying on another line struck him as demeaning and desperate. Hadn't Jacob hinted that he'd be a worthy suitor for his daughter? Or had he used her as bait, to lure him out here as a farmhand? He would show Jacob that he was worthy enough to be a part of the family. Felix had written out the words of the song phonetically, and each night in the bunkhouse, he went over them, so that he'd be able to stand on his own two feet at the Passover table and sing the way Felix had done, with manic abandon.

Privacy did have its advantages. And so did the pouring rain, which came upon them most days and nights, because it muffled his hopeful incantations.

TABLES COVERED IN white cloths had been pushed together in order to accommodate the guests. Two candelabra standing on either end shimmered inside the Weinbergs' house, enhancing the darkness surrounding them.

Jacob wore a yarmulke and a white long-sleeved shirt, the underarms stained with sweat, as he poured wine into a silver cup engraved with images of the Wailing Wall and the twelve tribes of Israel. He must have brought the cup with him on the ship from Europe. Karl had brought nothing but the jewels he'd stolen from his family.

"Slaves we were in the country of Egypt," Jacob solemnly intoned from the Haggadah. "We have worked with mud and rocks, and we were inhumanly beaten and mistreated."

They still worked in mud, and if there was a god, Karl thought, his intentions must verge on the preposterous to have led them all to a patch of tropical land once owned by the United Fruit Company. It was, as one of the settlers had said, a land of promise but far from the Promised Land.

"Slaves we were in the country of Egypt," Jacob repeated, rising to his feet and inviting Karl and the other guests to rise with him. "At all times of our existence potential enemies arose who tried to exterminate the Hebrew people, but the Almighty has saved us. Although we were thrown out of one country, He has provided us with another country. Despised by one dictator, another has offered us his protective hand. So, in this historic moment, let us raise our cups and drink to the health of our protectors and pray that the Almighty blesses the generous people and the ruler of this sunny island."

These last words provoked wry smiles from the table, because it had rained almost continuously for the past three days. December was when the rainy season usually came to an end, but the last downpour had even the locals, who usually took what came to them with equanimity, expressing surprise. The road to Puerto Plata was flooded, and they were cut off from town. But Karl welcomed the severance from the outside world; it made him feel safe.

And yet the matzohs, specially shipped to them from New York, had made it through to them for the Passover dinner. They were meant to make the colonists feel less isolated, to place them in the wider world, but their brittleness and fragility highlighted for Karl the precariousness of their position, of his position, not only in Sosua but in this household.

To his intense disappointment, Ilsa had invited another man to sit beside her at the Passover table, an older man in his early twenties or so, whose name, Walter, should have been enough to dissuade anyone from having invited him. Somehow, like the matzoh, he had made it past the flooded roads.

"Father, ask Walter to tell us how we came to be delivered, just like the Jews in Egypt."

Her suggestion was met with a smug smile from Walter,

who seemed all too pleased to tell the tale. Jacob nodded his assent.

"It's a curious story," said Walter. "Rafael Trujillo has a daughter, who he sent to finishing school in Switzerland. She was treated poorly by the other girls and was very lonely, until she met my first cousin Hannah. They became good friends and kept in touch, after she came back home. The General and his wife were so thankful for this kindness that when the troubles started, they gave our whole family visas. And that's how we came to live here, but maybe it's a reason why we are all here. He likes the Jews because my cousin was kind to his daughter."

So we should all be grateful to him, thought Karl. He spoke with a plodding, north German accent that Karl silently mocked but which he also respected for the manliness that seemed more suitable to their present environment. His own mother would have fainted if Karl had spoken like that, but she wasn't here: he was alone, and the proper world of Vienna, with its effeminate, cultured German, sounded wrong to him in this place.

Karl told himself that Vienna was larger than Hamburg, where Walter was from, and more important, but Karl still felt like a rube. Walter wore clean leather shoes with fresh laces and soles. His pants were creased. He wore an expensive watch that kept the pulsing beat of city time. It helped to be friends with the dictator. And Karl, what did he wear? Even on Passover dinner he, like most of the other colonists, wore a short-sleeved shirt, khaki pants and canvas shoes. The wide-brimmed hat they wore during the day had failed to keep the tropical sun from tanning their faces. Except for Walter. His face, his skin, was pale in comparison, and Karl sensed that this wasn't by accident, that it was a mark of urbanity that Karl had long ago lost.

Walter lived in the city. It turned out that not all Jews had to cluster in one small space on this island. Walter could come and go, while Karl was stuck here, at this table, on this farm, unable to venture beyond the roadway linking him to the outside world. Other Jews who had made it out of Europe earlier than Karl had been allowed to reside in the city, to live and work and trade, enjoying the pleasures of real shops and theatres and schools. It reminded him of Ilsa's descriptions of how she'd found bookstores and clothing shops and places to stop for coffee and a cold drink, served to your table by waiters wearing crisp white shirts.

Walter's family ran a commercial business that assisted in distributing commodities made in Sosua—made by Karl and the other colonists—throughout the island. They helped to place Sosuan cheese and pasteurized milk on the store shelves of Ciudad Trujillo. In turn, they brought valuable supplies to Sosua. The matzoh on the table, sign of a benevolent and thoughtful world beyond their shores, had more than likely been warehoused by Walter's family. His seat beside Ilsa was no accident, nor was his journey up here. The Weinbergs wanted a proper match for their daughter, and clearly ever since their trip to the city, they no longer considered Karl good enough for her. Even Jacob seemed to be taken in by Walter. All three of them were fawning over him, because he came from a good family.

But Karl's family had been better. We had more money, thought Karl, more *kultiviert*, more of everything than the Weinbergs and Walter. Karl would show them how much better he really was.

Jacob pulled one of the matzohs out of a small velvet bag embroidered in gold silk thread with the words *Cohen*, *Levi* and *Israel*. These were the names of families, and the bag another heirloom the Weinbergs had saved in the crossing from Europe, another piece of their past that could and would be passed down to their children.

He broke the matzoh into small pieces and spread the bitter herbs over each one before distributing it to his guests, saying a prayer before eating it. Then he turned his attention to Karl.

"We have a special moment before us. Karl is going to sing us a prayer, though he wouldn't tell me which one. It's a secret," he said, and Karl heard something too jocular in the tone for his liking.

Without clearing his throat, Karl began singing, but not as rhythmically or enchantingly as Felix, because he was nervous, and because he knew it wouldn't help, not with Walter there at the table. It was a long prayer, repetitive in parts; Karl stopped halfway through, but no one seemed to notice. The table clapped.

"That was very good," said Jacob.

And Karl, unable to help himself, looked at Ilsa with the same hope he had when putting a hand on the wall between their beds. But she and Walter were engaged in some private discussion, ignoring everyone else at the table not because they were children but because they were young and above the boring rituals and prayers that Felix had stupidly suggested would win her over.

The women helped Mrs. Weinberg serve the traditional dinner, and shortly thereafter, solemnity gave way to the common concerns of the community. Accountants, housewives, industrialists, traders, chemists—these were past lives. All now spoke with avid concern about the *coquillo* weed, which they fought against daily in the melon fields, and they spoke about the new Presser Shop installed in one of the two kitchens, where tomato sauce and sauerkraut, beet salad, carrot puree, peppers filled with sauerkraut and spinach puree, along with kosher pickles, were prepared and preserved in Ball glass jars. These were the foods they knew how to make, the foods that came from the lands they'd all grown up in and been thrown out of. Most of the goods were sent every week to the capital, in a slow attempt to introduce these new products to the Dominicans.

Their neighbour Mrs. Klamptra had recently hired a domestic labourer to help around the house. Karl had once ridden over to purchase some eggs from their chicken coop and found her berating the Dominican maid for failing to sweep the porch. "They're primitive," she had explained to him.

Local labour was a constant topic of discussion, and even though it was Passover, tonight was no different. What, asked Mrs. Klamptra's husband, was the point in working so long and hard at fencing pastures, digging drainage ditches, building homes, when such tasks could be better done by Dominicans? "The natives are better at these sorts of things."

"We didn't come here to exploit them," answered Jacob.

Such talk, Karl knew, made him uncomfortable.

"We're not exploiting them. We're giving them jobs."

Mr. Klamptra had actually laughed when he saw Jacob's flooded fields after the downpour. "Build an ark!" he had said. "You're going to need it."

"How can we of all people say such things?" asked Mrs. Weinberg. She did not like the Klamptras, who came from a lower station in life. Karl had heard her refer to them sarcastically as "shopkeepers," and again he wondered what she secretly thought of him.

"Because we come from a higher culture," Mrs. Klamptra declared.

"And that's why we should treat them decently. Don't you see? The natives are a very proud race. We mustn't be shown to lord it over them. It will cause us trouble."

And no one, thought Karl, wanted to cause trouble; it's what had led them to this place.

Sensing the conversation becoming acrimonious, Jacob steered it back to the more mundane issues of weeds and tractors, saying, as if it were a prayer, "We must learn to use our hands, not always our heads."

For all of Jacob's expressed concerns, he at times employed local labour, just like everyone else. He also employed Karl, who had helped to build his separate quarters so that he would no longer be a part of this house, a member of the family. Wasn't he, too, just a labourer they were exploiting?

"I think it's important to help the locals," Karl said. He directed this to Ilsa. He wanted her opinion. He wanted her to stop talking to Walter. "Don't you think so, Ilsa?"

There'd been a time when he and Ilsa could talk about things beyond the everyday. Karl still liked to ask her questions about what she'd learned in school, remembering the afternoon on the reef when they'd looked out at the ocean and beach and sky. He felt now that this was a mistake; it wasn't exactly that she'd begun to lecture him, but impatience, like some nasty insect, had crept into her voice and built a nest there. He could see that there was something in his earnestness that irritated her, and the more irritated she became, the harder he tried.

"Well, we certainly have no wish to harm them," she answered dismissively.

She resumed talking to Walter, who glanced at Karl with an expression verging on concern, as if he almost had time to consider Karl's pain, but then he went back to looking at Ilsa, and Karl knew that he was forgotten.

"Of course not," said Karl.

It wasn't because he was no longer in school, or that he wasn't smart or didn't work hard enough. The reason he wasn't good enough for Jacob Weinberg's daughter was that he didn't, like Walter, have a family. Thinking that he could become part of theirs had been a mistake. He might be invited in as a friend, certainly as a labourer, but he was alone, exiled without a tribe, because he'd rushed through the parting of the Red Sea without his family beside him. Hadn't he left his sister on the wrong side of the shore?

Jacob stood up once again. General conversation came to an end.

"The Haggadah ends on a note of triumph," he said. "Truth, justice and loving kindness are the enemies of slavery, tyranny and oppression. The weak may be overcome by the strong, but only for a while."

Everyone at the table began to speak in unison, and Karl found himself joining in, his voice mingling with theirs.

This is the power of Passover.

This is the lesson of history.

This is the story of freedom.

But Karl didn't feel free. He felt trapped and alone and wished to get away, to rejoin Felix in Sosua and, like some of the other men in town, to stop working so hard.

This wasn't his land, it wasn't his country, and it most certainly wasn't his family.

15 AARON PUT HIS COFFEE CUP DOWN on the table and knocked on his daughter's bedroom door. It was half past eleven in the morning. He'd left her watching television last night, unable to concentrate on the third episode of the fourth season of some television show that Petra couldn't tear her eyes away from. His father had gone to sleep a little earlier, but he wasn't awake either, which was unusual. Aaron had craved those lonely moments in the morning, when it was just him and a cup of coffee, but now that he was alone, he felt ill at ease, as if something was wrong.

He waited another half hour before returning to her door. All he had to do was knock harder, and she would wake up. He tried again. Not hearing a response, he stepped inside.

It was bizarrely immaculate, the bed made, curtains drawn, school books and pens carefully stacked on her desk. It looked a bit like a hotel room, except for the Obama poster up on the wall. The blanket and sheets were neatly folded and stacked. Even the pillows seemed to be plumped.

"Petra?" he called out, as if he might find her with his voice.

He rushed to his father's room and opened the door.

The bed was uncharacteristically messy, and clothes were scattered about the room. In contrast to his daughter's, this room looked like someone had made a quick escape.

He dialed Petra's number. It went straight to voice mail.

"Petra, what's going on?"

Without hanging up, Aaron got down on his knees to peer under his father's bed. It wasn't what he'd find that was important but what was missing. The old-fashioned suitcase of his father's, with a strap straddling its perimeter like a pant belt, was gone.

Aaron waited for another five minutes, maybe less, before calling again. He was forced to leave another message.

"I'm seriously worried. Call me right now."

Aaron phoned his mother. There was a chance Karl had gone to her house again. He should have checked with her first thing, he thought, and not worried Petra or offered her ammunition for accusing him once again of being neglectful. How had they just walked out of the apartment?

"Dad's missing," he said.

"Again?"

"You haven't heard from him?"

"No. I would have called."

"Petra seems to have gone missing as well."

"What do you mean by 'seems to'?"

"They both seem to have disappeared."

"Well, maybe they've just gone out for a walk. Have you phoned Petra?"

"She's not answering."

"That doesn't sound like her."

Lately, he wasn't sure anymore what his daughter sounded like.

He phoned Petra one more time, screamed another message into her phone and then waited for a few minutes, not in expectation of Petra answering but because he was filled with fear and unsure what he had to do next.

He phoned his ex-wife. "Petra wouldn't be at your place by any chance?" he asked her.

"No, why would she be?"

"Well, Petra and my father are missing."

"As of when?"

"They were gone before I woke up."

"When did you wake up?"

"Around ten-ish."

There was a pause, and in his mind's eye he saw her consult the Tag Heuer watch he'd bought her five years ago, a gift so successful it had outlasted him.

"But it's past twelve-thirty!"

"I know. I thought she was sleeping."

"How could they just walk out together without you hearing them?"

"I've been wondering the same thing myself," he said. Then he recalled how Petra had pleaded with him to keep watching the television show with her. She'd wanted to tire him out.

"Would you go up to her room and see if anything is missing?" he asked.

"Missing? Like what? Our daughter?"

As he told her about their daughter's oddly immaculate

room and his father's missing suitcase, Aaron heard Isobel's worried footsteps stop halfway up the stairs, as if she were going to say something to him, before resuming her march upward. Then the footsteps stopped, and there was silence as she entered Petra's room. Aaron saw it with her, the white duvet cover with the vertical blue lines, the blinds dropped down and turned against the sunlight, because for some reason teenagers become vampires and fear the light, the white desk in the corner, the wide-planked hardwood floor, slightly scuffed and strewn with shoes, jeans, socks and shirts. But maybe that wasn't what Isobel was seeing, because he hadn't visited the room since leaving the house, and it might all have changed, the way Petra had changed. The blinds certainly wouldn't be down. Isobel would have thrown as much light into the room as possible, in the hope of banishing whatever shadow was hiding Petra.

"Do you notice anything different?" Aaron asked.

"I don't think so. I've looked, but I can't really tell what's missing, or if anything's missing, because I'm not sure what she owns anymore. I used to always be in her room. I folded her clothes. I bought her clothes. But now I don't know."

"Neither do I," Aaron confessed. Had he ever known? "She wanted to spend time with her grandfather," he added.

"And you didn't want to spend any time with them."

This was unfair but, as he'd just lost his daughter and father, perhaps well deserved. The angrier she became with him, the more violently Isobel rummaged through their daughter's belongings. Drawers and closet doors were pulled open and slammed shut with ever greater grievance.

"I think some of her summer clothes are missing. Is that possible? Wait," said Isobel.

Aaron waited. He heard another set of drawers opened, then closed, then opened again.

"Aaron, I can't find her passport."

"That's impossible," he said.

But it wasn't, and at that moment they both knew it.

"She's supposed to keep it in the same place at all times."

"Yes, that was the deal," said Aaron, because he'd been around at that point to make it.

Petra loved having a passport and from the earliest age had insisted that she be the one to present it to whatever authority requested it. They'd let her keep it in her room, provided it was always in the top drawer of her desk.

"What about your father's passport?"

"I don't know if he has one. I've never seen it."

"Well, let's assume for now that he does."

"Okay," Aaron said.

"Where has he taken her?"

"Look, let's not get ahead of ourselves. Maybe Petra isn't even with my father."

"What do you mean?"

"Maybe she went out, left him in the apartment."

"So you're saying they're both missing, but not together?"

Put that way, Aaron had to admit that it didn't sound likely.

"Aaron, her passport is missing, and so is your father!" Her voice was rising.

His father had always been missing, thought Aaron.

The problem was that his daughter had chosen to disappear as well.

"Where are they?" Isobel demanded.

"Let me phone you right back," said Aaron.

Aaron had gone past cajoling or yelling at his daughter. Now the message he left her was just a plain statement of fact: "I don't care what you've done or why. Just call me and your mother back. Let us know you're okay."

The phone rang; it was his mother.

"Have you found them?" she asked.

"I think I know where they are."

"Are you going to get them?"

Aaron paused and wondered how to proceed on a topic they'd assiduously avoided all their lives. She'd never come to terms with what had happened with his father. Neither had he.

"Mom, I need to talk to you about a few things."

"What sort of things?"

The things of the past, thought Aaron.

An incoming call interrupted their conversation. "Stay on the line," he said. "It's probably Isobel." He switched over.

"I'm just talking to my mother," said Aaron.

"I'm in the Dominican Republic."

"Petra?"

Aaron pulled the phone away from his ear and looked at the screen. There was his daughter's name. And a photo of a young woman smiling back at him, taken on her fourteenth birthday, the year he and Isobel had separated.

"Dad, can you hear me?"

"Yes."

"I'm in the Dominican Republic," she said again.

"Are you kidding? How did you get there?" Now it was Aaron's turn to consult his watch. It seemed barely possible that she could already be so far away.

"By plane," she said. Even at this moment, she couldn't refrain from being a smart-ass. "We left at six this morning."

"What are you doing there?"

"You know what I'm doing here."

Aaron nodded, though there was no one to record his acknowledgement.

"Did Grandpa do this? Was he the one who took you down?"

"No, I did. I brought *him* down."

Aaron took a few considered breaths. "Well, now you both need to come back."

"We can't."

"This is not up for discussion."

Petra fell silent, as if she agreed with him. Then he realized she was crying.

"Grandpa has gone missing," Petra said. "I can't find him."

16 "I'D SAY 'WELCOME HOME,' ONLY this isn't home and you're not altogether welcome," Felix said when he first moved back to Sosua.

Karl hadn't been the only one to return. Within the year, close to sixty other settlers, having found life too hard, had broken their farming contracts and gone back to Sosua. As punishment, the DORSA officials in charge of them had offered inferior accommodation, and they were no longer separated by sex or even family. With the rumours of what was happening to the Jews in Europe came new pressures from New York that the colony needed to become self-sufficient, or at least not so great a drain on their resources. Money needed to be spent on Jews in far direr straits than them.

The Berbaums, with their two children, lived in the same barracks as Karl. "What are we, outcasts?" Gina Berbaum loudly complained to Karl. It was also a complaint against him, because her lack of privacy was something she acutely felt in those close quarters. Her husband had drawn a makeshift curtain around their beds, but during hot nights they needed to expose themselves if they were to remain cool. One of the children developed the awful habit of picking her nose whenever Karl looked their way, which disturbed her mother far more than it did Karl. She'd slap the child's hand away in fierce protest.

Yes, that's exactly what we are, thought Karl, outcasts, all of us, whether we worked the land or lived in town.

Felix, despite a second convalescence up in the mountains, didn't look well. He'd lost more weight, and the sun seemed to have lightened his hair without darkening his skin.

"I have the clap," said Felix, registering Karl's concern. "It's rampant here. Don't worry, there's no chance of you catching it."

Felix drew down the edges of his mouth to show, as a clown would, exaggerated sorrow for his friend. "You're a young man and you should be doing what young men in this world like doing."

"And what is that? Getting venereal disease and killing people? Because that's what young men are doing."

"Well, I don't suggest you go off and kill anybody. But you could find yourself a woman."

"I had Ilsa," Karl said. It sounded pathetic to his ears, and he was thankful for Felix's temporary silence on the matter.

He and Felix were standing in line outside the DORSA office, waiting for their pay. The settlement agency doled out the salaries once a week, along with special ration stubs for such items as cigarettes and soap. Lining up for their money, the colonists used the occasion to practise their English on the two Americans who wielded the authority to disperse it. Speaking of the weather while counting out the money tended to slow things down, but nobody complained, because it was accepted that English was important. Karl himself said only "Hello" and "Thank you" when he reached the front desk with its ledgers and stacks of money stored in a heavy metal safe that seemed to convey the solidity, weight and wealth of America. Felix was one of the few who took his money without uttering a word in English, German or Spanish.

After stuffing the money into their pockets and exiting, he and Felix went to purchase supplies at the *colmado*, located less than a minute's walk away, along a dirt road that continued to the beach. Constant use had substantially widened the path since the day, years ago, when Karl first walked down to the sea, and Ilsa took his hand beneath the water's surface. He should have understood right then and there that her interest in him was transitory.

Anyway, right now the beaches that mattered were far off in Normandy, their locations posted on a newsboard propped up on the *colmado*'s veranda. News of the world was typed on a sheet of paper tacked to a mango tree, but the occasional newspaper from the city made its way through, often a single copy, already well-thumbed and precious.

The upper and lower folds of the front page, pinned to the board like an exotic insect specimen, showed several maps, one of Western Europe, another of the northwestern shoreline of France, and a closeup of the actual beaches invaded by the Allies—Juno, Sword, Omaha. All the maps had bold arrows of various thicknesses thrusting eastward. Berlin was clearly marked.

During the past year, the sea off the Dominican coast had thickened with ships. Even the once empty skies were now filling up with flying metal and men. Karl had witnessed a fleet of heavy bombers pass over Puerto Plata on their way out to open ocean, the whitecaps seemingly whipped up by their thrumming engines.

No one ever spoke of following those arrows back home. Rumours of forced marches, starvation and death camps had reached the colonists without any aid of newspaper or radio and were generally accepted as truth. After all, as a group, they had been first to believe in the impending disaster and committed to escaping it. Everyone understood, most especially the administration responsible for handing out the money every week, that there would be many more Jewish refugees, perhaps millions, looking, as they once had done, for a new home.

Which made Felix and Karl and the other Jews milling about the *colmado* with their freshly dispensed money both an example and a burden. Passing over a few coins, Felix bought some Chiclets, for which he'd developed a mild obsession.

One of the Americans who only moments before had been doling out the money now spoke about the urgent needs of Palestine Jews, as if the colonists' good fortune were something to be embarrassed about.

"They need tools, clothes, food and money to buy land, but our resources are limited."

Their pleas were well understood, but the colonists had enough problems of their own to solve.

"We still haven't replaced the two trucks that were taken," one of them said.

"Stolen!" shouted another, as Felix leaned against the

colmado's veranda railing. Vigorously chewing his gum, he attempted a pose of studied boredom.

"We're working on getting them back or at least obtaining some compensation," said one of the Americans.

"We need those trucks to deliver our meat and cheese and milk. Otherwise everything will spoil."

The success of the Jewish colony depended on those trucks, and yet they'd had no choice but to hand over the keys and watch the officials drive off in plumes of petrol smoke.

"We understand, but remember that our brethren in Europe and Palestine and everywhere else in the world are suffering too."

Hal, the American, spoke with some exasperation, as if to spoiled children.

"The Allies have landed on the beaches of Normandy," he said. "The Russians are advancing. Europe is devastated, and support and finance will be needed for the millions of displaced Jews across the continent. This is not a welfare state."

They were all meant to make their own way eventually, to be profitable.

Hal had arrived from New York only four months ago. Along with the other Americans, he lived in private barracks with proper beds and finer sheets, shipped down to them by way of freighters from Miami and New York. Hal used hair gel that couldn't be found in the *colmado*, and his hair glistened with prosperity.

Felix hated Hal. "Trujillo brought us here, not you," he said.

"You must learn how to stand on your own two feet," said Hal.

It was an oft-heard comment, but Felix held an almost perverse belief in the opposite proposition. "Let them pay, that's my motto." Discussions about how their financial independence could come about had been going on for years and were especially pronounced after payday.

Felix pushed himself away from the railing and stood before the newspaper posted on the *colmado*'s veranda. He turned to Karl. "What will you do after the war?"

Such clear and confident certainty that all those arrows would eventually crash into Berlin left Karl momentarily speechless and reminded him of when his father had taken him to a museum. They'd stood before African masks, crossed spears, and shields covered in animal hides. His father told him, "You see, the treating of animal skins is an ancient and noble profession," but the physical facts presented to Karl had only deepened the mystery of what he was looking at. Who had owned these spears? What were the shields defending against? How did the shields and spears make it to Vienna? Had they been won in battle? Given as gifts? Were they stolen? He had so many questions, yet they'd already moved on. These primitive arts were meant to be looked at but not questioned too deeply.

If the arrows on the map were now like the strange spears he'd witnessed as a child, they also pointed toward something unknowable and primitive. The small, tropical world of Sosua, with its wooden huts and threadbare shops, felt more secure to him, more ordered and civilized than anything he recalled from the place he'd left behind.

"I haven't thought about it." Karl wasn't even sure he was able to envision the day when there might be a choice to stay or leave. The very idea felt threatening. Yet what he'd just said to Felix wasn't true: he'd chosen not to think about it every day.

"Have you noticed that everyone is learning English?" Felix asked. "The Americans will win the war and then everyone here will go to America." Felix stared at Hal, as if he were the full representative of that country and found it wanting.

"So why aren't you learning it?" Karl asked.

"I don't plan to leave."

He said this with the same tone of confidence he'd used for predicting the war's end. Karl was skeptical.

"But you don't like it here. At least, you always talk about how you don't like it."

"I hate the reason for being here but not the place itself. Besides, where would I go?"

"To America. You said so yourself. It's the future."

"Your future perhaps, but not mine." Felix pointed to the pinned newspaper with its striking arrows.

For all the suggested movement the arrows implied, he and Felix were stationary. Their tiny world was a form of shelter. They'd been hidden away.

"None of us is ever going back home, so I might as well stay here."

"Some of us might return," said one of the Belgian Jews who was standing on the porch near to them.

A new and hopeful expectation, especially among the Belgian Jews, who looked forward to early liberation, was taking hold of the colony. The war that pushed ever closer to Germany was also pushing toward them. They thought it possible that letters would soon make it out of liberated Europe, cross the ocean to reach them and that they, in turn, would write back to say they were alive and prospering.

Many of the colonists had been writing to their families for years. Karl had watched them as they sat on their beds, knees up, pencil in hand, or at a table in the dining room, bending their backs over a piece of paper, writing to those they'd left behind. These letters were more like diaries; though some colonists still slipped the folded papers inside envelopes they'd purchased at the *colmado*, they would not reach war-torn Europe.

At the same time, he and the other Jews created postage-stamp patches of cleared land that were never meant to be mailed or sent anywhere. Surrounded by mountains and forest and sea, they were cut off from the war and their past, which was the point of being here, the reason they were safe. Since returning to town, though, the outside world was moving inexorably toward him.

Felix had never left that world but had brought it with him like a poison.

"No one is going back," Felix announced. "There's nobody left. And we know it's true, because we're the ones who got out. We're the ones who knew. We're the survivors."

Felix popped a few more Chiclets into his mouth, and Karl was reminded of the sickly cows with their ribs sticking out in the field chewing cud.

"I've never told you what I had to do to get here," said

Felix. "And I've never asked what you had to do. There's a reason for our silence. It's like that with all the colonists. No one speaks about the past because it has no future."

Karl wasn't convinced this was true. If so, what about all the letter writers? *They* wanted to reach out and be found. *They* hoped for an ending. A future.

It was as if Felix were trying to chew away all the flavour of what they'd done so he could spit it out without remorse. Karl wondered about the compulsion. Why speak of not speaking about their past?

What would he, who'd never once sat down to write anything, have to say? Karl could speak about the machine-stitched American shirts, the good solid work boots he wore, the palm trees and tropical storms, and the babies born in Sosua who were proudly held aloft in their mothers' arms like ripe fruit that might easily bruise.

To actually address his family meant thinking about what might have happened to them. If they were dead, then he was truly alone; if they were alive, then he'd have to answer for his abandonment of them, especially his sister, who would no longer be a child. He wondered if he should write to her separately. She might understand what he'd done and why, but her tolerance—if that was what he was asking for—would be tempered by her experience.

What would she say to him, provided she could say anything? His last image of Trude was of her saying goodbye to him, knowing that she was being abandoned. To think of his family was to picture his father sitting by the window, the apartment bare of furniture and hope, his mother beside him stitching jewels into the lining of his father's coat, while Trude pleaded with her eyes that he take her with him, wherever he might be going. The worst of it was his own expression of reassurance that he'd look after her. Karl had saved himself. The jewels he'd stolen had brought him here to this tropical sanctuary. Now there was discussion of going home, of finding family, of a new life after the war.

"I'll stay here too," Karl said to Felix, in what he hoped was the same tone of finality Felix had used.

"No, this place isn't for you. You'd be better off going to Canada," said Felix.

"Canada?"

"It seems farther away, more removed and less important than America. I think there you could really escape."

Karl waited for him to elaborate on this unexpected thought, but Felix rubbed his hollow belly.

"It's lunchtime," he said.

Heading for the communal dining hall, they walked down the wooden steps of the *colmado* and onto the dirt road that had been so well trod over the years that, except for heavy storms, it no longer turned to pure mud after it rained. Farther from the sea, the soil was an oxidized red, as bright and boldly exotic as a tropical flower, but down here it was more the colour of the sand that was constantly being tracked into their sleeping quarters. Though it was common space and not hers, Mrs. Berbaum had scolded Karl more than once to take off his shoes and socks before entering their barracks. The soil of Sosua, which sustained and nourished them, managed to seep into everything, including their socks. Karl would rub his feet clean before getting into bed, but that didn't stop his sheets from becoming gritty. This insidious infiltration of nature infuriated Mrs. Berbaum. "What sort of place is this?" she'd ask. As with so many of her questions, Karl knew that in her mind it was the sort of place that didn't even deserve an answer.

He pictured her home in Vienna with its starched tablecloths and polished furniture, her children always clean behind their ears. That spirit of order and cleanliness found its strongest expression in the communal dining room. The long tables were beautifully set and spotless, their plates and cups without a chip or stain.

Some of the men here wore overalls, their sleeves rolled up as if eating, too, was work, while others wore shirts as spotless as the plates they ate off. Felix wore the same short-sleeved cotton top he used for the beach. "I'm on vacation" was how he would put it to Karl. Karl, who'd only just returned to the village and hadn't as yet been assigned a steady job, was also dressed in an in-between way, but whereas Felix seemed to enjoy his stand-alone status, Karl recognized the part of himself that wished to fit in. He would either acquire some overalls or get himself a clean white shirt.

In the dining hall, pretty women in light breezy dresses, their hair pulled back, served them. There was a rowdiness here that Karl always responded to. People complained and argued and laughed. At times like these, the community felt solid and strong, each person necessary for its continued survival.

As they made their way to two empty seats, Felix nodded in the direction of the open kitchen, where several Dominican women were cleaning up after cooking lunch.

"*Hola, Maricel. Hola, Paloma,*" Felix said.

"*Hola, Felix. Cómo estás?*" one of the women answered back.

Felix told the woman he was doing very well, which was a lie, because Felix was never doing very well, but he seemed genuinely happy to see her. "*Éste es mi amigo. Su nombre es Karl.*"

Karl said hello.

"How do you know her?" he asked, after they'd moved on.

"Maricel? The question is how do you *not* know her? Don't you think she's beautiful?"

"Yes, I suppose."

"You suppose?"

"I'm not sure. I haven't really looked."

He stopped, and Karl, following just behind, almost bumped into him.

"I'm sorry about Ilsa. I know you like her."

"She's found someone else," Karl answered, trying to sound worldly.

"Not found, but searched for," said Felix. "Mr. Weinberg, you believe him to be a man of the past with his faith in God and traditions, but all he cares about is the future. Do you understand?"

"Not really."

Felix sighed. It seemed always to be this way, Felix saying something and Karl not grasping it.

"The stink of survival clings to us. It's as odorous as

Italian garlic. Speaking of which, what I wouldn't do for a great plate of bolognese." Felix inhaled deeply, as if he could suck in the fragrance from across the Atlantic. "The war isn't ending just yet. You should get a woman," he said. "There are plenty to see, if only you'd bother. How about Maricel?"

Felix turned to glance at her, and Karl did too, but when she gazed back at him and smiled, Karl was deeply embarrassed.

"Don't be shy," said Felix. "We know you're not a virgin."

They may not have been served a good plate of spaghetti bolognese, but Karl enjoyed his heaping plate of rice and beans and chicken. As he ate, he had the sense that his own loneliness was a sweat stain he couldn't wash off. When Ilsa brought Walter into the house, he had felt the weight of family, the heft of it. He didn't belong to them, and he was happy to be back in town with people like Felix, who were also without family and alone. It was best to be with incomplete people, he thought.

"Go and say hello to Maricel when you've finished eating," said Felix.

He wanted to. Felix was right, wasn't he? The war wasn't going to end any time soon, and besides, he couldn't even imagine what would happen when it did. If every so often Karl felt the power of the outside world reach in and pinch him, if trucks could be confiscated, if Walter could come crashing through the front door of his happiness, if the General's limousine prowled the countryside looking for virgins, if there was an even darker and more brutal world lurking behind the lush foliage Karl found so beautiful, then it still felt safer than anywhere else he could imagine.

Perhaps it was his time to search for a future. All he had to do was walk over and say hello to Maricel.

Just then a great cloud of dust announced the arrival of the Jewish cattle ranchers, who rode in from the hills wearing wide-brimmed hats and stained shirts. They'd come to cool off in the sea and offered an excuse for Karl to postpone saying hello to the pretty woman. Slipping away from Felix, Karl followed the cattle ranchers and their horses to the beach. They were like cowboys in the American westerns he'd once seen as a boy at the Stadtkino cinema. They looked after nearly nine hundred head of cattle, the animals marked on one side of their haunches with *SS* for Sosua Settlement, an insignia that as Felix sarcastically pointed out was, by common consent, unmentioned by the colonists. Karl sometimes imagined the ranchers had come to assault and pillage this strange outpost in the sun.

At the beach, Karl took off his shoes and walked along the sand. The view was clear and sharp, and the gauze of humidity that usually wrapped the horizon in a milky haze had been stripped away to reveal a brightly naked world.

Floating out into water, the blazing sun overhead, the trees along the shore swaying in the breeze, Karl thought the land he'd left behind no longer seemed believable. How could he return, and what would there be to return to?

His fellow colonists might write letters, never to be posted, to those they'd loved and left behind, and a few might

237 | THE DICTATOR

even speak of reclaiming their wealth and past positions, but, in reality, nobody held much hope of returning. Most thought of finding a new life somewhere else. Felix had some strange idea of him going to Canada. Except for hearing of its soldiers battling in Italy and Normandy beaches, Karl knew little of it. He could list three of its cities, Montreal, Toronto, Vancouver, but he had no clear picture of them except that the last one was, like Vienna, surrounded by mountains. In school he'd learned about the Rocky Mountains and the Pacific Ocean. Perhaps he would go there. He couldn't imagine living in a city again, walking down paved streets in search of employment and a life.

He caught himself thinking about Ilsa, wondering if he could persuade her to come with him. But, of course, she would marry Walter and they would probably go to America after the war. They would leave this place. Karl was going to stay here, just like Felix, and this thought came to him at the precise moment he caught sight of Maricel and her friend, who after lunch had come down to play in the gentle waves that broke on the far side of the beach, where the Dominicans lived.

He shouldn't have been able to spot her so easily at such a distance, but it was one of those clear afternoons when sea and sky and all who inhabited the world in between stood out sharply. He was able to watch her in a way he could not, back in the dining hall. She was beautiful, her skin somewhat darker than that of her friend, as if she were marked out for something different, as if she were marked out for him, he thought. She was not wearing a bathing suit, something only the European women of Sosua could afford; she had on the same dress she'd worn in the kitchen, a blue cotton shift that clung to her body. It reminded Karl of his in-between clothes that weren't quite right either for work or the dining hall and that were now draped over some sea-grape roots on the beach.

Just then, Maricel waved at Karl and Karl waved back. Again, and against his will, he thought of Ilsa, because he had met her out here as well. Karl forced her from his thoughts. His future did not exist beyond this place, which he needed to make his own. Karl was a stranger; Maricel was not. Her wave to him was like a welcome to be a part of this place.

Karl remained on the beach until the sun started its slide toward the horizon. Moshe Baum, the eldest of the Jewish cowboys, his greying head bobbing in the water, said almost in a whisper, "Who among us would have believed we'd be bathing at one of the most beautiful beaches in the world?"

None of them, actually. But then, thought Karl, looking for Maricel in the emergent darkness, who would have believed any of it?

17 BECAUSE OF HIS PREVIOUS EXPERI-
ence at the Weinbergs' homestead, Karl was
given semi-permanent work in the dairy
factory. Since spotting the Jewish cowboys
while eating his lunch, Karl had dreamed of joining them up
in the mountains, but for now he milked cows and collected
the milk that arrived from the various dairy farms along the
north coast road. All the containers he pulled off the truck
looked the same, so he couldn't tell which of them belonged
to the Weinbergs.

The factory pasteurized and bottled the milk, which
was used by the colony and sold to Dominicans. The colonists also used the milk to make their Sosuan cheese. For
Karl, the excitement of creating the cheese had initially
distracted him from its rather bland taste. His mother had
adored a Tyrolean cheese so odorous it would stink up the
entire apartment. His family could afford a more provoca-
tive taste back then, before everything became dangerous.
The only thing anyone wanted to digest now was comfort,
something that was bland and pleasant.

Before work each morning, Karl filled his canteen with
tea from a large receptacle at the entrance to the kitchen.
Maricel was always there, and he received from her his rations
of bread, cheese, butter, sardines, salami, sugar, oranges and

bananas packed in the tin boxes that he carried in his backpack. He always said thank you, and she always smiled back. Karl knew—how, he wasn't sure—that if he wanted her, he could have her. And after days of milking cows and pasteurizing milk, Karl realized he wanted her. Why should he bother with Ilsa when he could sleep with a Dominican woman? He didn't need a white woman, a Jewish woman, to find contentment and pleasure. That would be like eating Sosuan cheese. Felix had told him as much, and the rabbi they'd brought down from New York had approved. Karl's interest was sanctioned by the community.

But he wasn't sure how to get close to Maricel. With Ilsa, things had happened gradually. He'd travelled with her from Europe, and she was the one who'd taken his hand that first day down at the beach. He'd worked for her father. They were Jews and spoke German. They suffered from the same problems and at times avoided the same subjects.

What of Maricel? He'd said hello to her and she'd smiled, but beyond that he didn't know what else to do. There were always people around in the kitchen, even early in the morning.

"She is always giving you extra food, so repay her in kind," said Felix, who also gave him directions to Maricel's family home.

After work, Karl decided to purchase a bag of groceries at the *colmado*—cheese, pork, rice and chocolate—and he trekked across the beach and then up a steep rise to Cherimicos, the Dominican village located on the coral headland opposite Sosua. He passed a church on the corner and then a series of wooden houses perched on cinder blocks, the quivering light from the hurricane lamps casting shadows along the narrow, unpaved road.

There was movement in both directions. Dominican women met settlers in Sosua, and Jewish settlers such as Karl came to Cherimicos. It was rumoured, too, that a few Jewish women had taken on Dominican lovers, but that was certainly not something Karl would have seen, because up until now he'd been on the other side of the beach and farther down the coast at the Weinbergs'.

He was surprised by the size of Cherimicos, though he had already observed how tropical countries can hide whole villages behind foliage. In his own way, Karl had kept his distance from the locals. He worked with them, conversed with them in his poor but functional Spanish, but until now it had all been conducted on his turf.

Karl followed Felix's directions, which were precise— take the second road after the church, turn right and follow the path until you reach the second from last home on your right—and he saw Maricel through the uncurtained window of her bare family home.

The door was open. He stood at threshold and offered the bag of food to Maricel's father, who wordlessly took it from him and placed it on the table. The father offered him a chair and they both sat down.

"Thank you for inviting me," said Karl, though in fact he'd invited himself, which he hoped was good enough.

"I have brought chocolate," he said, wanting to lay out its sweetness on the table.

Maricel, who did not smile, eventually took the bag of groceries and disappeared behind a thin curtain. She returned with a glass for Karl. Her father poured him some white rum.

"I don't speak very good Spanish," said Karl.

"I can understand you," said Maricel's father.

"I am Karl. Karl Kaufmann."

"I am Miguel."

Though there was already rum in his glass, Miguel poured himself some more and took a drink, not a large or aggressive gulp but a sip that indicated he might be searching for something to do with his hand. It occurred to Karl that he was shy.

"Where do you work?" Karl asked. "I have not seen you in Sosua."

"I work on a farm east of here. But my daughter, she works with the Jews. You pay her well."

Miguel smiled for the first time, and Karl wondered if he believed that it was Karl who actually paid his daughter or if he'd misunderstood because of his flimsy Spanish. Karl didn't know these people or how they thought. He was so far away from them that he felt dizzy and held in check a sudden urge to flee.

It was good that he stayed. Maricel soon returned from behind the curtain with the chocolate, its tin foil peeled back as if it had been delicately undressed. She served the two men, never sitting down herself, and though nobody said very much, Karl was infused with a sense of contentment as he tasted the chocolate and rum and basked in Maricel's attention.

When it was time to leave, Miguel shook his hand.

"Come back," Maricel said.

When he saw Maricel the next morning at the kitchen, he said hello to her as usual, and she smiled back. She gave him his rations, and after a day of labour, he went back to the barracks, showered, changed and returned, once again with groceries, to her home.

What struck Karl most about the house was the lack of window curtains. The place seemed bare without them. So about a week later, he arrived with curtains that had been used only briefly by a family in Sosua. They were white with red and blue stripes. One set was for the main room and the other for Maricel's bedroom window.

He'd returned to visit twice more before he spotted the curtains up on the windows, and he felt oddly proud of how cozy the house now looked when compared to the neighbours'. And only then was he struck by the fact that he hadn't as yet met Maricel's mother. Where was she? And how had he not noticed her absence on the few occasions he'd been there? Perhaps it was because Karl had become so accustomed to his own state of motherlessness that he apparently no longer saw it as abnormal for others to find themselves in a similar position.

"Where is your mother?" he asked her gently.

"She is dead," the father answered.

Karl felt his face flush in embarrassment. Should he have guessed this? Not asked at all?

"I am sorry."

"So are we," said Miguel.

A look of intense sadness crossed his face.

"My mother's name is Variola," said Maricel, and Karl was fairly certain she spoke in the present tense. The mention of her mother's name induced a smile so bright and open that it was as if she were casting sunshine into his eyes.

Karl let himself go blind. His own mother's name could not be spoken by him, in the present tense or otherwise. It had been years since he last saw her, and if the rumours coming out of Europe were true, he might never see her again. Dead. *Muerta*. He had this in common with Maricel.

She accompanied him on his walk back to Sosua that night. They strolled along the beach. It was dark, but they both knew their way along the worn path between the treeline and the sand. He took her hand, and she squeezed it.

"I thought you would never take it," she said.

They stopped halfway along the beach and sat down on a patch of surprisingly cold sand. Karl kissed her and then, for the first time since arriving in Sosua, and with only the second woman in his life, he made love.

Or he'd made something. It had been quick, and then he said goodbye and went back to Sosua, because he couldn't take her to the sleeping quarters he shared with the Berbaums and others. He imagined what Mrs. Berbaum, who yelled at him for bringing a smidgen of soil into the barracks, would say if she found a woman in his bed. She'd be hysterical.

Karl hadn't told Maricel he'd had only one woman before her, and one he'd paid for, and he hadn't enquired about her own sexual experiences, which he assumed by her actions to be more substantial than his own. As with so much else, though, he couldn't be sure. Up until that night, he hadn't even known her mother was dead.

AS THE VISITS continued, Maricel's father seemed to accept him the way he did the chocolate Karl brought to their table, as something worth admitting into their household. Karl would even lie with her on her cot, the mosquitoes buzzing around the net he'd bought for her, and gaze at her breasts and ripe hips, noticing how her dark skin was almost purple against his own. After all the time he'd spent on the other side of Ilsa's wall, wanting to touch her, there was now no barrier, nothing between him and Maricel.

Neither Maricel's father nor Mrs. Berbaum—nor anyone else, for that matter— interfered or commented upon his coupling with Maricel, though there was hardly any more privacy here than at the barracks in Sosua.

They never walked into town together. Karl would wake up at dawn, alone in her cot—Maricel left early for her job in the kitchen—and on his way into town, he'd pass the women gossiping at the communal water pipe as they awaited their turn to fill metal buckets and walk back across the beach to Sosua. Maricel was already working in the kitchen when Karl got there for breakfast. Nothing much changed in their routine—sometimes, for instance, he would watch a movie in Sosua and arrive at her house after she was already asleep, slipping quietly into her cot. Sometimes he spent the night at the dormitory, but he found that he no longer liked sleeping alone.

"Where is your family?" she asked him one night when they were in bed together.

He never imagined she would ask him this question. "I don't know," he answered.

"*Manman'm te Ayisyen*," she said.

This didn't sound Spanish. Karl didn't understand. Maricel repeated herself, and then, when Karl still looked confused, she said in French, "*Elle était l'Haïtienne.*"

My mother was Haitian.

As a child, he'd been given French lessons, but, like so much else in his life, that had come to an end under the Nazis.

"*Manman'm te Ayisyen*," she said again, and this time Karl understood that she was speaking Creole, a language Haitian cane-cutters spoke when they didn't want anyone else to understand them.

They were whispering, because they were in bed and it was late, but there was something other than the hurt of a lost mother that concerned him. There was something like fear in Maricel's eyes. It was as if the language she spoke was illicit and dangerous.

"One day she didn't come back," Maricel said.

"Where did she go? *Dónde fué?*" he asked stupidly.

"It was the Night of Tears," said Maricel. "I'm half Haitian. I am dark," she said. "*Oscura.* You see my skin. I am darker than many Dominicans, and that darkness is a danger for me."

My mother was Haitian. The explanation was inherent in those four simple words, but it took time for Karl to really hear what she had said, to piece the words together. She was not offering a clue for him to decipher but a bold clear fact. Maricel's mother was dark-skinned. And Maricel's skin, the darkness of it, marked her out. At night, when Karl reached out for her, he would notice how her skin lightened his own tanned body, but gradations of skin colour were not something Karl was attuned to. The Dominicans were all brown-skinned, some lighter, others darker, and while he noticed that the lighter the skin, the higher one's rank in government and business, even Generalissimo Trujillo, like Maricel's family—like many Dominicans—was *mestizo*, of mixed blood. Up until now, they had all been, to him, simply brown.

Karl had learned that Trujillo admired the colonists for their whiteness; it was one of the reasons they'd been brought to the country. But until now, he'd never properly considered the inverse: that Trujillo hated blackness, attributing many of the ills that plagued his own country to the dark blood flowing through Dominicans like an infestation.

"What happened to your mother?"

"I am taller than her now" was all Maricel had to say before she pressed her body into his and fell asleep.

It had never occurred to Karl that he too had grown taller over the past few years. He'd look down on his father, if he ever saw him again.

One day when Karl knew Miguel would not be home, he commandeered a vehicle and transported good chairs and a table to the family home. He didn't want Miguel to feel obligated by the gift or to object. Let the chairs just be there when he arrived home. Later, seated around the table, Karl asked him some questions about what had happened and why.

Miguel was born in Santiago, the second-largest city in the Dominican Republic, known for its rich agricultural land. The main road to the capital, Santo Domingo, ran through the city, and there was some trading that went on between Sosua and Santiago, but as with so much of the country, Karl had never visited the place. Before Maricel was born, her mother had found a housekeeping job with one of the land-owning families in Santiago. Miguel was already working for the family in the carpentry shop, helping to maintain the estate. They met and married, and shortly afterwards she gave birth to Maricel. Miguel found another job in the centre of the city, but Variola continued to work for the family, leaving every day before Miguel woke for breakfast and arriving home in time to prepare dinner for her family.

"One day she did not return," Miguel told him.

In 1937, branches of the military and police were called out to terrorize and herd the Haitians back across the border. Soon ordinary citizens began picking up rifles, guns, machetes or even common kitchen knives and doing their job for them, slaughtering as many Haitians as they could. Some families did what they could to hide and protect those who were being hunted, while others killed household servants who'd worked for them for years and even friends who were Haitian.

"That's what probably happened to my wife," Miguel said sadly. "But we will never know."

They never found her body. She just disappeared.

Generalissimo Trujillo wished to cleanse his country of Haitians who crossed into the Dominican Republic like a plague, unsettling the social order and worse, undermining its vigour with their negroid look—the same look Trujillo himself did his best to hide with whitening creams. His contempt metastasized into a nationwide slaughter.

After the fever of killing broke, Miguel was determined to leave the city that had killed his wife. For him it had been the Night of Tears, but the Dominicans, he said, had no name for what they'd done. Miguel never felt safe afterwards, not when his daughter was half Haitian.

"I heard a story about Jewish settlers who had come to my country in search of sanctuary, and I thought, 'What kind of stupid, crazy people must they be?' Then I read that they were white, from Europe, and I understood."

Miguel had brought his dark-tainted offspring to Sosua in the hope that the Jews' sanctuary might become his own. He did this at around the same time an American had come to Diepoldsau looking for young, strong Jews to farm a new land on the other side of the world.

"You are protected," Miguel said to him. "They will not come for you."

If Karl had learned one thing, it was that there was always someone coming for you. He felt safe here, but only up to a point. Who knew what the General might be thinking next year or the year after that, but compared to Maricel, he was safe, and so long as she was with him, she was too. Or so her father must have hoped.

The first time he'd spotted Maricel on the beach, Karl had thought she belonged to this place, when in truth, she was, like him, a foreigner. Her darkness was a sign of inferiority, a certifiable mark of an ancestry she couldn't scrub clean.

Lying on the cot that night, Karl placed his forearm next to hers and then entwined his fingers with hers; it was as if his white skin had also faded out his Jewishness. Nobody could see what he was. Underneath the covers, Maricel rubbed her hip against his thigh. He reached for her breast with his other hand and felt her nipple grow hard. She had small, perfect black breasts. Everything he loved about her, Trujillo despised. If they had children, they would be whiter than her, and their children's children might be whiter still. That was Trujillo's point, to clean up his country and eventually make it look like the one from which Karl and Felix and the other colonists had barely managed to escape.

"How many do you think died?" Karl put this question to Felix later, because Miguel had been unable to offer an answer. The death of his wife was enough; what more did he need to know about it other than that?

"Ten thousand. Others say more."

"Are you sure?"

"Yes, otherwise we wouldn't be here. C'mon, let's get going."

He and Felix, groceries in their arms, were on the road

251 | THE DICTATOR

leading out of town, which bent its way around the beach.
They heard the sound of the ocean beating against the sand.
It would be dark in less than ten minutes. Behind them, to
the east, lay Ilsa and the other homesteaders. In front of
them was Cherimicos and Maricel.

"I know you tried to tell me about it."

"Don't beat yourself up. No one wants to talk about
what happened."

"But you do."

"Yes, I do."

"You knew right at the beginning."

"At the very beginning, when we were on the bus to Sosua,
and you saw those Haitians working the sugar cane fields."

"I didn't actually know they were Haitians."

"But they were black."

"That didn't mean much to me."

"Remember when we got off the boat? That speech
about the white race, how we'd come to lighten the population? It didn't take long to figure things out."

"So why didn't you speak to me directly about it?"

"I did, and that's why you hit me, remember?"

"I hit you for other reasons." There'd been the play, the
white picket fence on stage, the Austrian songs, and Felix's
remorseless attack on all of it.

"Don't be so sure," said Felix.

They could have walked safely along the middle of the
empty road, but it struck Karl that they kept to its edge out
of respect for what it represented. This road linked them
to the outside world. They had travelled on it to reach this

place of relative safety, but the road also connected them to all the dangers from which they had escaped. One day when the war was over, Karl might take the road one last time and ship himself away to America or Canada, a place where a dictator did not rule.

"There's a lot I haven't understood," said Karl.

"Like I said, don't beat yourself up. There are a lot of people who do understand the truth but don't have the strength to lift it above their heads. Everyone here is without family. Even those with families, including the Weinbergs, are cut off. The Weinbergs were never strong enough for you."

It had never occurred to Karl to think of the Weinbergs as weak or in need of support, but looking back, he thought it possible that the loneliness he'd felt while living there might not have been his alone, that it was shared by all of them on that isolated pocket of land. What did Jacob Weinberg know of farming? The bemused smile he held for his cattle was perhaps nothing less than fear. And there'd been something desperate in the family trip to Ciudad Trujillo and in their eager welcome of the man who came to court Ilsa. The rituals of Passover had prevented Karl from seeing how fawning they all were to that German idiot, Walter. They needed something from him, Karl now understood. Their need showed weakness.

"I still don't have the full story. What are we all doing here? Tell me what you know, and I promise not to punch you again."

"I'm a weak man with malaria."

253 | **THE DICTATOR**

"And the clap, don't forget."

"That too, though that's been cleared up with penicillin. Me and the troops are fighting this dirty war together." Felix let out a hollow laugh.

For a moment, he'd been good and kind and thoughtful. Clearly it had taken something out of him.

"So tell me," said Karl.

"You have to go back to the old days in Diepoldsau. Remember how we worked those smooth Swiss roads? It didn't seem right that you and I should have had a hand in such perfection. One day Mr. Solomon Trone comes to a refugee camp in Switzerland offering sanctuary to Jews in some tropical country no one has ever heard of? Don't you think the whole of it was strange right from the beginning?"

Karl *had* thought it was strange, but so much had happened, most of it incomprehensible.

"Remember when the American mentioned a conference at Evian, France? It was about refugees, which meant it was about Jews. No one wanted them, least of all the Americans. And that's where our General comes in. Trujillo surprised everyone by offering sanctuary for a hundred thousand Jewish refugees. His problem was that he'd massacred Haitians, another persecuted people no one wished to help. Because the Americans were allies of Haiti and because they weren't exactly opening their arms to let in persecuted Jews, they were embarrassed on both counts, and so Trujillo saw his chance. Besides, he wanted white people to populate his country. Enter one Mr. Trone through the gates of Diepoldsau."

Obviously those hundred thousand Jews had never

made it over. There were just 650 of them, two of whom could now be found walking along a dark tropical road, each with a bag of groceries tucked under his arm.

"If you know all this, why do you want to stay here?"

"I told you. I don't have a home anymore. And I like it here."

"Even after what you know?" said Karl.

"You know it too. All of us do, including the Dominicans. But nobody wants to talk about it, and maybe that's the way it should be. We just carry on, maybe with some food under our arm and a girl to visit. And what can we do? I know what the man did, but maybe you can find some good in all of it."

"Who is this woman you are visiting?" Karl asked, changing the subject. He'd never met her and had never even asked after her until now, because he'd been so busy with his own problems and thoughts. It was also true that Felix was secretive and didn't appreciate questions directed at himself.

"She is someone I am seeing."

"Do you like her?"

"It's not a question of like."

Felix was too young to have lines on his face, but Karl could already see where they would appear. It was as if a thin sheet had been placed over him, hiding the wear and tear below.

"Then, what is it?"

"We might be travelling on the same road together, but our paths will lead us in different directions. Don't ever follow me."

Saying goodbye to the sweat-stained back of Felix as he marched farther down the road, Karl shifted the bags of groceries from one arm to the next, and in that moment, he noticed Felix do the same.

In some small way they were both helping other families. Maricel and her father had come to Sosua to make a new start and leave their past behind, just as Karl had done when he'd walked away from his own family. They were all in need of one another.

18

"SOSUA," AARON SAID TO THE TAXI driver.

Nearby was an armed sentry at the gates to the airport, and beyond him the mountains, their mottled greenery the same colour as the soldier's camouflage uniform. The soldier wore sunglasses with lenses so dark it looked as if he'd had his eyes plucked out.

The taxi turned left onto the main road and sped down a wide valley planted with sugar cane, their stalks brown and tattered on the upper reaches. After a few miles, Aaron noted how the sugar cane had been ripped out and replaced by a golf course that meandered with designed indolence toward the sea. People came here for vacations. In the distance were gigantic hotels and then more sugar cane fields. Ten minutes later, the landscape closed in on Aaron, as they left the wide valley behind and entered an area of green humped hills and scruffy villages. Smoke from burning leaves and rubbish rose into the afternoon sky like plumes of sewage.

Seated on the warm, worn upholstery of the taxi, windows down, the wind blowing through his hair, Aaron felt like he was stepping inside someone else's dream, a rushing, mysterious sequence of images that made little or no sense. He wanted to wake up and end this.

"You like merengue?" asked the taxi driver.

"I don't know," Aaron answered.

The driver shrugged. "People come, they want."

What Aaron most wanted was to find his daughter, and so he felt that the driver was in a profound way correct. The phone was in his hand, the aluminum body sleek and black and modern, refusing to absorb any of his sweat, and he resisted the impulse to phone her again. He'd spoken to her at the airport and had told her he was here and that he would meet her at the hotel. He'd also spoken to her mother and told her the same. Karl was still missing.

On Aaron's phone screen were the words he'd already scrolled through countless times since boarding his flight: *The small but growing town of Sosua, 18 miles east of Puerto Plata, is popular with visitors who come for the unusual European atmosphere. Founded by German and Austrian Jewish refugees escaping Nazi Europe, most of the original buildings have given way to modern development, but some of the town's original charm remains intact, with a Viennese patisserie, a synagogue, and a delightful, if rather busy, beach of fine white sand and calm inviting waters.*

There was something about this descriptive clarity that he hoped might soothe him, make him believe he was merely a tourist in hope of some sun, sand and a spot of history.

"He has a son. Your half-brother. There's a bank he sends money to." His mother's words came out in staccato bursts of anxiety after he'd told her that Petra and Karl were in the Dominican Republic. "All I know is that your father came to Canada after the war. He never really talked about what happened."

Neither had Aaron's mother.

Aaron spotted the billboards for hotels and soon the hotels themselves, as the cab turned left off the main road and entered the town, passing restaurants and shops selling sunglasses and fishing expeditions and real estate, until they reached the hotel where Petra was staying. He'd expected to see her waiting for him at the lobby; instead he met the concierge and allowed himself to be branded with a blue wristband, a prerequisite for admittance onto the grounds. Petra's room was on the second floor. Aaron took the stairs and then walked along a corridor overlooking the swimming pool. He searched for his daughter among the bathers and suntanners, but she wasn't there.

He knocked on the door of her room. "It's me," he said.

He was about to knock again, when Petra opened the door, and to his complete surprise, he slapped her in the face. She began to cry, not because of the slap, which wasn't very hard, but because she'd lost Karl.

"He's gone," she sobbed. "I shouldn't have brought him here. It was wrong. I'm sorry."

"It was a bit stupid," Aaron whispered gently into his daughter's ear, after she had buried herself in his arms. He'd last hugged her like this when she learned of the divorce. He hoped that one day they could be close like this without also dealing with some disaster, but for now, he greedily accepted this momentary gift.

"He wasn't in the room when I woke up this morning, and I can't find him anywhere. I've looked all over town."

They stepped inside, and the door swung closed with a thud, as if the spirit of Karl were getting back at Aaron for the times he'd locked his father inside the apartment. He glanced around the room: two queen beds, generic tropical prints on the wall, shelves, a television, and a balcony with an ashtray full of cigarette butts. He decided not to say anything to his daughter about the smokes.

"Grandpa is old. How far can he be?" he said, because Petra was still crying.

"I don't know."

"We're going to find him," he reassured her.

After making enquiries at the front desk—no, no one had seen Señor Kaufmann leave—they started their search on the street. Two girls, not much older than Petra, beckoned him over, and he pulled out his phone to show them a picture of his father.

"Fucky fucky?" they asked in unison.

He declined.

They followed up with a lesser offer. "Sucky sucky?"

Aaron once again declined and showed them his phone screen.

"*Mi padre*," he said, pointing to a photo of his father. It was of Karl eating turkey on a crisp Thanksgiving day. Now Aaron was talking to two prostitutes in the tropics. "He is lost. *Perdido.*"

The girls were sympathetic. They looked at the photo again but didn't recognize Karl.

He and Petra walked into nearby hotels and restaurants and shops, offering introductions and showing the picture. No one recognized him, but a few more girls attempted to entice Aaron with a blow job.

260 | DAVID LAYTON

"Prostitution is legal in the Dominican Republic," Petra helpfully informed him.

"I'm glad you did your research," he said, wondering why he'd done so little of it himself over the years.

There were dozens of hotels with names meant to enchant—Ocean View Hotel, Playa Beach Club, Pension Anneliese, Sosua-by-the-Sea. Situated away from the main drag were streets called Calle David Stern and Calle Dr. Rosen that recalled another aspect of the town's history.

They walked down toward the beach, past newly built shopfronts, most of them empty and smelling of damp plaster. Money-changers stood before stacks of multi-hued paintings with native themes of cane-pickers and swooping birds and sunsets. By the time they arrived at the beach, the late afternoon sun had begun its slide into the ocean.

"I don't think he'd be here getting a suntan," Petra said.

They made a short foray past plastic chairs and top-less women and then turned and trudged back up the hill, where, through the open door of a jewellery shop, Aaron spotted a man in his sixties standing behind the counter. They went inside.

Holding out the photograph, Aaron said, "This man is my father, Karl Kaufmann. I think he might have lived here a long time ago. I'm trying to find him."

The jeweller looked not at the photograph but at Aaron, as if in appraisal.

"Are you Jewish?"

His directness made Aaron uncomfortable. "Half," he said.

"Was your father one of the refugees?"

"He never spoke about it," he said, offering an apologetic shrug and wondering who or what he was apologizing for. Who his father was and what his son knew about it seemed none of this man's business.

"Yes," Petra said. "He was a refugee."

"Most of them left a long time ago, or they've died. I've been here since 1976."

"My grandfather isn't dead," said Petra. "He's lost."

A young couple came into the store and leaned over the display cases, speaking German. Aaron had noticed there were a lot of Germans in Sosua enjoying the "European atmosphere" of Calle Dr. Rosen and apple strudel that their forefathers had inadvertently introduced into this Caribbean island. Either that or they came for the girls. The jeweller took no notice of the young couple.

"A few of the children are around, but if you want any information, the person to talk to is Mr. Hesse. He came during the war and founded the school here, which they've named after him. He's one of the last refugees living here and knows everything about Sosua."

"Where can I find him?"

"That's not difficult. He's at the Britannia Bar every day for happy hour. You can't miss him. He turned ninety-nine a few weeks back."

They thanked the jeweller and made their way toward the Britannia Bar.

The growl of a plane flying overhead caught Petra's attention and, looking up, she said, "Isn't it weird how when

262 | DAVID LAYTON

you're on a plane, you just watch a movie or eat or even go to sleep like nothing's happening?"

"I suppose."

"Sometimes I feel like I'm just flying over, looking down at the world but not really part of it."

"We all feel that way."

"Do you?"

"All the time," Aaron said. "Just because you lost him doesn't mean that you're lost as well."

"What if we don't find him?"

"We'll find him."

Aaron spotted an old man sitting alone at a table who he assumed must be Mr. Hesse. The very fact of his presence there, as promised, was reassuring, as if finally a connective thread had been established. He looked ancient, with an almost translucent skin, the few remaining strands of grey hair slicked back over his sun-spotted scalp. He wore a short-sleeved, collared shirt with a pen in his breast pocket. Age had drained all the colour out of Mr. Hesse, except for his eyes, which were startlingly blue, like two precious stones he might have plucked from the jeweller's display cabinet. As Mr. Hesse fixed those blue eyes on the photograph, Aaron was startled at the resemblance to his father. These men, he was sure, came from the same past, the same place.

"We're looking for this man," said Aaron. "Have you seen him?"

Mr. Hesse laughed. "Not for seventy years."

"You know who this is?"

"Of course. People think all old people look alike. You're his son?"

"Yes."

"Well, talk to the other one. Maybe he knows." Mr. Hesse had reached an age when not getting to the point was an unnecessary expenditure of energy. "Abraham's probably still there."

"Abraham?"

"Your brother. He'll be at his shop," said Mr. Hesse. "Kaufmann's Rent-a-Car. It's not far."

Not far? For Aaron it might as well have been on the moon. How had his family name become intimately attached to a rental car company? he wondered. What was going on here? He had a brother, another family in a faraway place, but he was now *in* that place, and the truth was around the corner.

Mr. Hesse called over the waiter and spoke to him in Spanish. Aaron thought that he might be telling the waiter to take them there, but no, he was ordering another drink.

They took to the street again. It was past five, and soon the sun would be setting, but still it was insufferably hot. Aaron passed several stores selling bottled water, but he didn't want to stop, felt like he couldn't stop, that he was being dragged against his will. So when they reached Kaufmann's Rent-a-Car and stepped inside, he let his daughter approach the woman behind the desk.

"We're looking for Abraham Kaufmann."

"Abran is not here. Can I help you?"

At that moment, Aaron wasn't sure if anyone might help him, but his daughter must have thought otherwise.

264 | DAVID LAYTON

"Is there any way of reaching him?" Petra blurted out. "It's urgent."

"I'll phone," said the woman, dialing his number. She said some words of Spanish into the receiver and then told them to take a seat. "He said to wait."

And so they waited, each of them flicking through Spanish magazines, Aaron grateful that his daughter understood he didn't want to talk, that he didn't even know how to talk at this precise moment.

Ten minutes later, an immaculately maintained pickup truck pulled up, and out stepped a man in his late sixties with a plumpish, kindly face, dark skin and salt-and-pepper moustache partially shaded by the peak of a faded blue baseball cap.

"I'm Abraham Kauffman. How can I help you?" the man asked.

Aaron offered him the photo of his father and backed away, as if the picture were dangerous.

"Do you recognize this man?" Aaron asked.

Abraham Kaufmann took off his baseball cap and wiped his brow with his forearm, revealing, to Aaron's great surprise, a kippa pinned to his hair with a metal clip.

"Who is he?" Abraham asked.

"Does he look familiar?"

"No."

Maybe old men did all look alike, thought Aaron. But of course this man, if he was Karl's son, probably had no idea what his father looked like.

"I think this is your father," said Aaron, and added, "I'm his son."

"And I'm his granddaughter," said Petra.

"My father left when I was a baby. I don't remember him. This man is your father?"

"Yes."

"So you might be my brother." Abraham did not phrase this as a question.

"Half," Aaron answered. He was half of everything today. The question really was which half mattered.

And so there they were, Aaron staring at him for clues, resemblances that might bind them together. The colour of his skin, his fleshy nose and mouth, his dark eyes—all these must come from Abraham's mother, Aaron assumed. We don't look at all alike, he thought.

Just then Petra said, "You look like each other."

Her expression of amazement told Aaron she was serious. Perhaps Abraham saw the resemblance too.

"He's missing," said Aaron.

"It's my fault," added Petra.

"Don't worry," Abraham said, "Sosua is a small place. If he's here, we'll find him. Come."

They got into his truck and drove a short distance back into the heart of the town and then down a series of side streets.

"This was where I was born." Abraham parked the truck outside the entrance of a large hotel named The Sea Horse, and at first Aaron and Petra were unsure what he meant. "We sold the land fifteen years ago, and they built this hotel," he said. "I lived here with my mother and grandfather. They raised me."

Abraham walked through the wide, open entrance and

spoke to several hotel workers in the lobby, while Petra, seemingly exhausted by everything that had happened since her arrival, plopped down on one of the oversized wicker chairs.

"They've seen him," he said. "He came here earlier."

Petra jumped back to her feet. "What now?"

"I thought he might come back here," said Abraham, sounding pleased that he was right. As if Karl's presence offered some proof of patrimony, he added, "Our father built the house that used to stand here."

Whatever the difficulties, however great the distance, Aaron had never shared his father with anyone else. He was the singular offspring, the only one his father chose to ignore. Now there were two of them.

Aaron's eyes swept over the large lobby as if attempting to banish the polished floor and lobby desk and overhead fans and manicured ferns, so that he could return to this place as it must have been—a small house with a small lawn, perhaps a garden. He tried to imagine how it was furnished, the number of rooms, the woman his father had shared a life with, or a fraction of a life, but specifics were beyond his imaginative capacities. It certainly wouldn't have looked like any of the places his father had lived in recently, which, like his last one in Canada, felt stripped down, severe, with no space for wife or children, which was very much the point. Aaron reflected on the apartment he'd recently rented. That too had no proper space for family.

Aaron brought himself back to the moment. This was the world of "our father," the man he had spent a lifetime avoiding.

A group of tourists in bathing suits and with towels strung across their shoulders sauntered past them, speaking German.

"Follow me," said Abraham.

After exiting the hotel, they didn't return to the truck but instead turned right and walked down the street. Abraham stopped along the way to ask people if they'd seen an old man wandering around looking confused, or so Aaron assumed, since he didn't speak Spanish. Karl spoke it, and rather fluently, according to Petra, though Aaron had never heard his father utter a single word of the language.

Abraham led them to a metal gate embossed with a blue Jewish star. Beyond the gate was a stone path leading to a synagogue with front doors painted in the same inviting blue. The synagogue was also a small museum, and it was empty—one had the sense it was most always empty— except for the attendant, who knew Abraham and allowed them to enter without paying the entrance fee. They walked past walls of black-and-white photographs, the ones closest to the entrance offering familiar images of Jews being loaded into cattle cars but then giving way to something else altogether, of young men and women in their Sunday best alighting from ships, and of plowed fields and men on tractors and horseback, of crowded dining halls, and nurses in starched whites cradling babies in their arms, the caption reading: "A new Jewish community is born."

"I was circumcised in this synagogue. My mother and father were with me," Abraham said, forgetting for a moment that he and Aaron shared the same father.

"So you're Jewish?" asked Petra.

"Yes."

"My father is half Jewish," Petra said.

"But circumcised," said Aaron. As far as he knew, it had been done at a hospital. No rabbis and wooden synagogues for him.

"I'm not really Jewish at all," Petra said.

"No one can tell you what you are or aren't, Petra," said Aaron.

That was true—or Aaron hoped it was true—but his words sounded trite. He remembered that it had been a fleeting desire of hers to have a bat mitzvah, probably because she knew the recipient received money and gifts, or so he'd ungenerously thought at the time. Now he wasn't sure why he'd denied her the pleasure.

"Did Grandpa want you to be Jewish?" Petra looked at him and then at Abraham.

"I don't know what Grandpa wanted," Aaron answered. Then he too looked at Abraham, as if his half-brother might be able to shed some light on the matter.

Abraham didn't respond but stopped in front of a picture of two young men lying on the beach, heads propped on their hands, looking into the camera. The caption read: "Settlers on the beach." The one on the left wore a crooked smile; the other was Karl.

"This is our father," he said.

How many times, and for how many years, Aaron wondered, had Abraham come here to stare at the two young men in bathing trunks with white belts, one of them bronzed and youthfully skinny with slicked-back hair that appeared polished. This man was Abraham's father. Aaron was finding it difficult to imagine it was his father too.

Standing behind them in the water, a young blond woman in a one-piece outfit smiled directly at the camera as if pleased that the two young men on the beach were unaware she'd joined them in the picture. Behind her, one could make out a reef with breaking waves, and beyond that, looming in faded, ghostly grandeur, was a mountain that rose to the uppermost edge of the frame.

"He's not here," said Abraham. "But I think I know where we can find him."

19 THEY FOUND FELIX'S BODY OUTSIDE a small village several miles away from Sosua. A woman a few years older than him had walked into town and then rode with Karl and several other men in a Ford flatbed to show them the spot where Felix lay, the blood from the self-inflicted stab wounds pooling like oil on the saturated, swampish soil. Even in his last moments, Felix had refused to entertain the slightest knowledge of the land around him. He hadn't even bothered to find a better place to die.

They took him back to Sosua on the truck, his body covered in a sheet pinned down with their feet, and then they drove up the hill to the cemetery.

Felix wasn't the first suicide of the colony. There'd been two others before him, and their tombstones, along with those of the Balmuds' stillborn child and Otto Ruttenburg, whose death had inaugurated the cemetery's grounds a year before Karl's arrival in Sosua, comprised its occupants.

Now there was Felix Ziegler.

The cemetery was situated on a plot of land wedged between three homesteads. A low wall surrounded it to keep the animals out, and there was a high iron gate with half a Jewish star on either side, so that it was whole only when the gates were closed. Past the front entrance and to the right stood a wooden shed, its blue paint already fading in the sunlight. That was where the shovels were kept to dig the future graves. Like the wooden synagogue, the cemetery was a hopeful place in its claim of future deaths. The proof of the colony's continuation would be chiselled into the gravestones.

Karl counted at least fifty people at the cemetery, surrounding Felix's grave as if to claim him in ways they might have found difficult when he was alive. The soil was bright red, which made the grass seem even greener. The cows lazily chewed cud, while men threw dirt over Felix's body.

"We are all strangers in this new land," said the rabbi. "We have all witnessed great cruelty and suffered much sadness. Felix Ziegler lost his father and brother, both put up against a wall and shot for buying food on the black market, for trying to put food on their family's table."

How did Karl not know this, and the rabbi did? Karl had always relied on Felix for the truth, but the biggest truth of all had been withheld. Not only the suicide but the violence of his death shocked him. He thought he knew Felix, but he hadn't. And now, despite having Maricel, he was alone.

"We are here not to forget or even to forgive, but to carry on and make a new life for ourselves. But for some the burden is too much. Jews do not stigmatize suicide. It is a tragedy but not a sin."

Hadn't everything he and Felix done been in the service of their survival? Why end it just when the war was nearly over? Karl wouldn't even be here if not for Felix. It was Felix who had first spoken of the Dominican Republic, Felix who'd told him what to say in order to get here. And now there he was. And here was Karl, standing over his friend's dead body.

The men passed him the shovel so that he could be the first to scatter soil over the coffin. They were protective not only of Felix Ziegler but also of his friend, Karl Kaufmann.

"We know this must be hard for you," said the rabbi, who spoke with the assurance of someone echoing a community's voice. "He was a good friend of yours."

Yes, he had been. Karl saw in the eyes of everyone who surrounded him a measure of understanding but also pity. Felix had angered a great number of people over the years, and he thought that, if anything, he'd barely been tolerated. But Karl could see from the large turnout that Felix was one of them. All of them had kept their secrets. With everything that had happened to them, how could it be any different?

But one secret that hadn't been kept was Karl's friendship with the man he had come to bury. Everyone understood how close they'd been, and that emphasized for Karl how far he was from all those around him. That was the reason for the pity he saw in their eye. Perhaps it was just sympathy. Whatever it was, he saw that he was, like Felix, one of the wounded young men of the town.

At least he had Maricel. He'd come with no family and had received no formal education while living in Sosua. But he did have a Dominican woman. What did the men and women of Sosua think of that? What did Karl think of it?

"He was a good man," someone in the crowd said, and this was meant for all of them to hear, not just Karl.

Without Felix, there was no fixed centre to the place. It did not feel real. What, wondered Karl, would he do here? Standing in the afternoon light, the edges of the clouds tinged pink, the land saturated in green as if the grass were a high tide come to drown them, he threw dirt over his friend's grave and knew that he would leave this place.

THEY WERE ENTWINED, her black skin a bruise in the darkness. Karl felt responsible for Maricel, not so much for what had happened to her—that was beyond his control and not of his doing—but for what might happen to her in the future.

Rumours of war's end, of murdered Jews and visas to America ensured perpetual and growing anxiety for the people who lived in both towns. Esther, the concert pianist who'd forlornly stared at the tall buildings of New York while they were interned at Ellis Island, said it was already too late for her. Seating herself next to Karl at the cinema, she raised her arm in the beam of light and projected her fingers onto the screen to show how they'd been ruined by malaria and the ceaseless mopping of canteen counters. The Dominicans living in Cherimicos, where Karl now slept most nights, wondered what would become of their jobs and livelihood if the town of Sosua were to fold up, as it had done once before when it was an American banana plantation.

"Where will you go?" Maricel's father asked one night, while they were seated in the chairs Karl had brought from Sosua.

"I will stay here," he said, but he wasn't sure if Miguel accepted the lie.

Karl didn't know what was expected of him. He felt cut off, more so than when he'd lived on the homestead with the Weinbergs. He'd moved back into town then to feel less isolated. But now that Felix was dead, he wished only to please himself, to lie on the beach, to visit Maricel, to do as little work as possible, feeling all the while as if the quick-stroke arrows pointing toward Berlin were also coming for him. He floated, suspended, awaiting change. All he knew was that for the time being, he was safe and warm.

One night he asked Maricel if she would ever think of converting to Judaism. He'd asked her out of curiosity, but her immediate answer of "Yes" caused him to panic. Why ask her such a question unless he meant something by it? Had he? If he did go away, would he consider taking her with him? And what did it matter to him if she converted or not?

He found her pliancy disturbing and quickly changed the subject. "Have you ever seen snow?" he asked.

Maricel shook her head. Of course she hadn't. She would not even have experienced the cold of Mount Trujillo. He'd heard, from Felix and the others who'd convalesced from their bouts of malaria and dysentery and other tropical ailments Karl had managed to avoid, that there were pine trees up there, which Karl, sweating in the cot beside Maricel, found hard to believe. So how could she fathom snow? For some reason, he wanted her to understand.

"It's white. White cold flakes that fall from the sky."

He wiggled his fingertips as if to show her falling snow and dropped them on her warm body.

He began to speak of Austria and the home he'd come from, something he had not done with Felix or Ilsa or anyone else since arriving in Sosua. He described the high alpine mountains, and skating with his friend Erich Nussbaum along a frozen river, of scarves and gloves, not just fashionable but—and here Karl removed his fingers from Maricel's body and rubbed his hands together for effect—real winter gloves to keep your hands warm. That's what his father did, he explained, he made gloves. Maricel listened with acceptance and incomprehension. It must have seemed to her gloriously impossible.

And then Maricel told him she was pregnant.

The heat beneath the covers became unbearable and Karl flung off the sheet, revealing Maricel's belly. He looked at it. She was *pregnant*? The idea was preposterous; it was like imagining snow in the tropics.

"When?" he asked.

"Soon enough."

He'd meant when did she find out, not when would she give birth, but she took his hand and placed it on her belly, which he only now noticed was faintly swelled.

Maricel did not ask him if he was excited or happy. Either she did not believe such emotions were relevant, or she knew he did not feel either of these things. For his part, Karl did not ask her if she was excited or happy. He suddenly felt like a stranger to her. He'd heard reports of women in Sosua getting abortions in Puerto Plata, but he didn't know if it was true, and besides, Maricel was Catholic. Her Catholicism wasn't much like that of Austria—if it was, he wouldn't have found himself living in the family home of an unmarried woman pregnant with his child. Or maybe it was like that also in the small villages outside Vienna. He didn't know. Anyway, abortion was out of the question. His hand, which she placed on her belly, was meant to support her child's life, not end it.

"When?" Karl asked again. Time seemed important.

"Five months?"

That she wasn't entirely sure scared him. She seemed to know as little as he did about giving birth.

"Have you seen a doctor?"

Maricel shook her head.

"It's important," he said. There was a small maternity ward in Sosua, all starched white sheets and pillows, with nurses who wore uniforms even whiter than the sheets and caps over their heads like birthing crowns. Maricel shouldn't be lying here on a cot, sweating in the heat.

"I'll arrange something," he said, because that sounded right.

"I want the child," she said.

She'd misunderstood. Her directness surprised him and reminded Karl that he was, in many ways, out of his depth. Maricel wasn't quiet or pliant; she did not inhabit some place far from his own. It was possible he just thought that way about her, because it made him feel better.

* * *

MARICEL'S BELLY GREW inexorably, until it was impossible to ignore. Sometimes while they were in bed together, he would rub the tight drum of her belly and wonder how this could be happening.

"What if it's a boy?" she asked.

Karl wasn't sure what she was getting at.

"What do you want to do?" she said.

"About what?"

"Would you like him to be Jewish?"

His laughter surprised both of them. He realized he'd offended her, but what could he do? It was funny. Imagine what his family back home would think.

"You can't just choose like that," he said.

"Why not?"

He didn't have an answer. His Jewishness hadn't meant nearly as much to him as it did to Hitler. It wasn't something he'd chosen.

"Other children become Jewish," Maricel said. "They go to the synagogue."

It was a quick affair, nothing complicated or laborious. A few words spoken in Hebrew within the wooden synagogue, and then you became a Jew. Or Jewish enough, at least, to convert your children into Jews.

"Yes, I suppose they do. But it's not important."

"It isn't?"

He could tell that she saw neglect in his answer. In her eyes, he was already dismissing their child's prospects.

Karl was old enough to know that he was too young to have a child. For a moment he thought of talking to

Mr. Weinberg, but the fact that what he sought was fatherly advice was what kept him away. Besides, any meeting with Ilsa under these circumstances would be embarrassing, as if he'd gone off and fulfilled her doubts about him.

What he really wanted was to speak to Felix, who'd had doubts about everyone.

THREE WEEKS AFTER the end of war in Europe, Maricel gave birth to a son. There were celebrations, and while Karl would never mistake one for the other, they commingled in his mind, until he was unsure how to react to either one.

He did his best to avoid noticing how everything was changing. He still woke up each night to a sky that looked no different from before, though the clouds did seem, when he noticed them, to glide over him at a quickened pace. There were discussions in the community of expanding the single-dwelling guest house into a hotel. Petrol rationing would be abolished, and people would be on the move again. Tourists would want to come for the beach and cheeses and apple strudel, which were unique and worthy of a visit.

His son arrived in this world with a patch of damp hair, his skin lighter than his mother's or her family's. Karl noted this without prejudice or favouritism but was fully aware that he was grading his son's skin. His whitened child was a result of Trujillo's darkest wishes.

His mother chose to give him the name Abraham, which Karl found absurdly biblical and overwrought. "You can call him anything you like," Karl had told her.

"Give him a Spanish name, or a French one if you prefer." Maricel had chosen a Hebrew name and used it as if it were an amulet.

Eight days later, he was in the synagogue with Maricel and the rest of her family, who sat beside him watching with the awkward respect one exhibits in the midst of foreign rituals. His son, Abraham Kaufmann, was being circumcised. Maricel's father wore a kippa while clutching his straw hat against his stomach.

Karl stared at them, thinking that this was now his family, these black Christians who believed that a circumcised penis was the mark of a better life.

Karl would have laughed if he hadn't been so confused about what was happening. Hearing the howls of pain as his son's foreskin was cut off, Karl wished that he had the strength of mind to resist this ancient bond being foisted upon his baby.

"Children are a blessing," Jacob Weinberg said to him after the ceremony.

It was the obvious thing to say, and so it came out easily and with genuine enthusiasm, but Karl knew that Jacob would never wish this outcome for Ilsa. As if in understanding, no one in the community had spoken to Karl of marriage. All concern seemed to rest on his child, whose birth marked both the continuance of the community and its radical alteration.

"Be sure to come visit us," Jacob said, shaking Karl's hand goodbye.

"I will," Karl answered, though both of them knew he

wasn't going to make the journey out to their homestead any time soon.

"Ilsa is sorry she couldn't make it, but she is in Ciudad Trujillo at the moment. She sends her best. She's off to America to study," Jacob added, and then, as if unsure such news would be welcome, he said that she hadn't wanted to leave the homestead but that he'd insisted she go abroad. Karl accepted his explanation with a nod and felt as if once again he'd been left behind. It was possible he might never see her again.

As new parents, he and Maricel were given private quarters in town. He packed up his meagre belongings and had no one to say goodbye to, because the barracks by then were practically emptied out. The Berbaums had been relocated to private quarters, and for the last few months there'd been no one to tell him that he needed to take his shoes and socks off at the front entrance. Yet even without Mrs. Berbaum's steely orders, he had continued to carry them out.

"You'll be giving a lot of orders yourself. You'll see!" she'd said to him at the circumcision. That was her way of introducing fatherhood. "Not that anyone will listen." But Karl had listened, probably because he sometimes felt himself to be a child. He wasn't sure if he was ready to be listened to.

Plots of land were being developed along a new road cut past the synagogue, and the community gave him permission to build his own house, something he admitted would be beneficial and appropriate for his new family. A bulldozer was brought in to clear the area, but there was much more to do before his land would be ready for development. There was a question of proper surveyance, for instance, because his property line was triangular. After heavy rains, water tended to pool in the lower areas of his uneven land. That, too, needed to be studied, before he could even begin to imagine where to place the house. If he chopped down a tangle of trees and bush, he'd even have a view of the ocean.

War's end brought word of the slaughter in Europe. Karl was convinced his family had been murdered just like Maricel's mother. And yet he never felt he could share this tragic fate with Maricel. How would he explain to this woman who had never seen snow or Nazis what had happened or the part Karl had played in saving himself? When she proffered a milky breast to Abraham, it only made Karl feel that he had nothing substantial to give. He had betrayed his sister. He feared he was about to do the same to his child, and to Maricel, who remained calm and sturdy against Abraham's endless needs. Karl took to visiting his land, sometimes with a machete, others times with a shovel, in the hope of making a contribution toward his future home. He was determined to build that life, to start it now without delay, but instead he would stand there and listen to the sea, which he found calming.

Away from wife and child, he made a small clearing for himself on his property and brought a flat board on which to place his paper. The letter to his parents wasn't long, but it took him days to write. In it he spoke of where he'd been during the years he'd been away. He mentioned passage from Switzerland to Portugal, and the boat to New York and then onward to the Dominican Republic. He told them that he was a father. He said that he was in good health, pausing to consider whether he should ask the same of them. For Karl, it was as if he were throwing seeds onto soil flooded with rain. Every word he wrote seemed to be flushed away. He could see the ink dissolving before his eyes. "Your loving son," he wrote, ending his letter.

On the envelope, he wrote his parent's last known address: *497 Mariahilferstrasse, Apt. 41, Vienna, Austria*. He may as well have addressed his letter to God.

The letter clutched in his hand, Karl took a few steps up to the imaginary porch and let himself in to what would one day be his house. He walked through and out to his back patio. "I'll sit here," said Karl, and he squatted as if pretending to be seated on a chair and reached out for his cup of coffee. The men in Vienna sat at cafés drinking coffee; they did so after his own father had been banned from entering, and they probably continued to do so during the whole long war. They were doing so now that they were defeated, and therefore so would Karl, who had survived. He'd sit on his patio overlooking the sea and drink his coffee brewed and served to him by Maricel, his young son Abraham by his side.

People were talking about how one day Sosua would be worth something, when the tourists came. Of course, these were often the same people who were learning English so they could start a new life in America, but for a moment, Karl indulged himself in the absurd fantasy of running a hotel and becoming a millionaire.

He took his letter to the agency and the man in charge registered his name and that of his parents, dutifully writing them down in a crisp-paged ledger, one name after the next. When Karl was asked to examine the names and make sure the spelling was correct, he saw them all together again: *Bernard Kaufmann, Margarete Kaufmann, Trude Kaufmann.* Afterwards he posted his letter; just a few stamps were all that was needed to send it on its way, not a single person objecting to the impossibility of his actions.

He promised himself not to expect anything, but when nothing happened, Karl felt as if he were helping to bury three more bodies in the cemetery. Except on paper, they would never be together again.

A few months later, a truck filled with cinder blocks parked outside his property. Several Dominicans jumped off the backside of a Ford flatbed truck—it might have been the very one that transported Felix's body to the cemetery— and opened up the gate.

Maricel's father came to join the workmen, though Karl had not asked, and together they hauled earth and cement until the foundation blocks were in place and the floor frame squared off. They erected the wooden scaffolding. Then came the zinc roof, the new sheets, not yet oxidized, gleaming in the sun. One day they'd put on a proper roof with hardboard and tiles, but for now, this would do. Maricel busied herself with the grounds, cutting, pruning and, in a burst of optimism, planting new and tamer foliage to surround their property. Once it had been cleared, it was possible to imagine a proper yard. A finger of land jutting out to sea caught the surging waves. On windy days the sea spray burst into the air, catching the sun. This is where Karl built his bench.

The day came when a proper door was installed, something for Karl to open and close, and this time, he walked through a real home partly furnished with the two wooden chairs Miguel had insisted be placed in their new living room. Karl and Maricel, with Abraham in her arms, walked down to the edge of the property, along a path that was laid with flagstones quarried near Santiago, the town of Maricel's mother. As they sat on his wooden bench, Karl heard the Atlantic churn against the coral cliffs, eating away at them.

"The war is over," said Karl.

"We will be happy here," said Maricel. And then, as if registering his doubts, she added, "I want you to know that you're a good man."

A bursting wail from Abraham seemed to contradict her statement.

With Maricel's attention diverted, Karl turned his back on the house as if to make it disappear. Just as predicted, scarce funds were being directed toward Europe and Palestine, which meant that the Jews of Sosua needed more than ever to find a way to support themselves. He'd been transported to the other side of the world, given food and money and land; it was time to honour his circumstance, give it some purpose that felt right and personal to his life. The great work, which was survival, had been accomplished. Now came the task of living.

He'd built a house for his family. Now he could leave.

20 I T WASN'T EASY TO TELL FROM THE outside where exactly his house had stood, because everything on the street had disappeared, been disguised or moved around to such an extent that the only thing resembling his front door was a hotel entrance. It wasn't just Karl who was losing his memory but the town. Yet the house's original footprint—his footprint—was still here; it could not be removed.

Karl entered the lobby.

"Can I help you, sir?" a young Dominican boy in uniform enquired.

Karl tried to orientate himself. "I'm looking for my home."

"Do you remember your room number?"

Karl remembered that he didn't need a room number to find his own house.

"I don't have one."

"Are you a guest here?"

"I live here." Karl said this in Spanish. "*Vivo aquí.*"

"*Vive en la Republica Dominicana?*"

"*No. Aquí.*"

Here. Right here. That's where Karl lived.

He wasted no more time with the boy; instead he walked past the lobby and made his way toward the sea. Everything had changed but the crenellated coastline. It still met the sea with the same embattled scars. He recognized as his own the coral outcrop bare of vegetation. The hotel mustn't have known what to do with this piece of land tainted with sea spray and so had left it alone. Karl shuffled forward, trying to get just the right view from the bench where he'd once sat.

"*Kannst du mir mal noch ein Handtuch?*"

It was early morning, but already people were sunning themselves, including a woman with skin the colour and consistency of baked apple strudel. She called for another towel. His once modest patio had collapsed into a kidney-shaped swimming pool.

The man whom she addressed pulled one from a stack and then, as if suddenly called away, walked in the opposite direction. Karl fought an impulse to go over and explain himself to her. Did she know where she was? Was she here precisely because she did know? Her accent reminded him of Ilsa's boyfriend. She must come from the industrial north of Germany, but now she too was here, in his home.

So where was his home?

It wasn't back in Toronto either. He'd spent three-quarters of his life in Canada, but he felt more at home in a place where his home didn't exist. Buried somewhere were the flagstones leading to his house. He followed the path back to the lobby, and then, before more questions could be asked of him, he was out on the street.

He walked along the pavement, avoiding the sidewalk. He'd been walking these roads long before there was a need for such conveniences. Several houses, much larger and more solid than anything that had existed before, were situated behind hedges and metal fences. Another hotel followed and then, after he turned left into town, shops, apartments and rooms for rent. There was a sense of rambling prosperity about the place that he cherished, as if he'd had something to do with the outcome.

This was a proper town, with cars parked at the curbs and motorbikes patrolling the roads. It was a place with electric telegraph poles and telephones, air conditioning and swimming pools with fresh towels for the asking. The early morning sleepiness he observed in people he passed was an outcome of good fortune, not despair.

Karl, surprising himself, called out a *"Buenos días"* to the few people opening up their places of business for the morning. Without looking up, they returned his morning greeting. *"Buenos días,"* they called back to him.

One of them might have been his son.

The last photo that had been sent to him, a black-and-white picture taken when Abraham was still a boy, was so old that Karl had no idea who to look for. The one clue might be his skin colour. It would be lighter. But whose would he be comparing it to? His own skin? Ancient and withered, unable to sustain any pigmentation, even sun spots, Karl's skin could best be described as colourless rather than white. Dominicans, on the other hand, had a wide variety of skin shades. They were all mixed up, just like this town and its history.

Karl had sent Maricel money; Maricel had sent him back

photographs. At first she delivered some of both herself and their child, pictures of her holding up his son's hand to wave at the camera. The photographs were taken on the back patio with the hedges in the background, or in the house, the door always open as if waiting for his return. Did she believe he was coming back? Karl had needed an excuse to walk out the front door toward something resembling a normal life. He had promised to send for them when the time came. The time had never come.

After a few years, the photos Maricel sent were just of their son, as if she sensed she was disappearing from his view. Then, when he no longer even sent her the occasional letter, she stopped sending photographs at all. She knew what was happening, had probably always known but had hoped it might turn out differently. In the years after the war, one did not cohabit with a Haitian woman or father mulatto children circumcised by rabbis. There'd been no room for them in Toronto, no space that could contain such oddities.

The promise he'd offered Maricel was the last he'd ever made. He'd offered none to his Canadian-born son and none to Claire either. It was better that way, more honest and respectful.

He hadn't known what to feel, and so he felt nothing. What was the point? Maybe when his son grew up, Karl would think about bringing him to Canada, but that was far in the future, and when it was less so, he understood that he'd been using the idea to make his actions less ignoble. He wished his son well, as he did Maricel, and the money he sent every month would ensure the boy would be given a decent education and a good head start. The community of Sosua would help him, treat him as one of their own, even if Karl could not.

Karl never allowed himself to dwell on the photos. They were put away, and, in the course of the various moves he made over the decades, they, like Maricel, like his first-born, disappeared. Even if Maricel had wanted to send photographic evidence, she no longer had his address. He reasoned that any emergency—one that had to do with money—could be handled by his bank. They would give word if a problem arose. None ever did. Maricel had accepted her fate. Karl tried to do the same.

The money was sent, and it was received. Karl had another child, a boy, and he gave what he could to him, all the while attempting not to resent his existence. Perhaps this was how Karl had shown his paternal obligation, by neglecting his second son on his first son's behalf.

What had he thought, anyway? That he'd find his son in a house he'd left another century ago and say, "*Buenos días, mi hijo*"? Was he expecting his son to invite him in for breakfast? "*¿Le gustaría un café, Papa?*" *Yes*, he'd answer, *I would like some coffee*. And they would sit down at the table and enjoy each other's company in some utterly unbelievable way.

It was not that way with the son he knew, so why would it be any different with the son he didn't know? Well then, Karl asked himself, if that's the way it's going to be, what am I doing here? He'd come here for a reason, and he hadn't come alone. Petra was with him. He'd slipped out of the room early in the morning, when she was still sleeping.

She'd been up late the night before, overwhelmed by the heat and light and the promise it offered. She'd jumped in the pool after darkness fell, and he'd watched her from the hotel balcony, swimming in the lit water, wishing so much that it was his sister. He'd given her US dollars and told her that she could go out and explore the town. With money in hand, she'd cast him a dubious look.

"I'm worried about leaving you alone here."

"This is my home," Karl had said. "I can't get lost."

Now the sun reached higher in the sky. Karl was thirsty from walking on the road. He needed shade and something to drink. He'd find it at the *colmado* but everything had changed, and he was no longer sure of the way. Hotels along the cliff blocked his view of the sea and, with it, his ability to locate himself. He carried on walking in what he believed was the right direction and felt lucky when he spotted the administrative house where the Americans had their offices and doled out the weekly salary. It looked completely run-down. The galvanized roof was in bad shape, the shutters needed a new coat of paint, and there was furniture on the veranda, even a fridge, which upset Karl. The Americans weren't ones to let things slide like this.

He knocked on the door.

"*Dónde está el colmado?*" he asked the Dominican woman who answered the door.

She must have been in her late fifties or sixties and stared at him for a moment before turning to shout into the dark space behind her. "Danny!" She continued standing by the door as if to block his entrance, until Danny arrived, holding a slice of nibbled toast in his hand. Bread crumbs littered his poorly trimmed beard.

"What can I do for you?" he asked.

"I'm looking for the *colmado*."

Danny considered the question for a moment. "You Jewish?"

Karl had learned never to answer that sort of question. "Is the *colmado* close by?"

"That place hasn't been around for, like, fifty years. It was a night club for a while. But then it went out of business. It's a restaurant now. I don't recognize you. Have you come from America? I lived there for thirty years. I'm a musician. I've played all over."

He said this, Karl supposed, by way of apology for his current circumstances. Karl wished he hadn't approached. Where were the other Americans? he wondered.

"The *colmado* is just up the road," he said, pointing with his toast in the direction Karl had been walking. "But except for the building, there's nothing left. It's amazing the place is still standing." He stared at Karl.

Just like you was what Danny meant. Karl sensed his remark was hostile.

"You have family here?" asked Danny.

Petra would be up by now, worried where he was.

"Yes," he said.

"I'm Rebecca Berbaum's son. Did you know her?"

When Karl failed to respond, he added, "I'm not her first kid. She married a Dominican after Mr. Berbaum died."

Karl didn't think it possible. How could Mrs. Berbaum,

who wouldn't let Karl walk into the barracks without taking off his socks, give birth to such a sloppy and erratic offspring?

"I know her," said Karl.

"Yeah, she died eighteen, maybe nineteen years ago. My brothers live in the States. One's a professor at UCLA. The other one lives in Miami. A lot of the kids from Sosua live in Miami. They do business." Danny rubbed two envious fingers together.

"I need to get back to the hotel," Karl said. He shouldn't have left his room.

"I thought you wanted to go see the *colmado*."

"I'm going now."

"Go, then. And say hello to your family."

Karl felt thirstier than ever, but when he got there, the doors and windows of the *colmado* were shut tight. He might find something to drink in Cherimicos and maybe somewhere to lie down for a while. He set off. It was getting hot. Normally he took the road at night with Felix, travelling beneath a starry canopy, but in bright sunlight, there were cars and motorcycles honking their horns at him as they sped past. It was a long walk, and he was exhausted by the time he turned into town. Except that he didn't recognize anything and wasn't sure if he'd taken the right road.

Where was Maricel's house? The street before him was filled with restaurants, supermarkets, small bars with outdoor patios, wooden shacks that looked ancient but that he didn't recognize.

Fanning off from this street were other, smaller streets and laneways that spider-webbed their way beyond Karl's comprehension. He stepped into a small shop, but when he put his hands into his pockets, he realized he had no money.

Karl was sweating. He wiped his face with his shirt and nodded, to show the woman behind the counter that he was fully conscious and alert. He was lost again, as he had been in Toronto, and looking for home. He'd made a mistake last time, ending up at Claire's. He needed to make sure the same thing didn't happen to him again.

"*No tengo dinero*," he said.

There wasn't much else to do inside the shop if he wasn't able to buy anything, so he stepped back outside, and this time the heat hit him hard. He chose to walk back toward where he believed he'd just come from, and there he saw, a short distance away, a communal water pipe. There had often been women using it in the morning, a stack of metal buckets beside them ready to fill up, but now no one was there. Maybe, thought Karl, that was because it was so late in the morning. He turned on the tap, cupping his hands to catch the water, which at first was warm, but then, after he let it run for a moment, became refreshingly cool. He drank.

"Hey, old man! That water is no good!"

A young man from the village, someone Karl had never seen before, approached uninvited. Karl ignored him. He'd been drinking this water all his life. It had never done him any harm.

"Where you from?"

Why was everyone asking him this?

"I'm from here."

"From Cherimicos?"

"No, Sosua. *Soy de Sosua*."

"Ah," said the man. "You're a survivor."

Was that the word they used for people like him? If so, it was true. He was.

"What town is this?" asked Karl.

"You don't recognize it?"

Karl shook his head.

"This is Cherimicos."

That didn't seem right to Karl.

"Thank you," Karl said. He was developing a throbbing headache.

"Where are you staying? Do you need help getting back?"

Karl had no intention of telling him where he was staying. This man was most likely as untrustworthy and dangerous as the last one he'd spoken to. And then it occurred to him that he couldn't have answered, even if he wanted to.

He attempted to take his leave, but the man wanted to follow him out of a pretense of concern.

"Are you looking for something?" he asked.

Karl couldn't walk any faster, so he decided to slow down and keep silent.

Eventually the man gave up, peeling away from him after it was clear there would be no further conversation. Karl attempted to keep on even ground, so that he wouldn't tire himself out, but he sensed the need for a deeper, more thorough, plan than this. He needed to stop somewhere and take stock but was fearful of getting into any other conversations.

They all seemed to lead to the same questions: Where was he from? What was he looking for?

There was a church to Karl's left that he vaguely recognized—not the church itself, which was more prominent than the one he had in mind, but the path leading down to what he believed was the beach. If he was wrong, though, he would have to climb back up, a daunting task under current conditions. Karl decided to take the risk. Something about the light at the end of the path was familiar.

The sun retreated behind a canopy of thick foliage. A cooling stone wall followed him down the path that eventually turned into steps, which he carefully took one by one, until the scene broke out before him. He stepped onto the white sand and saw the mountain Isabel de Torres rising over Puerto Plata, just as it had that first day. The reef where he and Ilsa had played jutted out of the water. It was low tide. Karl followed the ribbon of sand but found it slow-going with his shoes on. He sat on the root of a seagrape tree and took them off. Then his socks. He planted his bare feet in the sand, digging in his toes where it was cooler. His body was ruined but not the beach. There was a breeze coming off the water, bringing with it the bright shouts of sea bathers.

Then he took his clothes off and walked into the water.

21

ABRAHAM DROVE RIGHT DOWN TO the beach, though it appeared this was not quite legal. Stalls selling bright paintings, wooden sculptures, water and snorkelling equipment lined the road to his left. Tourists and locals alike moved out of his way.

"When I was a kid there was nothing here," he said.

As he'd done when walking along the road, Abraham stopped at a few of the stalls and asked if they'd seen an old man shuffling by, perhaps on his way down to the beach. Aaron watched them shake their heads. Nobody had seen him. They parked the car in a sandy lot with puddles of water from recent rains and made their way on foot along a shaded path behind the beach. Many of the stalls had small kitchens and places to sit and eat. On the beach, hundreds of chairs lined the crescent of sand that stretched to the far cliff face. Dominicans, mainly kids, ran back and forth from the stalls to the chairs with drinks and food. Boats and sea jets bobbled close to shore.

Abraham stayed on the path, while Aaron focused on the back part of the beach and Petra walked along the shoreline. It was beautiful, but why would Abraham think his father would be down here? Karl was not someone who particularly enjoyed the beach or craved sunshine. On their vacations when Aaron was young, his father seemed to stick to the shade and hardly ever went into the water. "Come join us!" his mother would call out, but Karl would remain where he was as if to punish himself—or them, perhaps. Aaron had never been sure.

They carried on down the beach, and when they reached the end, Abraham pointed toward a narrow path with steps leading up to the houses that straddled the cliff.

"Cherimicos," he said. "This is the Dominican side of the beach."

"I don't think he's here," said Aaron.

"It's a big beach. We will walk back and maybe see him."

Aaron found this unlikely and wondered what the next step should be. He was dependent on Abraham's expertise, but then again, they were searching for a man Abraham hadn't seen since he was a baby. Abraham wouldn't recognize his father, even if he found him. What did this man know of Karl, of his movements and interests now or ever? If anything, Karl was sitting in some dark, air-conditioned room. Either that or he'd fallen into a ditch or manhole. Aaron stood beside Abraham waiting for him to make a move.

"So you are his son," he said.

"Yes, I am. And it seems you are too."

"And your mother? Where is she?"

"She's at home, in Canada. We all live in Toronto," Aaron said. "My mom and dad got divorced years ago."

"He was married?"

That was generally the precondition for divorce, thought Aaron.

"They were. I think the divorce might have had something to do with this place. With you. But to be honest, I'm not sure what they were doing together anyway. Dad was a bit absent after he left my mother. I saw him on and off. I guess for you, it's just been off."

All Abraham had was a photograph of a man on a beach—*this* beach, it might have been. Maybe that was why Abraham had brought them here.

"I found his clothes!" Petra shouted out.

Aaron ran to where she stood over a shirt, pants, socks and shoes lying on some tree roots.

"This was what he was wearing when I last saw him," said Petra.

Aaron was in search of a whole body and so had missed the clothing, which had been stashed with a measure of order—shoes lined up and facing the same direction, socks neatly tucked into the shoes—that indicated his father's habits. He turned toward the ocean and squinted.

"Where is he?" asked Petra. "I can't see him."

He put his arm around her. His father was out there, thought Aaron. It might be a fitting end for him, even perhaps the right one, but he couldn't bear how it would affect his daughter, who'd brought Karl down here. She would never forgive herself. For all their sakes, they needed to find him alive.

From the evidence of his clothes, Karl would only be wearing his underwear. Nothing in his father's character suggested he'd ever do such a thing, but Aaron needed to stop thinking that he really knew anything about Karl. It was Abraham who had been able to follow his father's tracks, trace him down to this beach.

"You see the reef?" asked Abraham. He pointed to a patch of darker blue some distance away from them. "There's a man standing on the rocks."

The light was fading, and Aaron couldn't really make out anything beyond a few bobbing heads out at sea, too far to realistically identify his father. Too far realistically to imagine his father ever swimming such a distance.

"That might be him," said Petra, heading straight for the water.

Aaron stripped off his shirt and sandals and was about to join his daughter, when he considered that there was another family member with them. His father's fate, if it actually was Karl on the reef, wasn't his and Petra's alone. He looked to his half-brother.

"We'll take a boat," said Abraham, but Petra was already swimming out toward the reef, so Aaron stripped off his shirt and joined her, the two of them swimming side by side the way it was when they'd bicycled together, Petra with training wheels, but it was different now because she was a strong swimmer and didn't need his help.

Petra shouted, "What are you doing out here!"—not to him but to Karl, who *was* the man standing on the reef.

Her grandfather didn't answer.

"What are you doing?" Aaron repeated.

His father was shivering despite the heat, his skin wrinkled from his time in the sea. He looked tremendously old but also vital, like some grand, ancient barnacle that refused to let go.

Abraham sped toward them in a boat, and when he

arrived, Aaron and his daughter manoeuvred its tip against the reef and then planted themselves on it. They did this without need of discussion or explanation, he and his daughter working on common instinct, as the three of them hauled Karl into the boat, doing their best not to scrape his skin or cause any bruising.

"Dad, what the hell were you thinking?" Aaron meant all of it, the whole trip down, but Karl took a more limited view of the question.

"I was looking for Maricel," he said.

"Who?"

"She died eleven years ago," answered Abraham, offering his father a towel.

Petra took it from him and rubbed the towel on her grandfather's back to get him warm. She was the only one who felt comfortable enough to touch him so intimately.

Waiting for Karl to recover, Abraham silently handed his father a bottle of water, which he greedily drank. Aaron caught his daughter's eye to confirm it wasn't for them to interfere between father and son. This was something Abraham needed to do in his own time. But he hadn't counted on Karl.

"I would swim with your mother right here," Karl said, looking at his son and then toward the shore.

"She took me to this beach many times," said Abraham.

"You know who he is, Grandpa?" Petra asked.

"Yes, of course. He looks like his mother."

Petra stared at Abraham's face. "He looks like Dad."

Yes, he did, thought Aaron. It was as simple as that. His

father's two sons here, together, an impossibility that could only exist in this place that had saved him. Looming before them all was Isabel de Torres, and beyond that mountain lay the world that for Karl had been full of threat and shame.

After drying off and putting Karl's clothes back on, they climbed into the truck with a tentative and forced politeness. Aaron and Petra sat in the back. Karl was up front with his first-born son.

"You will stay in my house," said Abraham.

He drove to Karl and Petra's hotel, where they collected their belongings and checked out. The glistening bodies soaking up the sun poolside seemed so far from his own predicament that Aaron, walking along the corridor with the three of them, found himself questioning if any of this seemed plausible. Maybe Abraham was a complete stranger called up to answer some need they all had of him. He even wondered if this was some sort of scam, or at the least a terrible mistake.

As they sped east of Sosua, the main road was busy with cars and taxis, motorcycles, delivery vans and buses of all sizes ferrying locals and sightseers, a constant rush of traffic servicing the tourists along the coastline.

"That was the Fleischmanns' farm," said Abraham, pointing to his left. "And the Strausses'," he added a moment later, pointing to his right. It went on like that for several miles, with him rattling off names. "That was the Katzes', the Benjamins', the Sichels', the Eichens'."

The lush land had all been converted to hotels and seaside apartments, none of it seemingly recognizable to Karl

302 | DAVID LAYTON

from the speeding car. Clearly the original inhabitants had left the land, sold it off and moved away, or they were dead. How many of them were left? Aaron wondered. Abraham continued to overlay the present with the past, until he mentioned the name Weinberg.

"Jacob," Karl said.

"Yes, Jacob Weinberg."

"I knew them," he said.

Abraham flicked on the right indicator and turned onto a poorly paved road that soon became a dirt path, the red soil looking bruised and angry at the truck's assault. There were plump cows, and skinny children whose wooden shacks offered sad contrast to the fertile fields, open and sunlit, as they made their way ever more slowly toward the Weinbergs' farm, which was no longer owned by the Weinbergs, said Abraham, all the family members having sold up and left the Dominican Republic over thirty years ago.

They parked beside a dilapidated and long-abandoned house, and Aaron kept a watchful eye on Karl as he moved toward the front door, which was a double-hung door, the bottom half closed and the top open. Aaron noticed a metal cup resting on one of the windowsills to the left of the front door and a patch of curtain lace, and he wondered if someone was in fact living there, or at least using it for temporary shelter from the sun and rain, but he returned his attention to Karl, who he feared might do himself harm, if he tried to walk up the warped and rotten front steps.

Instead, he walked around the side of the house, the rest of them following respectfully, not saying a word, until he stood beside a small window.

"That was my room," he said.

"You lived here?" asked Petra.

His father didn't answer and slowly continued around the perimeter.

Abraham pointed to an elevated patch of land behind the house, saying, "There's the well," and Karl responded, looking at the concrete drum with some interest.

Unlike imagining the house at the hotel, it wasn't too difficult to picture what life must have been like here back then. Even now it felt as if they were in some lost land, far away from all modern amenities. How had they survived out here? Not so much because of the practicalities of obtaining running water and electricity but rather the landscape, which was utterly exotic to a northerner's eye and somewhat menacing and mysterious. Yet it was also magical, with palm trees rising out of the open fields, like shafts of light plucked from the sun and planted in the ochre soil. Aaron felt that if he moved only a few feet away, he'd be lost.

Of course, that's how an outsider would see it. But the refugees who'd come from Germany and Austria had been outsiders too, and Aaron tried to envision it from their point of view, through Mr. Hesse's cobalt eyes, and through his own father's. Was the land something to conquer and overcome? Was it threatening or nourishing, or were such questions overly romantic, if not for the refugees in general, then for his father, whose most imaginative act was to clamp down on his imagination. That had led to the earliest of misunderstandings between them.

"There's the orange tree," said Karl.

Either the enormous tree was too old to be fruit-bearing, or it was the wrong season—but Aaron didn't see any fruit.

"Ilsa planted this tree," said his father. "She liked oranges."

Aaron didn't know who Ilsa was and looked again to Abraham.

"The Weinbergs were good to me," said Abraham. "They accepted me and always made me feel welcome."

Abraham did the same, when they reached his home, not more than a fifteen-minute drive from the dilapidated place his father once lived in. This was a two-storey, located in a solidly built residential area. Ana, his wife, was there to greet them, and they walked on spotlessly clean white tile floors to a living room furnished with plush, oversized couches and chairs covered in florid colours. It was spacious, with open views of the sea half a mile away and below them.

Ana explained their daughter was in Orlando, where she lived with her husband, but everyone would meet up, she assured them, as soon as it was possible.

Abraham must have phoned ahead, because she knew who they were and what they were doing here. In quick order, food was laid out on the table—rice, beans, salad and meat, which Karl tucked into with animated relish.

Aaron watched Abraham for any traits that might link him to his father and by extension to himself and his daughter. Despite what Petra had told him, he still didn't see the resemblance. But there was, in the way Abraham physically expressed himself, a subtle but definable similarity. Aaron noticed a precision in his movements, a methodical plotting in the way he moved food to mouth, and a particularity about his clothes, which, while not new, were carefully put together and cared for, projecting, as did his father, a certain elegance.

Afterwards, over coffee, Aaron was surprised to see Abraham take Karl's hand. There was an emotional frugality in the way he held it, a light clasp that could be undone at a moment's notice and that, precisely in its hesitancy, appeared to signify far more than if he'd taken a firmer hold.

And Karl was letting his hand be held, however lightly, however delicately. They were linked, and Aaron wondered how long Abraham Kaufmann had waited for this day to arrive.

"I have something to show you," Abraham said, getting up from the table. He returned with a paper document that he carefully pulled out of a cellophane cover. He unfolded it and spread it out on the table.

"This is my birth certificate." Abraham's index finger hovered over one of the signatures and then, after a moment of hesitation, gently tapped it twice. "This is my father's."

Aaron saw what he'd been trying to obtain from his father for the past two months, a simple signature of acknowledgement.

Abraham slid his finger across the page. "My mother," he said, stopping at another signature, this one less bold and sure of itself.

"She was a good woman," said Karl.

"I have another document," said Abraham. This one was framed and passed to him by his wife, who had taken it off the wall. "This is a Ketubah, a Jewish wedding certificate."

It was written in Hebrew, and again, there were two recognizable signatures.

"Do you remember signing this?" Aaron asked his father.

Karl acknowledged it was his signature on the document handed to him, but he did not remember signing it. The certificate was far more ornate than he could have imagined for a time when everything had been so stripped down. On either side of the Hebrew lettering, two trees were drawn, as if standing guard, their canopies joining at the top. It must have been handed to Karl at the synagogue and taken to their new home.

"I'm sorry that your mother died," said Petra.

"There's no need. She had a good life."

Aaron considered if he might ever be able to say that about his own mother. The wedding certificate before them meant that his father was a bigamist and Aaron a bastard. Such phrases seemed overwrought in this day and age, but for his mother they meant exactly as they sounded. The marriage had ended because in his mother's eyes, it had never actually begun. It wasn't just that Karl had once had another family—the man had always had *this* family. His half-brother was the legitimate son, the one with the signed contract. But for reasons he couldn't explain, Aaron felt immensely relieved, as if a burden of some kind had been lifted.

Karl announced that he was going to take a nap. He said this without knowing where he'd be sleeping, and Abraham stood up with his father to escort him to his bedroom. Aaron was tired too. It had already been a very long day, a very

long few days, in fact, and darkness had set in, but Petra
wanted him to go to the beach. Ana gave them towels and
told them the moon would guide them to the water.

They walked along a path leading toward the sea, the
two of them once more alone. They'd found her grandfather
and his family.

"I hope you aren't planning on ever doing something
like this again," he said.

"Not likely. We'll be able to visit here, don't you think?"
asked Petra.

"Do you want to come back?"

"Don't you? It's pretty amazing here."

"I guess it is."

The beach they found was a thin stretch of white sand
shaded with a few palm trees. They took a few tentative
steps into the dark water, their toes searching for unwanted
stones and rocks, but the bottom was sandy. This time they
weren't trying to rescue anyone, and they gently floated
out in the water, not talking but not keeping their distance
either.

When they returned to the house, Karl had taken a seat
on the patio, as if he owned the place, as if he'd lived there
all his life.

"Where is my jacket?" Karl shivered from non-existent
cold.

"You don't have a jacket, Grandpa."

"Why not?"

"You don't need one here."

Karl was quick to accept Petra's reply and returned to

his Spanish newspaper, which he'd propped in front of him. Placid and oddly content, he was a Dominican citizen who would, Aaron knew, remain here with his son until his last days.

Aaron and Petra found seats on the patio beside Karl, who soon put aside his newspaper, and the three of them watched in companionable silence as the moon shone on Isabel de Torres and the dark waters beneath.

ACKNOWLEDGEMENTS

I'D LIKE TO THANK THE ONTARIO ARTS COUNCIL for their generous support, and HarperCollins for their exceptional patience. The keen editorial insights of Jennifer Lambert, Gillian Stern, Jane Warren and Patrick Crean were all instrumental in making this book happen. Once on the page, Allyson Latta's keen eye made sure every word was accounted for. I'd also like to thank my agent, Sam Hiyate, for going well beyond the call of duty. The assistance provided by the Embassy of Haiti in London is also very much appreciated. Thanks as well to my brother, Max, and, as always, my mother, Aviva.

While entirely a work of fiction, this book is based on true historical events. For insight into those times, I am indebted to Marion A. Kaplan's *Dominican Haven: The Jewish Refugee Settlement in Sosua, 1940–1945* and Josef David Eichen's *Sosua: From Refuge to Paradise*.